P9-ELR-123

"Sometimes a story comes along that just plain
makes you want to hug the world. Your heart needs
this joyful miracle of a book."

—KATHERINE APPLEGATE,
acclaimed author of *The One and Only Ivan* and *Wishtree*

THE
REMARKABLE
JOURNEY OF
Coyote
Sunrise

THE REMARKABLE JOURNEY OF Coyote Sunrise

DAN GEMEINHART

SQUARE
FISH

HENRY HOLT AND COMPANY
NEW YORK

SQUARE
FISH

An imprint of Macmillan Publishing Group, LLC
120 Broadway, New York, NY 10271
mackids.com

Our books may be purchased in bulk for promotional, educational, or business use. Please
contact your local bookseller or the Macmillan Corporate and Premium Sales Department
at (800) 221-7945 ext. 5442 or by email at MacmillanSpecialMarkets@macmillan.com.

Library of Congress Cataloging-in-Publication Data

Names: Gemeinhart, Dan, author.
Title: The remarkable journey of Coyote Sunrise / Dan Gemeinhart.
Description: New York : Henry Holt and Company, 2019. | Summary: Twelve-
     year-old Coyote and her father rush to Poplin Springs, Washington, in their old
     school bus to save a memory box buried in a park that will soon be demolished.
Identifiers: LCCN 2018021834 | ISBN 978-1-250-23361-5 (paperback) |
     ISBN 978-1-250-19671-2 (ebook)
Subjects: | CYAC: Automobile travel—Fiction. | Fathers and daughters—
     Fiction. | Single-parent families—Fiction. | Grief—Fiction.
Classification: LCC PZ7.1.G46 Rem 2019 | DDC [Fic]—dc23
LC record available at https://lccn.loc.gov/2018021834

Originally published in the United States by Henry Holt and Company
First Square Fish edition, 2020
Book designed by Carol Ly
Title lettering by Michael Burroughs
Square Fish logo designed by Filomena Tuosto

7   9   10   8   6

AR: 4.7 / LEXILE: 730L

TO THE FOUR POINTS OF MY COMPASS:
KAREN, EVA, ELLA, AND CLAIRE

CHAPTER
ONE

There were big days and there were small days and there were bad days and there were good days and I suppose I could pick any one of 'em for my "once upon a time." But if I'm gonna be truthful—and truthful is something I always aim to be—then really there is only one best place to start this story.

It all started with Ivan.

Once upon a time, it was hot and I was sweaty. It was about five months before my thirteenth birthday, give or take. We were someplace in Oregon. Honestly, I don't even remember the name of the town, but I know it was on the dry, hot side of the state, away from the ocean. The whole world was so yellow and shining from the beating-down sun that you had to squint no matter where you looked. The blacktop of the gas station parking lot radiated the heat right back up at you so it felt like you were getting cooked from both sides. I suppose most barefoot people would've been hooting and hopping with that sizzling asphalt burning the bottoms of their feet, but my soles were used to it and I walked along easy as you please. My T-shirt was stuck with sweat to my back. The braid that hung down nearly to my blue jean belt loops slapped wetly against it as I walked.

The man behind the counter looked at my bare feet and

started to say something. "Miss, you can't—" but I knew where he was going with it before he started. That tyrannical "No Shoes, No Shirt, No Service" rule is pretty darn universal in America's gas station convenience stores. I just waved at him and cut him off. "I know, I know," I said, and kept walking. "I'll only be a minute."

I'd never been in that particular gas station before, but it was exactly the same as every other one, so really I'd been in it a million times. Rows of plastic-wrapped junk food. Walls lined with glass-doored coolers full of pop and beer and flavored iced teas. I walked past the metal racks of beef jerky and candy bars to the pot of gold at the end of my rainbow: the slushy machine.

There it was, humming in the corner next to the coffee dispenser and soda fountain. My mouth started watering as soon as I saw that neon-colored sugar slush swirling around under the big plastic dome.

There was a kid standing in front of it, looking up at the churning slurry with desire written plain and clear across his face. He was seven or eight and staring up at the left flavor, which was an unlikely pinkish color labeled "Wild Watermelon."

"Big mistake," I said, walking up next to him and grabbing a cup from the pull-down dispenser.

He jerked his head to look at me.

"What is?"

I nodded with my chin at the slushy he was coveting.

"Watermelon. That's a no-go. Never waste your time with anything that claims to be watermelon or banana flavored. It's a scam every time."

He squinted at me, clearly unconvinced.

"Doesn't matter anyway," he said. "My mom already said no."
He threw his head back dramatically. "But I'm *so hot*."

I yanked down another cup and held it out to him.

"Here," I said. "My treat."

The kid's face lit up.

"For reals?" he asked.

"Yep."

But then his face dropped again, just as quick.

"But Mom said no. I'll probably get in trouble."

I shrugged. "You're probably gonna get in trouble at some
point today anyway. You may as well get a slushy out of it."

He thought about that for a real short second and then
snatched the cup from my hand.

"But I really would think twice about getting watermelon," I
added.

My advice fell on deaf ears, and in a flash he was pulling down
the nob and squirting glistening pink slush into his cup.

I filled mine with the other flavor, "Funky Fruit Punch,"
which was the superior choice in every respect.

The kid looked me up and down as we walked toward the
cashier.

"You're wearing weird clothes."

I looked down at my raggedy blue jeans and grease-stained
white T-shirt.

"I'm basically wearing the same thing you're wearing," I
pointed out.

"Exactly," he said. "And I'm a boy."

"So?"

"So boys and girls shouldn't wear the same thing."

"Well, then you better change. 'Cause I ain't."

He had nothing to say to that, which was probably the right move on his part since I hadn't paid for his slushy yet.

I ignored the hostile, good-riddance look on the cashier's face when I paid. Like hot asphalt on bare feet, it was something I was used to.

Me and the kid walked through the jangling door and back out into the heat. The highway hummed not too far off in the distance.

The kid took a big slurping suck on his slushy straw. He swallowed and smacked his lips and nodded.

"Well?" I asked. "How's the Wild Watermelon?"

He ran his tongue over his lips, considering.

"Sweet," he said. "Weird. Not really like watermelon at all."

I nodded and took a suck of my delicious, flavored-as-advertised Funky Fruit Punch.

"Lesson learned, kid. Now you know."

He looked glumly at the phosphorescent pinkness in his cup.

I sighed. It's tough, seeing a kid get a bad break.

I held mine out to him.

"Here," I said. "Trade."

His eyebrows shot high.

"For reals?"

"Sure. I don't mind it all that much," I lied. "And you're the one who's getting in trouble. Better make it worth it."

We swapped slushies and I took a sip of Wild Watermelon. He watched for my reaction.

"I think," I said, "that the flavor designer at the slushy company needs to spend a little more time eating watermelon." The kid nodded. I tapped my slushy cup against his. "Cheers, kid. Enjoy."

He said, "Thanks," and I said, "You're welcome," and then he said, "You want a kitten?" and I swallowed a mouthful of syrupy slush and licked my lips and wiped a bit of juice off my chin with my arm and said, "What?"

"You want a kitten?" he repeated. He pointed to where an older boy sat on the curb next to a big cardboard box. "We're giving 'em away. Want one?"

I looked out at the big, beat-up yellow school bus parked next to one of the gas pumps.

There was no way I'd be allowed to get a cat. It was a no-go for sure. I sighed.

"Well," I said, "let's go take a look, at least."

There were five kittens in that cardboard box, and when I leaned over to look in they all looked up at me with big round eyes and triangle ears and I tell you I was smitten.

"Who're you?" the older kid asked, and the younger one said, "She bought me a slushy," and the older kid held out his hand and the younger one handed it over. The older kid took a slurp and smacked his lips and nodded and handed it back. "You wanna kitten?" he asked. They were as brothers as brothers can be, those two.

I eyed the bus again and cocked an eyebrow. He was nowhere to be seen.

"Well, I guess I don't know yet. It's complicated."

Both boys nodded. They had parents. They knew how it was.

"Go ahead, pick one up," the older boy said. "Take it for a spin."

I pursed my lips. They were awfully cute, those tiny things with their wispy tails and whiskers. I thought about how I could get away with it.

The kittens mewed up at me, squealing in scratchy little squeaks. That could be a problem.

"Which one's the quietest one?"

Without a moment's pause both kids pointed out the smallest one, a gray-and-white-striped puff of fur off by itself a little ways in a corner of the box.

"Something's wrong with that one," the younger kid said. "The other ones never shut up. But that one hasn't made a peep since it was born."

"Really," I said, and narrowed my eyes in approval. "She sounds just about right, then."

"It's a boy."

"It is?"

"Check for yourself."

"No, thanks. I'll take your word for it."

I crouched there, looking at that little silent white-and-gray furball.

He looked back at me. He had a very serious look about him. Solemn, even. Like maybe he had it backward and what he thought was happening was *him* deciding whether or not to pick *me*. He was not a kitten to be trifled with.

I set my slushy on the curb and reached in and cradled that little thing in my hand as gentle as I could. A hush fell over my whole self when I felt that trembling soul in my big clumsy hand. He was all fragile-feeling bones and feathery fur and racing, frantic heartbeats.

I held him right up to my face. He looked back at me, his eyes huge and ears forward. But he didn't make a sound. He didn't meow, didn't growl, didn't squeak, didn't wiggle. We looked deep into each other's eyes, me and that kitten. My heart got a little bigger with each beat.

I tell you, something changed when that kitten and I looked at each other. Something big. Either something in the universe that had been sitting still for too long started moving again, or something that was moving finally fell still. Either way, it was *something*.

You see, I'd walked into that gas station alone. And I'd walked out of it alone. Just like I'd walked into and out of gas stations alone every day for, like, years. And maybe, right then and there, holding that kitten, is when I'd just had enough of all that aloneness. It was a quiet moment, and maybe one that anyone watching from outside my heart wouldn't even have noticed . . . but I tell you it was a big moment all the same.

The kitten yawned, a jaw-gaping yawn that showed off his sharp needle teeth and scaly gray tongue and a decent percentage of his throat.

"Yeah," I whispered. "You're the one, ain'tcha?"

"So you want 'im?"

"Yeah," I answered through a little smile that was just growing on my face. "Yeah, I want him."

It was about the truest thing I ever said.

Now, I knew I'd never get permission to keep the warm little ball of perfection I was holding in my hands. It was a "no" without a doubt, and I knew it.

I knew he wouldn't be happy when he found out. But I also knew that the thing he was always saying was "wherever your heart wants to go, go there and don't look back." And where my heart wanted to go was definitely looking back at me with eyes that were bluer than a Blue Razberry slushy.

"Who's that weirdo?" the younger kid asked his brother, and even though I was still stuck in a love-at-first-yawn eye lock with the kitten, I didn't have to look to know who they were talking about. I glanced over my shoulder anyway, 'cause I now had a contraband kitten to keep concealed.

There he was, in all his glory.

Brown jeans with more hole than jean. No shirt, no shoes—there is no doubt he would get no service. Skinny, with bony shoulders and ribs poking out all over the place. Long, shaggy hair pulled back with a bandanna. A big, bushy beard that hung down almost to his collarbones. He was scraping all the bug corpses off the bus's windshield with the little squeegee on a stick that gas stations keep by the pumps, and he was half-dancing and whistling while he did it. He looked totally Funky Fruit Punch. Which he was, so . . . again, flavored-as-advertised.

"That," I answered, lowering the kitten to my belly to keep

him out of sight, "is Rodeo." Both kids squinted up at me. "He's my dad," I added.

"That dude's your dad?"

"Yep." I lowered my face and my voice and whispered, "But don't tell him that, okay?"

Both boys nodded with their serious, syrup-stained faces. They were the kind you could trust, those brothers.

I looked back at the bus, that kitten pressed up against my T-shirt. Rodeo was doing his cleaning shuffle all around the front of the bus. If I was gonna make this kitten-in-my-hand a kitten-in-my-bus, I was gonna need help.

I looked at the little kid, who was sucking hard at his slushy and still eyeballing Rodeo.

"Could you do me a solid, kid?" He scrunched up his eyebrows at me. "A favor," I explained, and he nodded.

"You see those back windows on the bus with the curtains that got stars on 'em?"

"Yeah."

"That's my room. I need you to—"

"That's your room? Like, your *room* room?"

"Sure."

"You live on that bus?"

"Yeah. So?"

"I never knew no one who lived on an old school bus."

"Well, you can't say that anymore, can you?" I handed the kitten over to him, gentle as could be. "Here's the deal. Ain't no way Rodeo is gonna say yes to this kitten. Yet, anyway. So I'm gonna go ahead and get on and go to my room. Meet me with the kitten at my window on the other side in like a minute. Okay?"

The kid looked at his brother. His brother shrugged and nodded, the kid looked back at me.

"So me and you *both* are gonna get in trouble today, huh?"

I grinned at him.

"Guess so. But heck, if kittens and slushies aren't worth getting in trouble for, what in the world is?" I grabbed my sunglasses from where they were hanging off my T-shirt collar. They were big, huge round brown things with thick plastic frames. One dollar at a New Mexico flea market, and worth every penny. I slid them on, turning the lights down on the world. "You ready?"

"Sure."

I sauntered up to the bus, sipping at my watermelon slushy like I didn't have a care in the world.

Rodeo looked over at me when I swung open the accordion door. He was scraping at a grasshopper leg with his thumbnail, his tongue out in concentration.

"No bananas?" he asked.

"No, sir," I said with a little salute, though to be truthful I hadn't remembered to look.

"Well, shoot," Rodeo said, and then flashed me that toothy smile that I could never help but smile back at. "On to the next stop, then."

I shot him a hand pistol and climbed up the stairs into the bus, all casual and slow. I walked past the rows of seats and Rodeo's little bed and then on through our living room, past the bookshelves bolted to the wall and the couch bolted to the floor and the garden of plants growing in planters bolted under a window. Through the windows I saw the kid walking toward the back of the bus, his hand covering a little lump under his shirt, his walk as easy and smooth as my own. He didn't even look in Rodeo's direction. He was a natural, that kid.

I pushed through the curtains into my room. It was hot and stuffy back there, but once we got rolling it'd cool down. I went straight to the window and pulled the curtain to the side. There was the kid, looking up at me with his mouth open and his hands full of kitten.

I pinched the latches with both hands and slid the window down with as quiet a *clunk* as I could manage. The kid reached up and held the kitten high. It hung limp in his hand.

"Huh," I said. Even with me leaning out the window, the kitten was still a couple feet below my hand. "Hold on a sec."

I ducked back inside and looked around. I pulled my old straw cowboy hat off the hook on the wall and shook my jacket off a wire hanger and then flattened the hanger out straight. The hat had a long braided chin strap and I hooked the hanger through it, then lowered the whole thing out the window.

"Go ahead and put him in the hat," I hissed, and the kid did. Careful as I could, I pulled the hat up, kitten and all. In a jiffy I had that kitten in my hands. He looked up at me as content as can be, like riding a cowboy-hat elevator up into a school bus was just a part of his daily routine. I was liking that cat more and more every second, and I'd liked him a whole heckuva lot to begin with.

I stuck my head back out the window.

"Thanks for the slushy," the kid said.

"You're welcome. Thanks for the kitten."

The kid shrugged, which I thought was appropriate.

I heard the bus door squeak and shudder closed. A second later that big ol' diesel engine fired up and shook my room with its rumble. The kid took a step back.

"Well, see ya, kid," I said.

"See ya," he said, and walked away around the back of the bus.

There was a big box of books by my bed and I tipped it over, dumping the books onto the floor. I sat the box between my bolted-in shelf and my bolted-in bedside table and set the kitten down inside. He looked awful small and lonely in there. So I folded up an old T-shirt and stuck that and a little stuffed dinosaur in there with him. He sniffed the dinosaur, looked up at me, and then laid down with a little plop.

I looked at the pile of books on the floor next to the box, and the shiny gold title of my favorite one caught my eye: *The One and Only Ivan*. It was a sign for sure.

"Perfect," I said. I reached down and scratched the kitten's head with one fingernail. He closed his eyes, leaning into it. "Ivan," I whispered. "That's your name. Ivan. Whether you like it or not. But I hope you like it."

Ivan sure didn't look like he minded it.

"Now, I gotta make sure Rodeo doesn't get suspicious," I said. "Stay put."

Rodeo had gotten up into the driver's seat by then. He slid his own sunglasses on and tossed a handful of sunflower seeds into his mouth, shells and all. I knelt on the seat behind him and leaned over his shoulder.

"Ready to roll, Coyote?" he asked me.

"Ready as rain," I answered with a grin. "Where we going?"

He disengaged the parking brake and flicked on the radio. Freaky hippie electric guitar wailed out of the speakers.

"Only one way to find out," he said. He slapped the dusty dashboard of the bus and shouted, "You ready, Yager?" He gunned the gas pedal, making that old bus engine roar, and then he popped the clutch and we started forward with a jerk. His head bobbed to the music and his lips pursed as he worked on tonguing those seeds out of their shells. "Give me a howl, Coyote!" he hollered through his mouthful of seeds.

I threw my head back and howled, a high and happy coyote wail that echoed off the riveted metal roof. I hoped Ivan would hear me and know I was still there. And I hoped like heck he kept his mouth shut and didn't try to howl back.

All the front windows were open and the air started moving around, fluttering the pages of books and cooling us down. I lowered my head and saw the two kids out the window, sitting on the curb next to a box that was one kitten short. They were both looking at me with curious wrinkles on their forehead. The little one was back to sucking on his—*my*—Funky Fruit Punch slushy.

I shrugged at them—the most fitting gesture, I thought—and threw them a big wave. They waved back, in unison. Good kids, those two. The kind of kids you almost wouldn't mind seeing again.

We pulled out onto the highway and the engine growled as it struggled up to speed. The black ribbon of road stretched out forever before us, just like it always did. I took a sip of my slushy and nodded my head along with Rodeo's to the beat of the music.

I had a kitten. Which definitely meant I had a problem.

But, heck. I already had problems. And now I also had Ivan. And that sure seemed like an improvement either way.

CHAPTER

TWO

*O*ne day. That's how long I was able to keep little Ivan a secret from Rodeo. One measly day.

I knew I needed to play my cards just exactly right. Rodeo is probably the nicest man in the whole world, but even his kindness has its limits. He never gets mean at all, but if he ever gets to a point where his kindness starts to wear thin, he just kind of goes away. He slips back into his own mind, polite enough but distant, and there's no getting to him. I knew I had to make sure to keep Ivan where he belonged: in the warm sunshine of Rodeo's kindness, not out in the cold.

I started laying the groundwork that very first afternoon. Once we were driving for a while, I slipped back to my room and cuddled and played with Ivan for an hour or so. Eventually, though, I tore myself away from his almost unbearable cuteness. I set him in his box and he looked up at me with those ridiculously blue eyes. "I gotta go up and work on the boss," I whispered to him. "He'll love you as much as I do by the time I'm done with him."

Ivan blinked at me. He didn't look all that convinced, but we were still getting to know each other and I wasn't all that good at reading his facial expressions yet, so who knows. I gave him a goodbye scratch and ambled up to the front of the bus.

Rodeo was sitting happy behind the wheel, bobbing his head to the music. He welcomed me with a smile and I knelt there on the seat behind him, looking out the windshield and singing along to the same old songs for a while.

I was just waiting for a chance, biding my time for the right moment to start my game, when Rodeo just up and threw me an easy pitch right over the plate.

"Give me a once-upon-a-time, Coyote," he said.

I knew a perfect opportunity when I saw one.

I squinted out the window and scrunched up my mouth, trying not to look too overeager.

"Mmmkay, got one," I said, resting my chin on the seat back in front of me and closing my eyes. "Once upon a time, there was a girl."

I heard Rodeo spit a sunflower seed shell into the empty Squirt bottle in his hand. "Always a good start," he murmured.

"Yep. So, this girl was a great warrior. She traveled from kingdom to kingdom, slaying dragons and killing giants and rescuing wimpy princes. She was totally hardcore."

"Nice."

"After a while, though, she got kinda tired of all that. So she built herself a castle. Right by the ocean. She made it out of, like, driftwood from the beach."

Rodeo snorted.

"Driftwood? A *driftwood* castle?"

"Yeah," I said, narrowing my eyes at him. "Driftwood. And seashells. And barnacles. And whale bones. But *mostly* driftwood."

"All right."

"But pretty soon, the waters off the part of the coast she was on started getting called haunted. Sailors crossed themselves and prayed when they had to sail through it. Ships went out of their way to avoid it."

"Why's that?"

"I'll tell you why, Rodeo. It was 'cause of the howling and the wailing."

"Howlin' and wailin'?"

"Yessir. Like you wouldn't believe. A horrible, heartbreaking sound. The kind of sound that'd make tears spring to your eyes like you were chopping onions. Some sailors even threw themselves overboard and surrendered their souls to the deep, that sound was so sad."

"Tragic." Rodeo *tsk*ed, shaking his head.

"You got that right."

"So this girl of yours in the driftwood castle, I'm guessing she sets off to vanquish this monster?" Rodeo asked.

"No, sir. No, she did not."

"Really?"

"Nope."

"Why not, sugar pie?"

"Because *she* was the wailing monster."

He took his eyes off the road a second to shoot me a surprised look.

"She *was*? That's a heckuva twist!"

"Yep."

"Well, heck, why'd she wanna kill all them sailors?"

"She didn't. She didn't even know all that was happening. She wasn't trying to drive no one mad or crash any ships. She was just sitting in her castle, moaning and crying, screaming all her sadness out."

"What was she so sad about?"

I swallowed and paused dramatically. This was it. My chance to really plant the seed. I looked straight ahead out the window. I concentrated and brought some tears up into my eyes, made 'em burn 'til they were blurry. I was kinda surprised at how easy they came. I waited until Rodeo got curious and looked over at me.

Then I shrugged. I blinked hard, feeling his eyes on me.

"She was just lonely," I said, all soft. "She didn't have any friends. She missed her family. Even *one* friend would've made her feel happy, even a little friend. A pet, even. But she didn't have one."

I sighed and looked away.

We rumbled along for a few minutes, our tires humming on the highway blacktop.

"Well?" Rodeo said at last, his voice kinda quiet and worried. "What next? Did she get a happy ending?"

I shook my head.

"I don't know," I said after waiting a breath. "I don't know. Loneliness is a terrible thing." I let that sit there a second, then I stood up with another sigh. "I'm gonna go read for a while." And I turned and walked all slow toward my room. I didn't look back, but I knew Rodeo was sitting at the wheel, eyeing me in the rearview mirror, his face all worried and scrunched up.

It was a good thing I was walking away. Because otherwise Rodeo might've seen my smile.

So I planted that seed and I let it set there the rest of the day. I watered it from time to time with wistful sighs and downcast eyes and a kinda overall downer attitude. I could tell it was having an effect on Rodeo. I caught him looking at me a lot, all concerned and confused.

That night after the sun went down, we stopped at a grocery store for dinner. Rodeo went into the bathroom and gave me that "it'll be a while" look, so I hustled and bought some cans of cat food and a bag of kitty litter and got it all out to the bus while I had the chance. I had the pet supplies stashed in my room and was back perusing the cantaloupes in the produce section by the time Rodeo came out, scratching at his beard and none the wiser.

When we got back on the road, I slipped into my room and set up pretty good digs for little Ivan: a shoebox filled with litter in the corner, shaded by a T-shirt on a coat hanger for privacy and odor blockage; a little plastic bowl for water and one for food; and a comfy little bed in my old book box. Ivan padded around me as I set it all up, sniffing and rubbing up against me, sweet as sugar and quiet as a mime.

He seemed just as pleased as punch with his new accommodations, too. He lapped at his water and sniffed at his food and took to the litter box like a natural. I never thought I'd be so proud to see another creature squat and piddle, but darn if I didn't have to sit on my hands to keep from clapping. Once he'd done his business and scraped litter over the top, I scooped him up and laid a big kiss right between his ears. He got to purring and rubbing his wet nose against my cheek and I tell you I was just about as happy at that moment as I had ever remembered being.

Rodeo always had a healthy respect for my privacy, so as long as Ivan kept his mouth shut and I kept his litter box smell under control, I figured I could keep that cat a secret just about until I was old enough to head off to college, or at least until I thought Rodeo was ready to be open-minded and reasonable about the whole thing.

That night, I pulled Ivan's sleeping box right over snug next to my bed. He looked up at me, blinking all slow and sleepy, and yawned a big curly-tongued yawn at me.

"Goodnight, Ivan," I whispered. We were still rolling down the highway—Rodeo liked to stay up late, driving deep into the night—and my bed rocked and swayed with the rhythm of the road, lulling me to sleep like it always did. My eyes started to blink closed.

But then: *scritch scratch scritch*. My eyes snapped open.

Ivan was sitting looking up at me, eyes wide and intense. He had one paw in the air and as I watched he did it again, flexing his claws out and scraping 'em on the cardboard walls of his bedroom.

"Goodnight, Ivan," I said again, but he shifted on his little rump and scratched again, a little louder, and cocked his head sideways at me.

I knew what he wanted. It was written all across his darn adorable face.

"No," I said. "You gotta sleep in your own place, Ivan, so I can keep track of you."

Ivan just looked at me, his eyes all kinds of blue and big and sweet.

He didn't meow. He didn't have to.

Now, something you should know about Rodeo is that he's got magic in his eyes. They're so deep and gentle and *kind* that folks just kinda fall into them. Time and time again, I seen it. He's tall and hairy and clearly not what anybody would call "normal," so folks always get pretty tight and wary and downright cold when he walks up. But then he looks at them with those eyes of his, and they just thaw right out and relax into a smile and next thing you know, them and Rodeo are best friends.

Turns out my little Ivan had the same magic in his eyes that Rodeo does. You looked into 'em and whatever "no" you'd been ready to say just kinda melted into a nice easy "yes."

I blew out a breath.

"Aw, heck," I mumbled, and reached down to pick him up.

Ivan slept all nuzzled up right against my neck, purring like a little lawn mower. He whimpered and kicked a little from time to time during the night with some mysterious kitten nightmares, but I didn't mind one bit. There ain't nothing wrong with waking up here and there to smile and cuddle up tighter with something warm that you love.

But, as Rodeo says, there ain't nothing in this old world that's gonna last forever except for Twinkies and Janis Joplin's voice echoing around the universe.

I woke up to a beautiful morning, all things considered. The sky was blue through the bus windows as I blinked myself awake. I didn't know where we were exactly, but I knew it was someplace with birds, because they were singing like a choir. I stretched a full-body stretch all the way to my toes and rubbed at the sleep in my eyes. But then I jolted still and my eyes snapped wide, and that peaceful morning feeling went rushing right out of me.

Here's what I realized: I was alone.

I sat up with a jerk and whipped my head around. Ivan wasn't in my bed. He wasn't on my pillow. He wasn't in his box.

"Ivan!" I hissed. Then again, as loud as I dared: "Ivan!"

I didn't hear any padding of paws or clicking of claws or sleepy head-shaking. My room was silent except for the carrying on of the birds through the window.

There was only one place Ivan could be.

"Holy heck," I swore, looking at the curtained doorway that led to the front of the bus.

My cat had busted loose.

I jumped up out of my bed and poked my head through the doorway.

Sparkling morning sunlight was coming sideways through the windows all down the driver's side. The bus was still and quiet. There wasn't a single wayward kitten or bearded hippie to be seen.

I tiptoed down the aisle, eyes darting around, looking under and on top of and inside everything, looking for a glimpse of Ivan's gray fluff. But my seeking eyes found nothing but our same old junk.

As I got closer to the front of the bus, I heard the soft, regular sound of Rodeo's sleeping breaths and saw his bare feet sticking out the bottom of the heap of blankets he called a bed. He wasn't tossing or snoring or turning the pages of a book, and that was all good. It meant I still had a chance to avoid the catastrophe I'd awoken to.

I crept right past Rodeo's slumbering form and up to the front of the bus. The driver's seat was empty, the door firmly closed and latched. I nodded to myself.

Ivan was still on board. I just needed to find him.

I turned back toward Rodeo, ready to give the bus and its various nooks and crannies a more thorough front-to-back search.

But before I could take even the first step, my body went stiff, my eyes went wide, and my heart stopped short like a motorcycle slamming into the back of a parked semi (which I actually saw once outside of Stevenstown, Missouri . . . not a sight you're likely to forget, I promise you). I froze where I was, breathless and unblinking.

'Cause I saw Ivan.

He was sleeping, calm and peaceful as a summer morning. Curled up cute as anything, with his little tail tucked right up under his chin.

It woulda been adorable.

If he hadn't been dozing tucked up right against Rodeo's sleeping neck.

CHAPTER

THREE

I woulda gulped, but I was afraid the noise would wake Rodeo.

I breathed in, quiet and easy as I could, and breathed back out. Rodeo is a reliably heavy sleeper—I once got six grapes into his mouth before he woke up—but even I knew this was gonna be tough.

I made my way toward Rodeo's sprawled body, one silent step at a time. The floor creaked beneath me.

"Quiet, Yager," I prayed soundlessly.

I snuck to within tickling distance of Rodeo's dirty-soled feet and shot 'em a quick side-eye. Walking around barefoot in gas station parking lots doesn't do the bottoms of your feet any favors on the cleanliness front, I promise. I made a mental note to do a better job of remembering to throw on some flip-flops in the future.

I crept past his hairy toes. He was laying sideways in his blanket nest, so I was able to shuffle myself right up to his middle.

His head was thrown back, his face turned away from Ivan. His mouth was wide open, and I spied a sunflower shell stuck in his beard. Despite all that, he looked peaceful, laying there snuggling unawares with my Ivan.

Peace don't last forever, though.

I leaned awkwardly over Rodeo, pinwheeling my arms for a second to keep from toppling right onto him, which would not have been ideal. I set my jaw, concentrated on my balance, and reached out with both hands for the kitten cuddled up in my dad's neck.

But then . . . well, shoot. Then it all went to heck.

Something musta made a sound. Maybe it was my heart hammering, maybe I was breathing too loud through my nose, maybe Yager creaked under my feet. I don't know.

But, whatever it was, Rodeo's eyes fluttered open. I stood still as a statue, hoping they'd settle right back closed.

Instead, they slowly widened and focused on me. His eyebrows furrowed.

"Coyote," he said, his voice hoarse with sleep. "What are you doing?"

I was standing over him, my hands reached out toward his neck.

"Nothing," I answered.

He blinked a few times and looked me up and down, still looming like a strangler over him.

"Coyote," he said again. "What are you doing?"

"Nothing," I repeated, although to tell the truth it sounded even stupider the second time.

Rodeo cleared his throat.

At that moment, Ivan opened his eyes. He blinked at me, just like Rodeo had. My heart stopped.

He yawned, one of his molar-showing monster yawns.

His yawn was soundless, but when he yawned his whiskers brushed up against Rodeo's neck.

Rodeo twitched and raised his hand to scratch at his neck.

"No!" I shouted, leaping toward them both.

I'm willing to admit it was not the smartest thing to do.

Rodeo, understandably startled to wake up and find himself being attacked by his deranged daughter, jumped and screamed and tried to scramble away from me.

Ivan, understandably startled to wake up and find his bed suddenly screaming and kicking, did what any cat would do in that situation: He dug all ten of his razor kitten claws into the nearest object.

Which, of course, happened to be Rodeo's neck.

The results were both instantaneous and dramatic.

There was a high-pitched screeching sound that at first I thought was coming from Ivan, but then realized was actually coming out of Rodeo's mouth. He leaped to his feet with the most speed and athleticism I'd seen him muster since the time he surprised a raccoon in a campground outhouse.

Ivan, superstar kitten that he was, managed to keep his grip on Rodeo's neck through all the screeching and the leaping. Once Rodeo had shot to an upright position, Ivan decided he'd rather not be attached to a screaming, vertical hippie. He disengaged and leaped down to land on the nearby horizontal, silent couch.

There was a moment of breathless quiet; Ivan stood with his back arched and all his fur puffed out, looking about as fierce as a two-pound cotton ball could look. Rodeo stood with wide eyes and bleeding neck, panting and leaning away from Ivan like he was a king cobra about to strike. He was wearing nothing but a ratty pair of tighty-whities and a look of utter shock.

I saw my chance to take control of the situation.

"Oh," I said to Rodeo with a casual smile. "You're up!"

Rodeo blinked at me, still breathing fast through his nose, then shook his head.

"What . . . What . . . What in the . . ." He rubbed at his neck and his eyebrows shot up when he saw blood on his fingers.

"Rodeo," I said pleasantly, "this here's Ivan. Ivan, this is Rodeo."

Rodeo shook his head again.

"Who the hell is Ivan?"

Rodeo's breathing was starting to settle down a bit and his eyes looked slightly less frantic, so I figured it was a good time to forge ahead.

"Ivan is my kitten. I've been meaning to have a talk with you about him."

"You have?"

"Yes, sir. But I was waiting for a chance for you guys to be formally introduced. Which I guess is right now."

"Well, Coyote, you picked a helluva way to introduce us," Rodeo said, dabbing tenderly at his neck.

"I didn't exactly pick it, Rodeo," I pointed out in my defense, "and your screaming sure didn't help things." But Rodeo shot me a pretty clear look, so I changed course quick.

"Look, I'm sorry. I'll admit this wasn't the ideal way to bring up the subject of getting a kitten."

"You think?" Rodeo asked in a tone I thought was unnecessarily nasty.

"Easy, man," I said, holding up my hands for calm. "The eggs are already broken, so we may as well enjoy the omelet."

"Enjoy the omelet?"

"You know what I'm saying. Let's make the best of this."

"And what exactly is this?"

"This is me. Getting a pet."

Rodeo sighed and closed his eyes and started to shake his head, so I jumped in quick.

"Now, listen. I know we've had this conversation before, but this time is different. Ivan and me have really gotten to know each other over the last eighteen hours. He is unusually restrained and dignified for a cat of his age. An old soul, Rodeo. A fellow traveler." I could hear my words speeding up, the desperation seeping into my voice. "He was born for the road, and we're already fast friends. You won't even notice him, Rodeo, I promise. He won't be any bother to you, and to me he'll be . . . he'll be . . ." *Everything*, I wanted to finish, but my words cut off.

Rodeo *tsk*ed his tongue and rubbed his bearded jaw.

"Pets, Coyote," he said, shaking his head. "Come on. You know this. Pets, they're a no—"

He was gonna say it. I saw it coming a mile away. Rodeo was gonna pronounce pets a no-go, and once Rodeo decided something was a no-go, he never wavered on it.

"I need him," I cut in, before he could make it official. It wasn't something I'd planned on saying. It just came out. I knew there were plenty of fancier arguments I could make—arguments about how lonely I was, or how responsible I'd be, or how I'd take care of him all the time and all that—but in the crush of the moment, all those arguments ran away. And I was just left with three dumb little words, hanging there in the air right between Rodeo's "no" and his "go."

Rodeo stopped, his mouth hanging open. His eyes crinkled up.

"I need him," I said again, softer. There was a little break in my voice that surprised me, a tightness in my throat I wasn't expecting. A wetness to my eyes I had to blink away quick.

Rodeo looked into my swimming eyes.

"Yeah," he said. "And that's the problem, sugar. It ain't good to need things that you can lose."

"*Please*, Rodeo," I said, and I said it right into those ever-loving eyes of his.

"Aw, honey pie," he said. His voice wasn't much more than a whisper.

I didn't say anything.

He blew a big breath out through his lips.

He stepped toward me and reached up with a thumb and wiped at a tear that was tickling down my cheek. He shook his head again, but this time there was a smile hiding in his beard.

"Well," he said, and held out his hands. "Let me see the little guy."

I didn't dare let the little flutter of hope in my heart take wing. But I stooped down and scooped up Ivan—who'd calmed down back into a normal kitten shape and size.

I placed Ivan's warm little self into Rodeo's grubby hands.

Rodeo cupped him in his hands, turned him around nice and

easy, and then held the kitten up to his face. Ivan's whole precious little body nestled in one of Rodeo's palms.

Ivan sat, happy as you please, in Rodeo's hand. He took Rodeo's unblinking gaze and gave it right back to him. He didn't meow or tremble or purr or wiggle. That wasn't Ivan's way. And Rodeo didn't *oooh* or *aaah* or make kissy sounds. That wasn't Rodeo's way. Those two just stood there a minute, looking at each other.

But something must've passed between them, between that skinny kitten and the scruffy hippie.

I saw it in Rodeo's eyes. They didn't go distant. They sparkled and softened.

He blew out a resigned breath.

"Darn it, Coyote," he said, but he said it soft.

That little hope in my heart stretched its wings just a bit wider.

His eyes left Ivan's and found mine.

"We'll give him a test. Two hundred miles."

My hope started fluttering for real. Mile tests were something Rodeo and I did from time to time, trying something out: a new album to listen to, a different flavor of air freshener, whatever. It was a waiting period to see if we liked something, to see if it fit with our distinctive scene.

"A thousand miles," I countered.

"Five hundred," he said. "Final offer."

I stuck out my hand and he shook it with his free one. Ivan perched in his other hand the whole time, watching the negotiation.

"Thanks, Rodeo. You won't regret it."

"Well. We'll see about that. He wakes me up like that again, he's heading straight out the nearest window."

I grinned.

"That was quite a launch you pulled off there, old man. You darn near hit your head on the ceiling."

"It was *not* funny," he said, but I could see him fighting his own smile.

"You were shrieking like a dang car alarm," I added through a laugh.

He shook his head, but his smile broke through clear this time.

"I thought a badger had snuck on the bus and gone for my jugular," he said. "Took ten years off my life."

"Aw, it's good for you. Gives your heart some exercise."

Rodeo snorted, then narrowed his eyes appraisingly at Ivan.

"Don't get too attached, pudding pop. Five hundred miles. That's all he gets."

I reached out and took Ivan back, holding him warm against my stomach.

Rodeo wiped his hand off on his belly. Please—like Ivan had any germs Rodeo had to worry about catching.

Rodeo jerked his head toward the front of the bus.

"Write down the mileage. The sooner we can get to five hundred miles and bid this bundle of trouble farewell, the better."

I rolled my eyes.

"Put some pants on," I said. "I'm in the mood for biscuits and gravy."

CHAPTER

FOUR

Well, no surprise: I was right about just about everything. Ivan fit in with me and Rodeo like a slice of cheese between two pieces of bread.

He made himself right at home, Ivan did. He slept wherever the heck he felt like and whenever the heck he felt like it. He roamed and rambled around the bus, sniffing and investigating and generally just being adorable.

Now that he was out in the open, I gave him an official tour of his new home.

"This here is a 2003 International 3800 bus," I told Ivan, cradling him in my arms. "Her name is Yager." Once upon a time, our home had the words "VOYAGER DAY SCHOOL" painted in black on her yellow sides, but when we'd bought her, Rodeo had scratched most of those letters off to give her a new, less institutional-sounding name. She was long and sturdy-looking, with a handsome hood sticking out in front of her like the prow of a boat. Yager was *not* one of those flat-nosed buses. No, sir. Those may be all right for getting back and forth from school, but they're nothing that anybody would call a *home*.

"And this is the cockpit," I continued, holding Ivan out so he could see it good. He took a look at the driver's seat and the dashboard and the big ol' steering wheel. There was a white ceramic sculpture of a pug on the dashboard, looking out at the road before us. We called him the Dog of Positivity, and Rodeo insisted he was a sort of canine guardian angel, keeping us happy. Ivan gave him a curious sniff. Rodeo, sitting in the driver's seat, slid a snotty look at Ivan and said, "This is my zone right here, cat. Stay out of it," but I just turned and whispered into his ears, "He doesn't mean that, Ivan. You go wherever you want."

Behind the driver's seat were two rows of bus seats, the only ones that Rodeo had left in when he'd converted it to a full-time residence. Behind the second row was Rodeo's blanket pile on one side and our kitchen area on the other. We didn't have running water or anything, so it was really just a cupboard and a counter and a big cooler where we kept milk and stuff. Ivan seemed especially interested in the cupboards of food, but I kept us moving.

Next to the kitchen was our garden, which was a shelf against the window that had a bunch of tomatoes and lettuce and stuff growing in pots. I also had a couple of pots of sunflowers going, and they were looking great . . . about four feet tall and each one holding up a gorgeous, bursting yellow flower that leaned over toward the sunlight. I don't think there's about a darned thing in the whole world that's more happy and hopeful than a big blooming sunflower. Ivan, sniffing and batting at the nearest bloom, seemed to agree. He's a smart one.

Across from the garden was a big bolted-in armchair we called the Throne. I can personally vouch that it is a fantastic reading chair—soft enough to lean your head back and relax, or big enough that you can lay sideways and drape your legs over one of the arms if you feel like it. It was conveniently located next to our main bookshelves, which were always crammed full with a rotating selection of me and Rodeo's favorite books.

In front of the shelf was the couch, a giant, cushy flower-print number. It was ancient and threadbare and most of the springs had been broken since the '80s. It was hideous and monstrous and absolutely perfect. It was the kind of couch you stretch out on and then all of a sudden you wake up and it's an hour later and you never even realized you were falling asleep.

Then, of course, there was my room. I got the whole back of the bus, with the dangling curtain giving me my privacy and space. It wasn't big, but it was mine. It had room for me and my bed and a bookshelf and my clothes, and since that was all the stuff I had, that was all the space I needed.

"And that's it," I said, plopping down on the couch with Ivan. "Your new home. Whaddaya think?"

Ivan's baby blues were looking right into mine. He rubbed up against my chin and purred, which I took as a stamp of approval.

I could see pretty soon that Rodeo was getting fond of Ivan, though he sure tried to hide it from me. The first time Ivan tried to settle into Rodeo's lap while he was driving, Rodeo made a big deal about pushing him off and griping about it. Later, though, I looked up from where I was reading and saw Ivan curled up in Rodeo's lap, eyes all closed and happy, with Rodeo's dirty fingernails scratching at his head. I wanted to jump up and gloat about it, but I knew better; I'd won a battle, but it was best to hold off 'til I'd won the war.

Ivan soon found his favorite spot for when we were on the

move: He stretched out right up on the dashboard, pressed up against the windshield, basking in the sunlight and lazily looking back and forth between Rodeo singing behind the wheel and the world blurring by outside the window. Rodeo acted like he hardly noticed his new driving partner, but sitting close one morning I heard Rodeo mutter when Ivan ambled up and leaped into his spot, "Oh, there you are!" and I smiled wide but kept the little victory to myself.

Then there was this: The night before we hit five hundred miles, we were camping on a dirt road in the middle of nowhere, somewhere outside Steamboat Springs, Colorado. We'd had a fine night, singing together by a campfire with Rodeo strumming away at his guitar and me at my ukelele, soaking in the coolness of the night air and the spectacle of the stars shimmering above us. Ivan sat on my lap the whole time, dozing or blinking into the fire. When it was shut-eye time, though, I somehow lost track of him in all the in-and-out of getting our chairs and whatnot back aboard the bus . . . and like that, he was gone without a trace. I was just about sick, running all around, shouting his name, throwing all sorts of fits. Finally Rodeo got me calmed down and put me to bed, telling me he was sure Ivan'd be back by morning, once his belly got empty. I couldn't sleep, of course, but knelt on my bed with my head sticking out my bedroom window, whispering his name into the night. That's what you do, right? When someone you love is gone? You call their name out into the darkness? Then, just like that, I heard him: meowing up at the front door. My heart was a sugary burst of fireworks and I bolted for the front, but stopped short at my doorway curtain.

'Cause I saw that Rodeo had beat me there. The bus was dark except for the small yellow glow of Rodeo's bedside lamp. He already had the door open, and I saw his head disappear as he bent down to pick up Ivan. He shut the door and stepped up by the steering wheel and I saw that he was holding Ivan close, tight up against his chest, and then he dropped his mouth to kiss the top of Ivan's head. Then, just barely across that dark distance, I heard Rodeo murmur, "Welcome back, compadre. You had us worried sick, buddy." Rodeo gave him another kiss and set him down gentle and I slipped back behind my curtain. I was smiling to myself in the shadows. *Us.* Huh. Now, that "us" was really pretty darn interesting. Yessiree, it was. The thing was won and I knew it right then, and it was only a matter of waiting for the odometer to make it official. A minute later Ivan poked his nose through the curtain and then the rest of him followed and he jumped up and joined me on my bed. I grinned at him and scratched his stupid wandering-away-and-worrying-me-sick little head. Ivan, guiltless and unapologetic as a cash-flush con man, closed his eyes and leaned into my fingers. "Well, Ivan," I whispered, "I think you did it. I think you found yourself a home."

And, sure enough, he had.

Because this was how it all played out. We rolled right through Ivan's five-hundred-mile moment. And we didn't say a darned thing. We just kept rolling, Ivan right there with us, and that's just how it was.

We both knew it, of course. I'd pointed it out that morning, when we'd started driving.

"Four hundred miles, Rodeo," I'd said. "Ivan'll hit five hundred this afternoon, likely."

Rodeo sipped from his Styrofoam cup of coffee.

"Mmmm" was all he said, blinking all slow and acting sleepy like it wasn't a big freaking deal.

We'd taken our time that day, not really racking up the miles. Stopped for a long lunch, dawdled in a tree-shaded park, pulled over for a swim in a muddy river.

But then, well after lunch and closer to dinner, it happened. The odometer ticked right over the number we both knew was exactly five hundred bigger than it had been when we'd had that early-morning bleeding-neck conversation. It was a number I'll remember to my dying day: 248,845. I was not-so-casually leaning over Rodeo's seat when that last little white five rolled onto the meter, then held my breath for Ivan's last mile, eyeing that digit 'til my eyes burned from not blinking, and then it did it: ticked from five to a beautiful six. That was it. Ivan had ridden with us for five hundred miles.

I looked out of the side of my eye at Rodeo, who was still sitting there all nonchalant, one hand draped over the steering wheel, the other picking at something between his teeth.

"Rodeo?"

"Mmm?"

I opened my mouth, ready to just flat-out ask, but then I reined myself in. Rodeo was well aware we'd hit five hundred. He was playing possum, and I knew from experience that Rodeo was sometimes best approached in a sideways direction.

I cracked my knuckles and looked away, playing my own casualness against his.

"Give me a once-upon-a-time," I said lightly.

I saw him hide a smile in his beard.

"All right. Let's see." He screwed up his eyes in thought and took a swig of root beer. Then he nodded and switched off the radio. "Okay, honeycake. Here we go. Once upon a time, there was a crow and a sparrow. The sparrow was a pretty little thing, with bright eyes and a sweet nature and the prettiest song you ever heard. The crow, though, he was an ornery old cuss. He'd lost one eye, and he was missing feathers here and there, and he had a wing that was busted and all bent, so he couldn't fly. He just hung around in their old tree, singing with the sparrow and eating whatever measly bugs he could find in the branches. But they were tight, these two, and through wind and rain and, heck, even *hurricanes*, those two stuck together."

Rodeo took another swallow of his root beer, and Ivan chose that opportune moment to come toddling up with a yawn and hop up on Rodeo's lap. Rodeo didn't even look down, but he scratched gruffly at Ivan's head and kept talking and didn't shoo him down.

"So one day, old Crow sees something down there on the ground under the tree. It's . . . It's . . . a french fry."

"A french fry?" I asked dubiously.

"Yes, a french fry. Dropped, no doubt, by some careless girl with bad habits such as dropping french fries and interrupting stories. So, old Crow decides to go get this wayward fry. But he can't fly, right? So he hops down, branch to branch, and then finally that last long drop to the earth, and he lands with one helluva clumsy crash. But he grabs it and looks up and realizes: 'Well, crap, I shoulda thought that through.' He's feeling pretty hopeless down there, flightless and stranded, but then who shows up?"

"A hungry fox?" I guessed.

"No. It ain't that gruesome a story. It's Sparrow, of course. And that sparrow? Well, she was something else. All heart, that one. And she got right up under big ol' crotchety, broken-winged Crow and she beat her wings something fierce and at first nothing happened, but then Crow, he started flapping his wings, too—best he could, anyway—and with the help of that remarkable little sparrow, darned if that old crow didn't fly again for the first time in a long time, right up into the branches of that tree. And there they sat, the crow and the sparrow, side by side, up in the bright blue sky where they belonged, sharing that french fry. The end."

I nodded thoughtfully.

"Not bad, Rodeo. Not bad. That crow must've sure loved french fries, though."

Rodeo shook his head.

"Nah," he said, still scratching at Ivan's head. "He didn't at all, really."

"What? Then why'd he flop all the way down to the ground to get one?"

Rodeo looked down at the perfect kitten in his lap, then back out at the highway winding its way through Colorado pine trees.

"'Cause the *sparrow* loved french fries, Coyote. And the crow loved the sparrow."

I smiled then, just to myself, and sat back in my seat and blew out a big sigh I'd been kinda holding in since that odometer had ticked over to that magic number.

That Rodeo, he's something else. From time to time he can be darn near clever and poetic in spite of himself.

CHAPTER

FIVE

We stayed that night in a campground at a place called Turquoise Lake, in Colorado. It was a real, honest-to-goodness campground, with numbered camping spots and picnic tables and crusty metal fire pits.

The second we came to a stop in an empty camping spot I was out the door, Ivan in my arms, ready to go exploring. I wandered down to the lake, sniffing at the smells of cooking hot dogs and toasting marshmallows, dodging the kids zipping around on bikes.

I steered clear of the kid-crowded gravelly beach full of splashing swimmers, knowing Ivan wouldn't appreciate all that ruckus and horseplay. Instead, I found a little quiet spot off by itself, where the lake lapped up under the shade of some trees. I kicked off my flip-flops, sat down on a log, and slipped my feet into the coolness of the water. Ivan wriggled out of my hands and stepped with cautious paws along the log, bobbing his head curiously at the water.

"Oh. My. God."

The voice made me just about jump out of my skin. I jerked back so fast I nearly tumbled backward off the log. It rocked underneath me, and Ivan crouched low, digging his claws into the wood.

Once we were both steady, I looked up to where the words had come from.

There was a girl about my own age, sitting up in the tree above us. She was resting in the crook of two branches, a book held open on one knee. She had round horn-rimmed glasses and a look of utter seriousness on her face.

"Sorry if I scared you," she said. "But that is the cutest kitten. I. Have. Ever. Seen."

I smiled up at her.

"That's probably true," I said back. "They don't come much cuter."

"Can I hold him?" she asked, and I shrugged and nodded and she closed her book with a snap and hopped right down to join us. I scooped up Ivan and held him out to her. She tossed her book back into the bushes and took Ivan nice and gently, just like you oughta.

She spun him around so they were facing each other. Ivan hung limp in her hands, looking her right back in her wide eyes.

"Oh, man," she breathed. "I'm, like, *dying* from the cuteness. What's his name?"

"Ivan," I answered. "After the book. You know, *The One and Only Ivan*?"

Her eyes shot sideways to me.

"Are you kidding me? That's, like, my favorite book."

"Me, too!" I said, warming right up to that girl. There's

nothing like a good book for bringing folks together. I jutted my chin at her book lying in the bushes.

"Whatcha reading now?" I asked her, and she answered, "*Anne of Green Gables*," and I said, "Oh, lord, I *love Anne of Green Gables*!" and she grinned at me and cocked her head and said, "Wanna come to our camper for dinner? We're having tofu sausages," and then she saw my are-you-serious face and she assured me, "They're way better than they sound . . . Pretty yummy, actually," and I shrugged and said, "Sure," and then I asked, "Can I bring Ivan?" and she smiled and said, "You *better*!" and I laughed and stood up and we headed off together and that was that.

Sometimes making friends is tough, and sometimes it's as simple as finding someone who loves books and kittens as much as you do.

The girl's name was Fiona, and even though she gave me a look when I told her I went by Coyote, she didn't make a big deal out of it—always a good sign in a human being.

We spent the afternoon mostly at her family's site, playing with Ivan and comparing favorite books and avoiding her little brothers.

Her family was her mom and her dad and her two little brothers, Alex and Avery, who were kinda annoying but mostly cute, and Fiona was right: Tofu sausages, if you put enough ketchup on 'em, aren't half-bad.

After dinner her dad took the boys down to the lake to burn off some energy, and it was just me and Fiona, sitting around the table and talking. Fiona's mom puttered around, tidying up the campsite and jumping into the conversation from time to time. It felt like a family. Like a sister and a mom. I liked it. I wouldn't have been willing to admit right then that it felt like that, or that I liked it—but it did, and I did.

Fiona and me mostly just gabbed about books, but we also covered other important topics like favorite pizza toppings, the worst songs on the radio, and national politics. Ivan scampered around us, sniffing for food and batting at anything that caught his eye.

I was having a fine time, right up until Fiona heaved a big yawn and griped, "Man, I'm tired. Avery and Alex *claim* to be afraid of the dark whenever we're camping and they kept the flashlight on practically all night. So annoying."

"I know all about that," I said, pulling Ivan back from the bag of marshmallows he was sniffing. I guess I was all swept up in the relaxed family vibe they were throwing off, 'cause I kept talking without even thinking about it. "My sisters used to always keep the hall light on and—"

But then I caught myself. And I stopped quick and tried to think of something to change the subject, but it was too late.

"I didn't know you had sisters!" Fiona's mom cut in with a smile. "Are they here camping with you?"

"No, ma'am," I whispered, shooting a careful look up at our campsite. I squeezed Ivan into a tight hug and kissed his head before letting him go.

"Where are they?"

I swallowed. Looked up toward Rodeo and our bus. I knew I shouldn't answer. I knew I should come up with an excuse and make a gracious exit. But there was no way Rodeo would be able to hear me. And maybe I didn't *want* to leave my new friend and her nice mom. There's nothing wrong with that, right?

So I answered her. With the truth. But it came out stuttery. And still at a whisper.

"They're . . . They're dead, ma'am. They were killed in a car accident five years ago."

I could feel Fiona and her mom's eyes on me but I kept mine on Ivan, waiting for the night to slide back into the nice, easy normal it had been before. Come on, Coyote—as if.

"Oh, dear. Oh, I'm . . . so sorry. That's just awful. How . . . awful."

I wanted to say something breezy and light and I even opened my mouth, but for once I came up short.

Out of the corner of my eye I saw her mom put her hands on Fiona's shoulders, pulling her close in a little from-behind hug that made me sort of ache in a weird, quiet way.

"I just can't imagine," her mom said, her voice faltering. "If something ever happened to Fiona or the boys, I'd just . . . Well, I don't even know. I can't imagine how your mother dealt with such a loss."

I flicked a ball of tinfoil, sending it skittering off the table. Ivan scrambled after it in hot pursuit. I kept my eyes down, on Ivan.

"Well, then, I guess she was lucky, ma'am. She died in the accident, too, so she didn't have anything to deal with. I suppose the loss was all me and my dad's."

There was another silence, stiff and heavy. I wished Fiona would say something. I could feel her looking at me still, wordless, and I didn't like it.

I ain't broken. And I ain't fragile. And that's that.

Finally, I managed to swallow down whatever feelings had gotten stuck in my craw.

I brought my eyes up, wide and daring and ready, to meet Fiona's and flashed her a smile.

"Hey, wanna come see our site?" I asked.

Fiona was biting her bottom lip, but she raised her eyebrows and gave me an eager nod.

"Where is your family staying, honey?" her mom asked, and her voice was different than it had been all night and I was ready to get out of there, away from her careful voice and sympathetic eyes.

"We're just three spots up. The end spot up by the campground host."

Her mom's eyebrows shot up.

"That big yellow school bus? That's *your* camper? How hilarious!"

I wasn't exactly sure what was so hilarious about it, but I nodded anyway.

"Yes, ma'am. That there's Yager. Built to carry up to fifty-six children and a driver, but we've retrofitted her, of course, and taken out most of the seats."

"That is just so . . . *interesting*," her mom said. "What an idea! Do you camp in it often?"

I shrugged.

"Mostly during the summer. The rest of the year we usually just pull off and park in a parking lot when it's bedtime."

Her mom's smile dimmed noticeably.

"You mean, you . . . you *live* in that bus? All the time?"

"Yes, ma'am. Have for the last five years."

"You don't . . . have a home?"

I frowned.

"Of course we do. It's parked right up there."

"Oh. Yes. Well." She cleared her throat. "So it's just you and your dad, living on the bus?"

"And Ivan," I said, holding him up with a smile.

"Of course," she said back, but her smile looked pretty thin at the edges and her voice was more careful than ever. She stretched her neck a bit, looking up toward our site. "Is that your dad there? Up on the table?"

I stood up, and sure enough there was Rodeo, sitting up top of the picnic table, strumming away at his guitar. He was shirtless, naturally, and he'd untied his hair from the sloppy braid he'd had it in all day, so it was poofed out all wild and frizzy around his head.

"Yes, ma'am," I said, setting Ivan on my shoulder. "But don't tell him that." I looked away from her frown, down to Fiona. "Come on, I'll show you my library."

Fiona started to stand up, but her mom still had her in that backwards hug and she kept her hands on her shoulders, holding her down.

"Actually, hon, it's pretty late. Time to start getting ready for bed, I think."

Fiona scowled.

"What? Come on, Mom! It's not even dark yet!"

"I'm sorry," her mom said firmly, then looked at me. "But maybe you could come down and join us for lunch tomorrow?"

I knew the game. I'd seen how she'd looked at Rodeo, and I knew how he probably looked to her. It wasn't her fault, not really. She hadn't met him yet, hadn't gotten close enough to look into his eyes. She didn't know that if she actually did meet him, Rodeo'd probably become one of her very favorite people. I didn't hold it against her. None of us knows what we don't know, I guess.

"Thank you for having me for dinner," I said, and I gave her a real smile, too.

"Wanna swim tomorrow morning?" Fiona asked.

Now, here's the thing: I knew I wouldn't be doing any swimming in the morning. Rodeo had his heart set on some eastern Carolina barbecue, and we were making tracks that way as fast as we could. We'd be pulling out the next day before sunrise, when Fiona and her family would still be asleep.

But here's another thing: I know goodbyes. And I hate goodbyes. The best kind of goodbye is the kind you don't even say.

So I smiled at Fiona and gave her a big nod.

"Absolutely."

She grinned at me.

"Awesome. Come down after breakfast."

"You got it. See you then."

I thanked her mom again and gave Fiona a hug and then walked off up the road. And that right there was the perfect goodbye in my book. Easy-cheesy.

I walked back up to my freak dad and our hilarious, horrifying home and I didn't have downcast eyes or any sort of heavy heart. Nope. It was all right. It was all right. There was nothing to cry about. There was *nothing* to cry about.

Sure, I woulda liked to have had another day there. Sure, I woulda liked to hang out with Fiona and talk about books and share secrets and build forts. Sure. But that didn't matter. We always kept moving, Rodeo and me. That's the way it was. That's the way it'd been for years. That's the way it was gonna be always, I thought. That's the way it *had* to be, I thought.

I had no way of knowing right then that it was all about to change. In a huge way.

CHAPTER
SIX

It was weeks later that it happened, and hundreds of miles away.

It all started at three o'clock in the afternoon on a Saturday, which I know for sure because I call my grandma every Saturday at noon, Pacific time zone, no matter what. Rain or shine, no matter what middle-of-nowhere place we happen to be at, I call her and we chat.

Now, Rodeo wants nothing to do with cell phones and our bus don't exactly work with a landline, so obviously I have to be the one to call her. Which means that every Saturday around eleven o'clock I start keeping my eyes peeled for a pay phone. Since everyone's got a cell phone in their pocket these days, pay phones are pretty tough to find. You have to find *just* the right kind of gas station—usually an old one with flickering lights and a wooden counter and dusty cans of chili on the shelves. If there's no pay phone to be found, then I gotta start asking strangers if I can borrow their cell phone. It's not as tough as you might think, if you pick the right kind of person. Find an old lady with a nice face and smile wrinkles all around her mouth and ask her if you could please borrow her phone to call your grandma, it's a yes darn near every time. Say "excuse me" and "ma'am" and it's practically a guarantee. They just about fall all over themselves trying to snatch their phone outta their big ol' purse, and half the time they end up showing you pictures of *their* grandkids.

That's what I did on that Saturday when everything started going crazy. We'd driven late the night before and I'd just reluctantly woken up from an afternoon nap, so I was dead on my feet and yawning when I managed to find a woman with a cell phone she'd let me use.

"Hi, Grandma!" I said, plenty loud so the lady who'd loaned me the phone would know I wasn't scamming her.

"Hello, honey!" my grandma answered, sweet as an oatmeal cookie. "Oh, it's so good to hear your voice!" It was the same thing she said every Saturday, but it always gave me a happy little tingle.

"Where are you this week?" she asked.

"Ummm . . . Hold on a sec." I covered the phone with my hand and asked the phone lady, "Excuse me, ma'am. Where are we right now?"

"You're outside of Naples, dear," the woman answered with a nod and a face-wrinkling smile.

"Uh-huh. That's Florida, right?" Last time I'd been paying attention we'd been in Alabama, so it was a fair question.

Her smile flickered a bit and her eyebrows furrowed.

"Of course."

"Thanks," I mouthed, then turned around to get a little privacy.

"Naples, Florida," I told Grandma.

"How is it?"

"Hot," I answered. I looked around. "This gas station has showers, which is nice. Rodeo *really* needed one."

"Hmm. And how is your dad doing?"

"*Rodeo* is doing all right," I answered, gentle but firm. I love my grandma something fierce, but she refused to call Rodeo "Rodeo," and not calling someone what they want to be called seems fairly indecent to me. "Well, just as all right as he always is."

"Um-hmm," my grandma said. She knew Rodeo, so she knew what I meant. "And how's little Ivan?"

"Not so little!" I said. I'd taken to sending pictures of Ivan to Grandma from time to time, like postcards. "He's grown a ton since the last you saw. He's not hardly a kitten anymore at all. He's tall and slender and regal and all kinds of smart. You'd love him."

Grandma laughed softly in my ear.

"Yes, I'm sure I would, dear. Maybe someday you could come back this way and I'll get a chance to meet him."

It's what she said almost every Saturday, and just like every Saturday I had to kind of dodge it. She knew as well as I did that that'd never happen.

"Yeah, maybe. For now, though, I'll take another picture and get it in the mail to you tomorrow."

My grandma sighed—she didn't even try to hide it—and said, "All right, dear. That would be lovely. I do miss you, though, sweetie, so much."

She said that every Saturday, too. Her voice was getting that familiar sad, wistful sort of flavor it always did, so I knew it was time to wrap it up.

I took a steadying breath and blinked a few times, then rolled my eyes. Grandmas can be so emotional sometimes.

"Well, I better let you go, Grandma. It's hot as Hades here, and I know Rodeo's eager to get moving so we can roll down the windows and cool off a bit."

"All right, baby. Be sure and send me that picture of Ivan, now."

"I will," I said, stepping back toward the old lady waiting patiently for her phone.

"Oh, wait, honey," Grandma said quickly. I thought she was just trying to keep me on the line, and I didn't mind that one bit. "I've got some kind of sad news about your neighborhood."

"My neighborhood?" After years of driving around so aimlessly, it sounded weird to think of a neighborhood as mine. It sounded weird to think of *anything* as mine except for a bus, a bearded weirdo, and now an exceptional cat.

"Yeah. Remember that little park at the end of the block?"

"Of course." It'd been five years since I'd seen it, but I didn't even have to close my eyes to picture it, with its picnic tables and rusty old swing set and, most of all, the corner of it that was all wooded and overgrown and wild-looking.

"Well, I'm afraid it's going away, dear," Grandma said with a sad click of her tongue.

Everything stopped. Everything inside me, everything outside me. My eyes locked on the cigarette butt I'd been eyeing, still smoking on the hot asphalt by my bare feet. My lungs caught in mid-breath. My fingers froze on the phone, clutching it in a death grip. I forgot about the old lady watching and pretending not to listen in, blurred out the sights around me.

"What?" My question came out as a raspy croak.

"They're taking it out, the whole thing," she said, her voice regretful but casual, like it was no big deal, like it wasn't the worst thing I'd heard in maybe five years. "They're putting in a new intersection, doing some sort of street expansion. There are so many new houses since you've left, so much more traffic." Her voice droned on while my mouth went dry as day-old powdered doughnuts.

"All of it?" I managed to ask, thinking of that wild little forest in the far corner, that green-shadowed bit of wilderness that held secrets and memories and magic.

"Yes, I'm afraid so."

"When?" I choked out.

Grandma sighed.

"Next week. They've already got it all roped off, with the bull-dozers and whatnot parked and waiting. They put signs up, giving notice. They're tearing it all out on Wednesday."

"Wednesday?!"

Grandma paused a beat. I think she was a bit startled by my panicked shout, but I wasn't in any state to be all that tactful or diplomatic.

"Yes, dear. Are you all right?"

"They can't do that."

Grandma paused again.

"Well, they *can*, dear. No one's that happy about it, but it *is* city property and the city *is* growing, so—"

"I'm coming back," I said, and I'm not sure which one of us was more surprised by my words.

There was another beat of silence, and in that pause all the sounds around me came rushing back in, the cars and doors and brakes and voices, but I didn't care. My eyes rose from the cigarette to Rodeo sitting on the steps of the bus about fifty feet away, happily scarfing down a banana and petting Ivan on his lap. I knew exactly, precisely what he would say, but I didn't care about that, either. My brain unfroze and for a second I thought about where we were, in Florida, and where that park was, way up in Washington State, and I calculated the miles in between and the hours between then and Wednesday and I didn't care about that, either.

All that happened in the time it took my grandma to suck in a quick, sharp gasp.

"What? What did you say, dear?" Her voice was surprised and startled and colored just here and there with something I hadn't heard in it in quite a while: happiness.

I took in a lungful of air and blew it out through flared nostrils. I always flare my nostrils when I'm determined or terrified, so I flared them double right then in that parking lot. I looked down and stomped out the smoldering cigarette with the sole of my bare foot.

"I said I'm coming back," I said, looking back to poor unsuspecting Rodeo sitting there with my cat.

Then I said something I hadn't said in over five years.

"I'm coming home."

CHAPTER
SEVEN

*H*ere's a once-upon-a-time for you.

Once upon a time, there were three girls. Sisters.

Once upon a time, there was a mom.

And, once upon a time, there was a box.

"It's a memory box," the mom had said. And the three girls and the mom had filled it. With pictures. With notes. With letters. With memories and locks of hair and little treasures. Little pieces of themselves and little pieces of each other and little pieces of their life together.

And then, together, they'd buried that box. They'd buried it under the roots of a tree in a shady, wild corner of a park, and they'd put a big stone on top to mark it and to keep it safe.

"We'll come back," the mom had said, "years from now. And we'll dig it back up. Together."

And they'd all promised, all three sisters and one mom, had promised to come back for the box of memories. They'd grinned at each other through the spring sunshine and held up their hands and swore in solemn whispers that, no matter what, they'd come back for that box.

And then, once upon a time that was only a few days after that box was buried, everything came apart. In one terrible moment

of squealing tires and shattering glass, everything came apart.
And instead of three sisters and one mom, there was just one girl.

One girl, mostly alone and completely heartbroken.

A sister without any sisters. A daughter without a mom.

But a girl with a memory.

And a girl with a promise.

A promise she would do anything to keep.

CHAPTER

EIGHT

I squinted across the parking lot at Rodeo, sitting innocent and unawares on Yager's steps.

I chewed my lip to the point of hurting. This was gonna be tough. Come on, Coyote—this was gonna be darn near impossible.

For Rodeo, going home was a set-in-stone, hard-as-dried-concrete no-go. We hadn't been back since we'd left five years before. We hadn't *talked* about it or even mentioned it in all that time. We weren't allowed to. Just like we weren't allowed to talk about my mom, or my sisters. Couldn't say their names. Not ever. They were ghosts, and they were ghosts we weren't allowed to look at.

So if I waltzed up to Rodeo and told him I wanted to go back home to dig up a memory box of my mom and sisters, we'd get to no so fast I'd get a sore neck.

I was gonna have to play this one just right.

Now, I was pretty good at playing Rodeo. I'd been doing it for years. But he was a tricky bird to play. You *could* say that learning to play Rodeo was like learning to play a guitar, if the guitar had thirteen strings instead of six and three of them were out of tune and two of them were yarn and one of them was wired to an electric fence. He's a handful, is what I'm saying. And the tune I was gonna have to play wasn't anything simple like "Mary Had a Little Lamb."

I looked at him. I swallowed. I considered. I chewed my lip a bit more.

I couldn't just have my grandma dig up the box. There were, like, thirty trees in the corner of that park. I couldn't ask my grandma to go digging holes under thirty trees in August. I had no way of describing which one it was to her . . . I'd have to be back there, looking around, to have any chance of even finding it myself. Plus, it was *my* box. My memories. Shouldn't I be the one to save it?

So, I absolutely one hundred percent needed to get to Washington State. Rodeo absolutely one hundred percent would refuse to take me. It was a puzzler.

Then it hit me. Rodeo absolutely one hundred percent would not take me *on purpose*. I just had to get him to take me to Washington State without him knowing he was doing it.

My pulse bumped up a notch. Now *that* . . . *that* I might be able to do.

I ran through the options in my head. Pictured the map, dredged up some memories, went back through the files in my brain.

Then, I smiled. Small and quick.

"Yep, Coyote," I murmured to myself. "That just might work."

I put on my most casual of faces and ambled over to Rodeo.

He popped the last bit of banana in his mouth and flashed a mushy yellow grin at me.

"You ready to go, pretty bird?"

"Whenever," I shrugged, cool as anything. I stretched, looked up at the Florida sun, rubbed my stomach. "I'm hungry."

"Yup. 'Bout that time. What sounds good?"

I looked at the ground, then up at the clouds, my lips pursed in a perfect portrayal of thoughtful consideration. Then I snapped my fingers.

"I got it. I know *exactly* what I want."

"Lay it on me."

I squinted at him, screwed up my mouth, nodded.

"Yep. I'm sure of it. Only one thing I want."

Rodeo's eyes darted to the side, then back to me.

"Oooookay. And it is . . . ?"

"A pork chop sandwich."

Rodeo blinked at me. Then he peered at the parking lot world around us.

"I don't know, little pigeon. I don't think any place around here will have—"

"No, Rodeo. I don't just mean I want *a* pork chop sandwich. I mean I want *the* pork chop sandwich."

"You mean . . ."

"That's right, old man. I want *the* pork chop sandwich. From Pork Chop John's Sandwich Shop. In Butte, Montana." A lot of people don't know it, but a pork chop sandwich is one of the world's perfect foods. And a lot of people also don't know it, but the world's best pork chop sandwiches are in Butte, Montana. And even more folks don't know it, but the best place in Butte, Montana, to get a pork chop sandwich is a little place called Pork

Chop John's Sandwich Shop. I knew it, though. And so did Rodeo. I looked him right in his eyes. "I just had myself a Dead Dream."

Now, if any normal folks had heard me say those words, they might've been concerned. But Rodeo . . . he wasn't normal folks. When I told him I'd had a Dead Dream, he grinned at me, wide and bright.

Dead Dreams were a thing for us. It was an acronym. When one of us—and let's be honest, it was usually Rodeo—got a strong, undeniable hankering for something and it just couldn't wait, we called it a D.E.A.D. Dream, a "Drop Everything and Drive" Dream. Didn't matter where we were. Didn't matter what we wanted, or how far away it was. Rodeo loved 'em. He'd had a D.E.A.D. Dream once for a fish taco from a specific taco truck he loved in San Diego. We were in North Dakota at the time. Didn't matter. There were some songs sung and a lot of coffee drunk and a ton of miles covered and three days later ol' Rodeo was noshing that taco and rolling his eyes with pleasure. "Was the taco worth the drive?" I'd asked him, and he'd wiped some taco juice off his chin and said through a mouthful, "It ain't about the taco being worth the drive, woodchuck; the question is, was the drive worth the taco?" I had no idea what he'd meant, but that's Rodeo for you.

So when I told him in that Florida parking lot that I had a Dead Dream for a pork chop sandwich in Montana, Rodeo was too excited to notice it was a bald-faced lie.

"You calling it?" he said, jumping to his feet. "For reals?"

"Cross my heart," I said, and he held up his hand for a high five and I gave him a good hard one and he threw back his head and *yeehaw*ed and then said, "Well, heck, let's hit the road, then, sugar bun," and spun on his heels and climbed up onto Yager.

I stood there for a beat or two. The fake smile I'd plastered on my face went stale and rotted away.

I'd gotten us started. If I could get us to Montana, that was most of the way to where I really needed to get. As long as Rodeo never got a whiff of my real dream, I could get us most of the way there. But if he ever did figure it out, he was gonna hit the brakes fast and forever.

I took a breath. Blew it out. Flexed my fingers.

"You got this, Coyote," I whispered. "Piece of cake."

But it wasn't. And I knew it, even as I put that smile back on and climbed up onto the rumbling bus.

I had to get myself, and a bus, and my dad, all the way across the country in less than four days. And I had to do it without my dad noticing.

CHAPTER
NINE

I spent the next hour or so on the couch, hunched over our wrinkled and crinkled old highway atlas. I traced my fingers over highways, checked distances, calculated miles, estimated drive times. Ivan sat beside me, switching back and forth between dozing off and batting at the pencil I was scratching notes with.

We *could* make it.

Using some old dental floss as a tape measure, I added up the miles.

"Three thousand six hundred miles, more or less," I told Ivan. He yawned at me. I agreed. It was doable. "If we say an average of sixty miles an hour, that's a mile a minute. Three thousand six hundred minutes. That would be, let's see . . ." I did the long division, just like Rodeo taught me out of the old textbooks we used for my homeschooling. "Sixty hours. There are . . . ninety-six hours in four days. That gives us thirty-six extra hours for sleeping and eating and stuff. We can make it. Just in time."

I gnawed on the crumbly remains of the pencil's eraser. Yawned a big ol' I-was-awake-most-of-the-night yawn. Looked at Rodeo, up behind the wheel.

"I just gotta keep him driving. And, of course, completely unaware of where we're going."

I closed the atlas. Tucked my notes into the pages of the book I was reading.

"Hey!" I called out to the front of the bus. "How you doing? Need anything?"

"Just peachy, prickly pear! I can almost smell that pork chop sandwich!"

"All righty. You let me know if you need any company!"

I leaned back into the comfy-ness of the couch cushions. I knew I should go up and get to gabbing with Rodeo, but my heart was all aswirl. I hadn't thought about that box for . . . shoot, I didn't know, *years*.

Ivan stepped onto my lap, turned a few times, and then settled in. His warmth was calming.

I closed my eyes, and then I gulped, and then I let the memories play behind my eyelids. I wasn't supposed to. *There ain't no use in looking back, Coyote*, Rodeo always said. He used to be able to tell when I thought about them—my mom and my sisters. I'd get quiet, I'd get sad. He'd shake his head, his eyes all watery. *No, baby. Don't go back there. Your happiness is here, now. You gotta leave all that behind.* But I never could, the way that he could. I just got better at hiding it. Better at looking at those forbidden memories in secret.

And I'd thought that was enough. That I could hold them in my heart, tucked away behind my eyes, and it'd be enough. But that had all changed when my grandma told me about the park. It changed when I remembered that day years ago, and the box, and the promise. Secret memories just weren't enough anymore. They never had been, maybe. But now I knew it.

At some point, without even realizing it was happening, I drifted off into sleep.

I dreamed about warm hands soft in mine, and shoulders touching, and whispered promises, and a family waiting for me to come home.

I woke up with a start. Not quite an oh-my-god-my-secret-kitten-is-gone-and-my-crazy-dad-is-gonna-find-him kind of start, but close. I didn't know how long I'd been asleep. It felt like evening and the light was kinda gray and it smelled a little like rain, but I wasn't worried about dim light or precipitation. I was worried about the fact that the bus I was lying in wasn't moving.

I jumped up.

Rodeo was sprawled in his bed, bare feet sticking out of the blankets. The secondhand clock we had hanging above the windshield said seven o'clock. We'd only made it four hours before the lazybones decided to take a break. I kicked one of his grubby feet. Not mean, just urgent.

There wasn't much of a reaction, so I bent down and grabbed his foot and shook it like a dog killing a snake.

Rodeo's head shot up, looking . . . well, rather pissed off.

"What are you doing, Coyote?" His voice was thick with sleep and confusion.

"Excuse me?" I asked. "What do you think *you're* doing?"

He blinked at me, looked down at his blanket-covered body, then back up at me.

"Sleeping."

"Exactly. And we got miles to cover, papa bear. Get your butt up."

"Coyote," he started, and it was generally never a good thing when he started a conversation with my name and then a pause. "I drove for, like, twelve hours last night. That kinda thing can make a fella tired, you know. I have to sleep sometime, kid. This Dead Dream turns into a nightmare pretty quick if I fall asleep behind the wheel and we slam into a highway overpass. And unless you got a driver's license, honeybear, this bus is gonna have to stop moving when I do. Now leave me be. Those pork chop sandwiches aren't going anywhere."

He rolled over, pulling the blanket dramatically over his head.

I cursed myself silently. I never should've let myself fall asleep.

I craned my neck, looking out the windows.

"Where are we?" I asked. When there was no answer, I kicked at the blanket and asked again. "Where are we?"

The blanket growled.

"*I* am in bed. *You* are standing over me shrieking like a damn harpy. That's where we are."

"No, like where are we *actually*?"

The blanket blew out a sigh.

"Florida, still. Tampa, I think."

"We're still in Florida?!"

"Yes. Good night."

I stood there looking down at the grumpy lump, chewing on my lip. I squinted out the windows and saw a gas station just up the road with a little diner attached.

"I'm going out," I announced.

"Thank god."

"When I get back, we're leaving."

"When you get back, the door's gonna be locked."

I rolled my eyes. Like I didn't know how to break into Yager.

I grabbed our atlas and a wad of cash from our money box by the garden and slipped into my flip-flops. Ivan was curled up dozing on the dashboard and I gave him a quick head scratch on my way out the door.

I wasn't in the mood for sitting around and waiting, but there's something about the smell of hamburgers and french fries that'll make a soul feel a little more all right about settling for a bit. I made sure to grab a seat by the window so I could see Yager, then took a gander at the menu. The diner was small, but they knew what they were doing. They had all the right things on the menu and the food came out quick, hot and salty. I popped a salty fry in my mouth and considered my problem.

As irritating as it was, Rodeo had a point; he probably was gonna have to sleep from time to time. I'd have to meet him halfway on that issue. But we had a lot of miles to cover and precious little time to cover them in, and there was no halfway on that one: Either we made it or we didn't, and I was determined that we would.

So I had a bit of a dilemma on my hands. Looking at the atlas didn't help. It showed me *where* to go but not how in the heck to get there. I sat there, chewing and pondering and wishing I was old enough to drink coffee.

Now, here are some things I don't generally believe in: fate, astrology, angels, magic, or the mystical power of wishes. Sorry, I just don't.

So there ain't no easy explanation for what happened next. But that's all right, 'cause not everything in this world needs to be explained. We can just chalk it up to luck and call it good.

Here's what happened: I was sitting there, wondering how on god's green earth I was gonna get us to Sampson Park before the bulldozers fired up, when I heard the following words from the booth behind me.

"Tammy, you *know* I wanna get there. Of *course* I do. But I'm broke. I got no money for a bus ticket. How am I gonna get all the way across the country with no money?"

I stopped mid-chew.

In the diner window to my side, I could see the reflections of our two booths.

In the booth behind me was a black fella wearing big, round black-framed glasses. He looked young-ish, not a teenager anymore, but not too far away from it, either. He was wearing a white tank top undershirt and an old-fashioned bowler hat on his head. All he had in front of him was a chocolate milkshake, and he was hunched over, whispering into his phone.

"Yeah," he said. "Uh-huh. Of *course*. You know that. I'll figure something out. No, baby, don't say that. I *will*. I promise. Well, I don't know yet. I'll catch a ride or something. No, no . . . Come on, don't say that, I'll—"

But then his words cut off. He sighed and set his phone down.

Tammy, whoever she was, had hung up on him.

I swallowed the bite in my mouth, then nodded to myself. I picked up my plate and the atlas and slid out of my booth, then walked around and plopped down on the seat across from the milkshake dude.

His eyebrows went up and his mouth dropped open.

"Hello," I said.

He narrowed his eyes.

"Um . . . hello?" he said. "Do I know you?"

"Not yet," I answered. "Where you headed?"

The guy looked around. He was probably looking for a parent or something, unaware that my version of a parent was asleep on an old school bus.

"Excuse me?"

I took a bite of my burger and chewed, talking around it.

"I'm sorry," I said. "I'm being rude. It's just that time is of the essence and I was trying to get straight down to business." I set down my fork and held out my hand. "Coyote."

He looked at my hand, then back up at me.

"Excuse me?" he said again.

"My name is Coyote. It's a pleasure to meet you." I stretched my hand out an inch closer to him.

"Oh. Your *name* is . . . Okay." He still looked a little unsure, but he reached out and shook my hand. "My name's Lester."

"Listen, I couldn't help but overhear your conversation with Tammy."

"You know Tammy?" Lester asked.

"Of course not. But I think I gotta handle on your situation. Where you headed?"

Lester leaned back, sizing me up. He shot another look around the diner, then took a sip of his milkshake.

"Boise," he answered.

"Boise, Idaho?" I asked.

One corner of his mouth went up.

"There another Boise I don't know about?"

I grinned at him.

"Good point."

I shoved a few fries in my mouth and flipped the atlas open to the big map of the whole country at the beginning. My eyes darted from Florida to Boise to Washington State. I nodded. Then I looked Lester up and down. He had a nice face, friendly and open. There was a duffel bag sitting on the seat next to him. I didn't see a rifle or shovel or human leg sticking out of it.

I swallowed the fries and grimaced.

"Man, those are salty," I complained, looking around for a glass of water. Lester saw me looking and slid his milkshake across the table to me.

And that sealed the deal, right there.

Now, I tend to like folks with nice, friendly, open faces.

And I tend to like folks who eat nothing but a milkshake for dinner. I think it really says something about their openness to life and their general philosophical outlook.

But I *definitely* like folks who offer to share their milkshake with someone they just met.

I took a strong sip of his shake and smiled.

"So, tell me something, Lester," I said, licking the milkshake off my lips. "You got a driver's license?"

CHAPTER
TEN

I roused a distinctly grouchy Rodeo and poked him into a bleary stumble down the bus steps and into the dusky light of the parking lot with plenty of repeated promises like "I got someone you gotta meet," and "It'll be worth it, I promise."

Lester was waiting with his duffel at his feet, and his face got increasingly doubtful with every step Rodeo took down into the waking world. I'd made Rodeo pull on jeans and a T-shirt, but saying he looked halfway presentable would be more than halfway generous.

Rodeo was still Rodeo, though, and he wasn't the type to be inhospitable.

"Howdy," he said with a nod at Lester.

Lester gave him an up-and-down look.

"Hi, there," he replied.

Rodeo rubbed at his face and then looked at me.

"So?" he asked. "What's up?"

"I'm glad you asked," I began. "This here's Lester. We're giving him a ride to Boise."

Rodeo said, "What?" at the same moment that Lester said, "Now, wait a minute," and I held a hand up to each of them and said, "Easy, easy, easy, fellas."

I turned to Rodeo.

"With two drivers we can get to that pork chop sandwich faster. And we got plenty of room, right?"

Rodeo shrugged and nodded. He was generally pretty laid back about giving folks a ride when they needed one.

"Exactly. Well, Lester here needs to get to Tammy and quick, and she just happens to be in Boise. He's in a pickle, and we can help."

"Who's Tammy?" Rodeo asked.

I waved my hand impatiently at him.

"You need to focus, Rodeo. This is important."

"Okay," Rodeo agreed with a dazed squint. Something else I'd learned through the years is that just-woke-up Rodeo is crabby and irritable, but woke-up-about-two-minutes-ago Rodeo gets pretty darn compliant. I was in the golden window of opportunity and I needed to close the deal.

"So, we could use another driver and he needs a ride to Boise, which we just happen to be passing through."

"Hold up," Lester cut in, "I never agreed to—"

"Oh, I know," I said, pivoting to Lester. "Now, *you* have both a desperate need to get to Tammy and a desperately empty wallet, am I right?"

Lester sniffed and looked away, but nodded.

"All right. I know this crusty heap of ugly don't look like that prime of an option," I said, "but it's the only option you really got."

"Easy on Yager, now," Rodeo protested. "She gets us where we need to get to."

"I wasn't talking about Yager, Rodeo. I was talking about you."

"Ah" was all Rodeo said, and he scratched tiredly at his beard.

Lester narrowed his eyes.

"Who said I don't have other options?"

I rolled my eyes at him, then looked around. There was an old guy shuffling along, walking his dog on the sidewalk at the other side of the parking lot.

"Hey!" I shouted at him.

The man stopped and looked over at us.

"Are you going to Boise?" I hollered.

The guy looked left, then right, then back at us.

"Me?" he asked.

"Yeah! You going to Boise?"

The man looked both ways again, then cocked his head at me.

"No?" he answered.

"That's what I figured," I called, and waved him goodbye. He shook his head and kept walking.

I shrugged both palms at Lester and gave him an I-told-you-so look.

"See? You got any other options for free rides to Boise?"

Lester looked at me, eyes wide and mouth open. And then Lester did something wonderful.

He laughed. A big, deep, from-down-in-his-belly laugh. He shook his head and he laughed and it was perfect, because Lester's laugh was just like Rodeo's eyes: It invited you right in and set you at ease.

I realized I was smiling without ever planning on it, and a quick glance showed that Rodeo was smiling along, too.

"You're crazy," Lester said, still shaking his head. He wagged a finger at me. "You. Are. Crazy."

"A little bit," I agreed. "But all the best people are." I looked over at Rodeo. "Go ahead. Ask him the questions."

Now, Lester is not the first person we ever offered a ride to. Far from it. We'd given all sorts of folks rides to all sorts of places over the years. Traveling from gas station to gas station like we did, we often ran across wayward souls who needed some help. And Rodeo is the helping sort; he just is. But he don't let just anybody on board Yager with us. He always asks 'em the same three questions first, and they get a yes or a no based on their answers.

For the record, I have no idea what the right or wrong answers are. But Rodeo seems to.

Rodeo nodded and cleared his throat. He stepped closer to Lester.

"All right. It's a pleasure to meet you, Mr. Lester. I'm Rodeo. This here is our home, Yager. The worthless cat sleeping on the dashboard is Ivan. And that girl there who talks more than she should and knows less than she lets on is Coyote." Rodeo lowered his chin and looked slow into Lester's eyes. Lester looked back and I saw it happen, saw him fall into the kindness that he saw in Rodeo's eyes, saw his whole body ease up a little. "Are you interested in traveling with us for a ways?"

Lester smiled. He shook his head and laughed a little in his throat.

"Well. Yeah. I guess I am, more or less."

"Good. We'd be happy to have you. After you answer our questions. Ready?"

Lester shrugged and nodded.

"Okay. What is your favorite book?"

Lester answered without hesitation.

"*Their Eyes Were Watching God.* Zora Neale Hurston."

Rodeo smiled. Good answer. It was one of Rodeo's favorites. There was a tattered paperback of it on the bookshelf in the bus behind me.

"Okay. And what, Lester, is your favorite place on this planet Earth?"

Lester pursed his lips. His eyes wandered from Rodeo, drifted someplace far away. A look came over his face, a thoughtful kind of look. A private sort of smile played across his lips, but soft and small.

"There's a beach," he said, and he sounded almost like he was talking to himself. "In Georgia. We used to go there, in the summers. When I was a kid. Meet my mama's family. We'd play all day in the water. Me and my cousins, my brother and sister. We'd play right through the sunset. Splash in the dark. One year, there was fireworks. I don't think I ever saw my mama smile the way she smiled when we were there at that beach every summer. Never heard her laugh like she did there. Like she was a kid again."

There was a beat of stillness. Lester's eyes cleared, and came back to Rodeo.

"There. That's my favorite place."

Rodeo took a deep breath. Held it. Let it out slow through his nose. His voice, when he spoke, was a hoarse whisper.

"Last question, Lester. What," he said, "is your favorite sandwich?"

Lester squinted at him. Then he answered, just as quick and sure as he'd answered the first question.

"The pulled pork sandwich at Stamey's Barbecue in Greensboro, North Carolina."

I smiled again. A pulled pork sandwich is a good answer to just about any question. I looked quick to Rodeo.

Rodeo's eyes were on me, his head to the side.

I raised my eyebrows at him.

Rodeo nodded once, then all at once a smile broke across his face. Rodeo was like that: When he made up his mind, his face knew as soon as his brain did. Sometimes a little before, to be honest.

"Okay," he said to Lester, "you just got yourself a ride."

Lester sighed and shook his head, but then stooped and picked up his duffel bag.

Rodeo's face darkened.

"Hold up." He eyed the duffel bag in Lester's hand. "One last question: You got a snake in there?"

"A snake?" Lester exclaimed.

"We picked up a hitchhiker in Reno once who was carrying a big ol' duffel like that," I explained to Lester, "and . . . well, things got weird."

Lester shot me a look, then looked back at Rodeo.

"No, man. I ain't got no snake in my bag."

Rodeo smiled and yawned and then pushed open the bus door.

"Welcome aboard, compadre. Make yourself at home, and help yourself to the tomatoes."

Lester shook his head again—I think he was seriously wondering what he was getting himself into, which was just one more sign that he was an insightful and perceptive sort of person—and then threw his duffel over his shoulder and stepped toward our bus.

"What was that about a pork chop sandwich?" he asked me, but I just shook my head and waved him inside and said, "Long story, Lester. Welcome aboard."

And that is how Lester joined our homeward journey.

CHAPTER
ELEVEN

"So," I said, taking a bite off an apple and then offering it to Lester, "what's the story with Tammy?"

Lester shook his head in a "no, thank you" to the apple. Me and him were sitting on the couch in the back. Ivan was purring in my lap. Rodeo was up at the wheel, muttering to himself. The Lester introduction had woken him up enough to get in a few more miles before handing the keys over.

"Uh . . . long story," Lester said in answer to my question.

He was sitting pretty stiffly on the couch, his back straight, his eyes bouncing around our home, his arms around the duffel he held in his lap. He looked decidedly ill at ease, and I could see second thoughts passing like clouds over his face. Some of them looked to be darn near third or even fourth thoughts, so I figured I'd better put him at ease with some stimulating conversation and fresh fruit. Oh, and with a cat. Cats relax folks. That's just the truth. So I scooped Ivan up out of my lap and handed him over to Lester.

"Here. Could you hold him? My legs are going to sleep."

Lester gave Ivan a less-than-super-excited look, but slid the duffel off his lap and took him. He set him down on his legs and Ivan did some sniffing and turning but, seeing as how he's the best cat in the world, he settled right on in and Lester gave him some pets and I could see right away that he started to relax a little.

"We got time, Lester. What are we talking here? Girlfriend? Sister? Wife?"

Lester looked me up and down, deciding on whether or not to answer me.

"Come on," I said. "We got to get to know each other. I introduced you to Rodeo. Now you introduce me to Tammy." I held the apple out toward him again.

Lester shrugged, took the apple and bit off a chunk, and handed it back to me and then said through his chewing, "Girlfriend, I guess. Maybe."

"Girlfriend you guess maybe? Huh. You guys sound close."

Lester gave me a glare.

"It's complicated," he said.

I took a crunchy bite and shook my head as I passed the apple.

"Nah. Love is never as complicated as it seems."

Lester's eyes twinkled.

"And you know all about love?"

I picked at a bit of apple skin between my teeth.

"I know plenty."

"Really?"

"Yes, as a matter of fact. You see those books over there on the bottom shelf?" I pointed with the apple at the bookshelf. "Those are all mine. I got even more in my room. I've read every single one of 'em, some of 'em *twice*. And see the top shelf? Those are Rodeo's books. *Grown-up* books. I've read most of those, too.

And every book ever written is about love, really, whether it knows it or not. So, yeah, I know a thing or two about love."

Lester blinked at me and pinched his lips together in one of those smug, know-it-all smirks that grown-ups have that can just about drive you crazy, but I forged onward.

"So . . . based on your answer to my first question, I'm guessing Tammy is either a used-to-be-your-girlfriend or a you-hope-she'll-be-your-girlfriend-someday. Which one is she?"

Lester took two more bites of the apple before passing it back and answering.

"Both, kinda," he said.

"Ah. I get it. She broke your heart, left you alone, took off for Boise. I seen it a hundred times."

"Really."

"Yup. So, did she leave you for another fella?" I reached out for the apple, but Lester got all stone-faced and finished it to the core in three more monster bites.

Lester sighed. One of those why-is-this-happening-to-me-and-how-can-I-get-out-of-it kind of sighs. He dropped his head and fixed me with a stare.

"You're not gonna drop this 'til I give you the details, are you?"

"Absolutely not."

He sighed again, but the second time was more of an okay-fine-let's-get-this-over-with kind.

Then he filled me in.

Lester Washington played the upright bass in some sort of bluesy-rootsy band called the Strut Kings, which sounded cool as heck in my book. He straight-out lit up when he talked about music and the Strut Kings. It was like how Rodeo gets when he talks about taco trucks, but even more, which is saying something. You could just tell that Lester and music were like me and Ivan, and me and Ivan were like macaroni and cheese, so it was really a meant-to-be-together kind of situation all around.

Now, Tammy in Boise apparently had other thoughts. Lester was a little stingy with the details, but I got the impression she wasn't super interested in the broke-as-a-joke-musician-living-his-dream-and-trying-to-make-it-work scene. He had some communications degree from college that she thought he should be doing more with, but when he left the full-time job he hated to spend more time on his music, she left him. And then she left the entire state of Florida.

I'm not gonna lie—I wasn't all that impressed with Tammy. But, I told myself, I hadn't heard her side of the story.

"She says if I wear a tie, she'll wear a ring."

I looked at him blankly.

"If I get a real job, she'll marry me," he explained.

"What about the Strut Kings?" I asked.

Lester shrugged.

"Boise's got bands, I bet. I could probably play on the weekends or something."

Now, I don't know about most folks, but I can't imagine only having cheese on my macaroni on the weekends. But love's a crazy thing. I know that. And if Tammy was the one for Lester, then I suppose there's worse things than moving to Boise to get her back. It kinda made me think, actually: What Lester was doing for Tammy was . . . really something. He loved her, so he was biting the bullet and doing something tough because it mattered to her. It was nice, him doing that for her.

"Okay," I said, once he'd given me the lowdown. "Well, I wish you luck in winning her back, Lester."

Lester worked some apple bits out of his teeth with his tongue.

"Thanks. Glad I got your support."

"Sure thing. So, tell me. Boise is an awful long way to go for somebody that already broke your heart. What's so great about her?"

"Why should I tell you that?"

"'Cause it's good practice, man. You're trying to woo her back, right? You better get this stuff down. Lay it on me. What do you love about Tammy?"

Lester sucked on his teeth for a second, then rolled his eyes and leaned back on the couch and looked me in the eye.

"She's got this great laugh," he began. "Sounds like music. She's just about always in a good mood, and when she's not, she snaps herself out of it pretty quick." His eyes drifted away from mine and a little smile started to play on his lips. "And when someone's feeling down, she'll do just about anything to cheer 'em up."

His eyes came back to me.

"That," he said. "That is what I love about her."

I shook my head.

"Nope, Lester. If you want me to believe it's worth taking you all the way across nine states, you gotta do a lot better than that."

He pulled his head back.

"Excuse me? What's wrong with that?"

"All you gave me is reasons why *anybody* might love her—heck why *I* might love her if I met her. You didn't say anything about why *you* love her."

Lester screwed up his eyes doubtfully at me.

"Okay, look," I explained, pointing up at the front of the bus. "Look at Rodeo up there. There's plenty of reasons anyone might love him if they could get past that greasy doormat he calls hair: He's kind to everyone, he helps strangers, he's a gold-medal listener. That's all great stuff, right? But that's different than why *I* love him."

Lester snorted.

"Then why do *you* love him?"

I thought for a moment.

"I love Rodeo because if tomorrow I spit in his face and threw all his favorite books out the window and called him all the worst words I could think of, he wouldn't love me one little bit less." The bus rocked and swayed underneath us. I kept my eyes on Rodeo, on the back of his shaggy head bobbing to the music. "I love Rodeo because on the worst day of my life he held me and held me and held me and held me and didn't let me go." I tried to clear my throat but kinda failed, so I went on in a scratchy sort of whisper. "I love Rodeo because if I didn't love him, he'd fall apart."

I looked out the window, blinked a few times, filled my lungs with air and then emptied them. I could feel Lester watching me. I counted ten cars whiz past us in the other direction, then looked back at him.

"That's whatcha gotta do, Lester. Don't tell me why she's perfect. Tell me why she's perfect for *you*."

Lester was eyeing me in a thoughtful, intense kind of way. To tell you the truth, it reminded me of Ivan . . . which was only more points in Lester's favor.

"That's a lot of wisdom for a kid to drop," he said at last.

"I'm almost thirteen. And it ain't my wisdom, either."

"No?" Lester smirked. "Whose wisdom is it?"

"It's . . . It's . . . It *was*," I dropped my voice to a whisper and kept an eye on Rodeo. "It was my mom's." Talking about her at all was a strict no-go, and doing it on board Yager was like farting in church. But something about Lester's listening eyes— and something about the secret mission I was on at that very moment—made it easier to walk away from that rule, at least for a minute. "She had me and my sisters write letters to each other one day. We had to say what we loved most about each other. And it couldn't just be something nice about them—it had to be unique and special to us, what *we* loved about each other. She had to write the words for my little sister, but we all did it. Me and my sisters sat down and we wrote what we loved about each other."

Lester looked around the rattling bus.

"Where they at, your mom and sisters?"

I picked at a thread that was trailing out of a seam in my jeans.

"Oh," I answered, trying to pluck the thread out without unraveling any more, "they're dead, Lester." My eyes flashed up quick to Lester. I liked that he wasn't making some syrupy sympathetic face, liked that he didn't look away, liked that he didn't cluck his tongue or bite his lip or anything stupid like that. "But I'm glad we wrote those letters."

We passed a semitruck and for a few seconds we were lost in the rumbling thunder of the tractor-trailer.

Up at the front, Rodeo stretched dramatically and let out a flamboyant yawn.

"Whoo-hee!" he hooted. "Put a fork in me, y'all. I am done." He slapped his face a few times and then flicked on the turn signal and steered Yager off onto an exit ramp. The bus shuddered around us as it slowed down from highway speed.

"Looks like it's your turn to drive," I said, poking Lester's knee and standing up, holding myself steady with the arm of the couch.

Lester was still looking at me.

"What'd your sisters say?" he asked. "What'd they say they loved about you?"

"I don't know. We never read the letters."

Lester blinked.

"What did you do with them?"

I stepped past him, heading toward the front of the bus and a badly needed bathroom break.

"We put 'em in a box and buried 'em in a park," I answered.

In retrospect, what happened next was at least partly my fault, but I'll never admit that to Rodeo 'cause I don't wanna let him off that easy.

It all started with Rodeo and Lester arguing over a map.

We were at a random gas station somewhere outside Gainesville, Florida. The sun had set and it was starting to smell like nighttime. There was still a little purple glow on the western horizon, but it was dim and fading fast; darkness was on the way.

Lester had just been given the briefing on how to handle Yager—though Rodeo was more than a little reluctant to hand over the keys—and was getting ready for his first shift behind the wheel. I came wandering back from the gas station bathroom, snapping my gum and humming a little song, to find those two bickering out in the parking lot, waiting for the pump to finish filling our tank.

"I'm telling you, man, you gotta start using a phone," Lester was saying in an argument I could've told him was a lost cause. "Using a paper map is crazy."

Rodeo was smiling serenely, the open atlas in his hands.

"Yeah, brother? What can your phone do that my map can't?"

"Are you kidding?" Lester sputtered. "Everything! Check this out." Lester stepped shoulder-to-shoulder with Rodeo so Rodeo could see the screen. "I can just type in where I wanna go, and it'll tell me the whole route. Turns and everything. Shows me how long it'll take. It even tells me if there's construction or delays or anything."

My interest was piqued.

"Lemme see that," I said, and elbowed my way into their huddle. The candy-bright screen before my eyes was a revelation. I'd always seen folks playing on their phones, but I'd only ever used phones I'd borrowed to make phone calls. On Lester's phone was a map, all colorful and clear. There was a blue line from where we were to a glowing red pushpin labeled "Boise." It said right there on the bottom of the screen, "36 hours (2,504 miles)." No dental floss or long division required. It was a miracle.

I did the math real quick. We still had sixty hours until Wednesday morning came along. Plenty of time, I figured. Not a lot of wiggle room for wandering or lollygagging, but we were on schedule.

I beamed up at Lester and Rodeo.

"This is fantastic," I said.

Lester nodded.

Rodeo scowled.

"Aw, take the knife out of my back, sweetie pie! You gonna abandon me for this heartless piece of technological soul-poison?"

I could tell Rodeo was in a dramatic mood, and my mind was too bubbly with maps and timelines to engage.

"I'm going to bed," I lied, knowing full well I was gonna lay in my room and strategize a way to get us from Boise to home instead of Boise to Butte. I leveled a finger at Rodeo as I walked away. "And now I want a phone for Christmas."

Rodeo howled in theatrical horror and I left them to their conversation. I was walking up Yager's steps when my stomach gave a little rumble. I shrugged and grabbed a few bills from our cash jar and changed direction, back down the stairs and off the bus and toward the gas station. Behind me, I heard Rodeo making some loud point about how *he* didn't have to *plug in* his *map*, but I shook my head and kept walking.

And it's that darn stomach rumble that got me in a heap of trouble.

See, 'cause I didn't look back over my shoulder. So I didn't see Rodeo taking the gas nozzle out of Yager and putting it back on its cradle. And I didn't see Rodeo and Lester climbing back into Yager, still talking maps and phones. I didn't see the door closing behind them.

What I did see, though, when I came back out a few minutes later with a mouthful of CornNuts, was an empty parking lot and not a bus or a hippie in sight.

CHAPTER
TWELVE

Some folks might think that a kid like me, living on the road and whatnot, would be unfazed by being left behind like that. Seeing as how gas stations and mini-marts are pretty much my natural habitat, it might seem like I'd just shrug and roll my eyes and sit down to wait for the two idiots to figure it out and come back for me.

Here's the problem with that theory, though: It ain't true. The fact of the matter is, as flaky as ol' Rodeo is, he'd never once come close to doing anything like this before. Up until that moment when he and Lester left me behind in Gainesville, Florida, I hadn't been more than a couple hundred feet from Rodeo in five years. I hadn't hardly been out of his sight for longer than a bathroom break since I was seven years old.

So, what I'm saying, basically, is that when I walked out and saw the bus gone, I wasn't, like, super calm about it.

There were a couple of seconds of confused blinking, and then the freak-out began.

I sputtered and coughed, choking on the CornNuts in my mouth. My stomach somersaulted, and not in a fun, roller-coaster kind of way. My breathing got fast and shallow and I dropped the bag of CornNuts and ran out to the sidewalk and looked both ways desperately. No bus in sight. I spun around and hopelessly scanned the parking lot again, like maybe I'd somehow missed an entire school bus the first time.

I hadn't.

"Okay," I said, and my voice sounded so high and scared it actually kind of freaked me out more. "Okay. Okay okay okay. Oh god. Okay. Oh god." I closed my eyes and made myself take a deep, long breath. I opened my eyes again.

Still no bus.

I went through it all in my head. How they'd seen me climb up into the bus, but then I'd slipped back off. How they'd both been distracted by their maps-versus-phone conversation. The curtain that blocked off my bedroom. They must've thought I was back there, reading or sleeping.

"Rodeo'll figure it out," I said out loud, trying to make my voice sound calm and in control. "Trying" is the operative word there. I could hear the terrified tremor in my voice. "He'll realize what happened. He'll know exactly where I got left behind. They'll come straight back and Rodeo'll have that gas pedal pressed all the way to the floor. They'll come roaring up any minute." I nodded to myself, but my hands were shaking and I felt like I was one bad swallow away from puking up my CornNuts. Because I knew that maybe it *wouldn't* be any minute. Rodeo was bone-tired and probably wanted to lie down, and Lester was most likely focused on driving Yager. Rodeo had just filled up with gas, after all—and, sweet fancy catfish, what if it was, like, twelve *hours* before they realized they'd left me behind? Then it'd be *twenty-four* hours before they got back. Rodeo didn't have a phone. Lester did, but I didn't know his number.

I was lost. And alone. More lost and more alone than I'd ever been, ever.

And Rodeo, wherever he was up the road, was gonna wake up . . . and I wasn't gonna be there.

"Oh, lord," I breathed. "This is gonna kill him. He is gonna lose his ever-loving *mind*." My stomach knotted with worry.

I looked around. No restaurants. No parks. No public libraries or nothing. Just a gas station all by itself next to a highway off-ramp. It wasn't even a nice gas station. There was one old car parked at the far corner of the parking lot, and it looked like someone was sitting in the driver's seat; other than that, the whole scene was pretty dang desolate.

The coming darkness that had been no big deal back when I wasn't completely and totally alone suddenly seemed like kind of a pretty darn big deal, after all. I swear, as I stood there, the last little bit of sunset purple turned to black. I gulped. I wasn't just alone and forgotten . . . I was alone and forgotten *at night*. One of the tears stinging in my eyes got heavy enough to drop, dripping warm onto my cheek.

A pair of headlights pulled off the highway onto the exit ramp, coming my way. I was caught for a minute in the headlight glare as the car turned into the gas station and I squinted, rubbing quick at my wet cheek. The car, a red SUV, rolled past me and I saw the woman in the passenger seat look twice at me and crane her neck. Her brow furrowed, and her lips moved like she was saying something to the man driving. I suddenly realized how I looked, standing there sniffling by myself in the dark by the side of a highway. Kids alone at highway rest areas and gas stations attract attention, from both bad dudes and overprotective, oh-my-god-is-that-girl-okay-honey-we-should-call-the-police types.

I didn't like the look the lady had given me. She looked like the get-involved type. I couldn't leave, though. This is where Rodeo'd come looking for me, whenever he did. I needed to stay here, but I needed to stick out less, and quick.

What do perfectly normal, happy, and not-at-all-terrified-or-abandoned-or-in-any-danger-whatsoever kids do at gas stations?

"They buy slushies," I said out loud, trying to work the shakes out of my voice and blink the wetness out of my eyes. I nodded to myself and then spun and marched back into the gas station, keeping my eyes straight ahead and a casual, completely calm smile on my face as I walked past the SUV that was parking in front.

The cashier shot me a curious look when I came back inside, but he was too busy petting his mustache to cause any problems. A kid I hadn't noticed before was browsing in the chip section, and he glanced at me as I walked past him. I made my way to the slushy machine in the back corner. It whirred loudly, churning one garish bright flavor.

"You gotta be kidding me," I muttered, reading the label. "Wild Watermelon."

It was a no-doubt-about-it rotten piece of luck for the universe to toss on top of my current heap of troubles, but I heard the door jangle open as the SUV woman walked in behind me, so I grabbed a cup anyway. I pulled the spigot and filled my cup with the frozen atrocity and turned around and sure enough, there was the lady standing right behind me with a worried look on her face and her phone in her hand.

"Hello, dear," she said, her brow crinkled in concern and her voice careful, like I was a cornered deer she was trying not to spook.

"Hi," I said, moving to sidle past her. She shifted quickly, though, just enough to stop me.

"I'm sorry, but is everything okay?" She was looking with wet, hungry eyes into my face, searching for clues.

There were a couple of ways to play this. I went with bravado.

"No," I answered. Her eyebrows shot up and I saw her eyes glisten with excitement. She opened her mouth but I barreled on, not giving her a chance to talk. "Climate change is wreaking havoc on our planet," I said. "The coral reefs are dying. Species are going extinct at a terrifying rate. Honeybee colonies are collapsing. And have you heard about the deforestation of the Amazon?" All those *National Geographic* magazines that Rodeo made me read were paying off. I shook my head and took a suck of my slushy, which tasted even worse than I'd feared. "The world is a mess, ma'am. Everything is definitely *not* okay."

The lady's eyebrows scrunched in confusion. I moved to squeeze past her but she moved again, plainly trying to block me now. "No . . . No. I mean, are *you* okay?"

"Oh, me? I'm just peachy. Excuse me."

She didn't budge, though.

"Where are your parents, dear?"

I gritted my teeth. She was more persistent than most.

"My dad's just up the road getting gas. He'll be back in a minute."

The woman frowned.

"This is a gas station. Why didn't he just get gas here?"

Dang. The distracting flavor of chemical watermelon was throwing me off my game.

"He's . . . a bargain shopper. It's five cents a gallon cheaper at the next exit."

"Then why did he leave you here?"

I clenched my jaw, then held up my cup.

"For the slushy," I said.

Her eyes narrowed.

"They don't have slushies at the next gas station?"

The woman wasn't letting go of this bone, and I was running out of lies. She clearly wasn't going to let me leave, so I turned and headed the other way, toward the back of the store.

"I gotta go to the bathroom," I said. My armpits were hot and tingly. This was not going according to plan.

The bathroom was single occupant with a locking chain, thank goodness. I wouldn't have put it past the lady to follow me right in and wait outside the stall.

I splashed some cold water on my face, then crept back to the door. Leaving the chain locked, I eased the door open and peeked through the crack.

The lady was up at the counter, standing next to a beefy guy with a shaved head who I assumed was her husband. She had her phone up to her ear, and I could just make out what she was saying.

"Yes, ma'am. All by herself. At night. And she's been crying. I don't know, maybe twelve or thirteen? No, ma'am. She gave me some story, but I can tell she's lying. Yes, ma'am. Yes. I'll keep her here until the officers arrive."

My heart thumped. I clicked the door closed and leaned my forehead against it.

"Son of a biscuit," I whispered.

Police, generally speaking, were not big fans of Rodeo's and my lifestyle. Anytime cops started asking questions, they got suspicious real quick. They always seemed to think I was some sort of kidnapping victim or something. I'll admit Rodeo does kinda look the part of an unhinged criminal at times, but that's a real judging-a-book-by-its-cover situation. Sometimes it took hours for the police to let us go; one time, in Denver, it took two *days*, a call from my grandma, and a call to the sheriff in our old hometown before they finally believed Rodeo wasn't a child abductor and let us go. And I didn't think the fact that Rodeo had abandoned me at night was gonna be super helpful in us talking our way out of this one. I didn't have a couple days to waste this time, either.

The watermelon slushy, never all that soothing in the best of circumstances, turned to sour nausea in my stomach.

I jumped back when there was a soft knocking on the bathroom door. Not even a *knocking*, really. More like a fingertip drumming.

Man. That lady wasn't giving up.

"Occupied," I said in my most don't-mess-with-me voice.

The knocking came again, even softer. Like someone was trying to keep the knocking a secret.

It didn't seem like the kind of knock the nosy lady would do.

I turned the knob and opened the door a sliver.

I didn't see anyone there. Until I looked down.

It was the kid I'd seen earlier, but he was crouched down outside the door, looking up at me with big, serious brown eyes.

"I can help you escape," he said.

CHAPTER

THIRTEEN

"This is the, um, bathroom," I whispered, not wanting the lady to notice me.

The kid frowned up at me. He was Latino, and he was wearing blue jeans and a white T-shirt. His hair was cut in a tight-to-his-scalp buzz cut. He looked about my age.

"I know that," the kid whispered back. He jerked his head toward the front of the store. "That lady called the cops on you."

"Yeah. I heard."

"You need help?"

I rolled my eyes.

"Not from them."

"No," the kid said with a shake of his head. "I mean *because* of them. You need to, like, *escape*?"

I realized then that he was crouching down so the lady couldn't see him past all the shelves of snack food.

"Escape" sure seemed like an awful dramatic word.

But, hey, if the flip-flop fits . . .

"Yeah," I said, crouching down so I could whisper to him rather than at him, "I guess so."

The kid nodded.

"Okay. There's a window in the men's room."

I just looked at him.

"Big enough to crawl out," he clarified. "My mom's in our car at the back of the parking lot. Just tell her Salvador sent you. I'll meet you out there in a minute."

I reached up and unlatched the chain, then eased the door open just wide and long enough to duck out and close it behind me.

Once I was crouched down next to him, Salvador reached out for my slushy.

"But first, give me that."

"What? You're making me *pay* for your help? With a slushy?"

"No," he said like I was an idiot. "You haven't paid for it." He fished a wallet out of his back pocket and showed it to me. "I'll buy it and meet you out there."

"Oh. Right. Thanks."

Salvador took the slushy from my hand and stood up, then strolled all casually toward the front of the store. I scurried bent over and ducked into the men's room.

Sure enough, there was a little (but big enough) window over the sink. I generally wanted to spend as little time as possible in a men's room, so I didn't do any dawdling. I climbed up onto the sink, wrenched the window open as quietly as I could manage, and then wriggled through and swung myself down to the black asphalt below. I scraped my stomach pretty good on the way down, but considering that it was in fact my first time crawling out of a men's bathroom window, I think I managed the operation pretty well, all in all.

I saw the car—the same one I'd noticed earlier—parked at

the back of the parking lot. I ran through the evening gloom over to the driver's-side door.

A woman looked out at me, wide-eyed. I smiled encouragingly and motioned for her to roll the window down. She did, about an inch, which I thought was fair since she'd just watched me shimmy through a bathroom window.

"Hi," I said, a little breathless. "Salvador said I should come to you? And . . . hide in your car?" I thought it was probably smart to leave the police out of it at this point.

The woman's face was kind but understandably uncertain.

"Hide? In my car?"

"Yes," I said, and smiled again, even bigger. I pointed to the back seat, where I saw a couple of suitcases and duffel bags piled up. "Can I get in?"

She looked me up and down again and didn't make any move toward unlocking the car. I didn't blame her, not one darned bit, but the clock was ticking.

I looked over my shoulder, scanning the highway and parking lot nervously. No sign of the nosy lady or the police. Yet.

"Please?" I said. Then I thought of what Rodeo would do with those magic eyes and that soul-deep kindness of his. I dropped the cheesy smile and looked right into her eyes, serious and honest. There was plenty of kindness there, plenty of warmth back behind her confusion. I saw it there in her eyes and shined it back at her with my own. "Please?"

Her face softened, just a bit.

"Is Salvador in trouble?"

"No, ma'am."

"Are *you* in trouble?"

"No, ma'am." I looked back over my shoulder. "Look, I promise it's nothing all that bad. But could we, like, talk about this once I'm in your car? Please?"

The woman's frown tightened, but then I heard the *clunk* of the doors unlocking. I slid a duffel bag out of the way, jumped into the back seat, then closed the door and ducked down out of sight.

"Thank you," I said. "Thank you, like, a *lot*."

She just shook her head.

"So . . . what are you hiding from?" Her words had a nice Spanish accent to them that made them sound prettier than normal words. I hated to follow up her pretty talking with the ugly truth of my own situation, but it didn't seem like a time to be lying.

"Um . . . the police."

Her head snapped back to me so fast I jumped.

"Ex*cuse* me?"

I got ready to try and explain, but at that moment Salvador came walking up and opened the door and plopped into the passenger seat.

There was a fierce back-and-forth between him and his mom in Spanish. She gasped and shook her head and spat something that sounded an awful lot like a Spanish curse word when Salvador mentioned the *policía*. She shot a couple quick questions at him, then he looked back at me.

"You're not a thief or something, are you?"

"Nope."

She asked me the next question.

"You're not a runaway or anything illegal like that?"

"No."

"So . . . what's up, then?" she said. "Why are you hiding from the cops?"

"It's kind of a long story," I said. "My dad . . . *forgot* me, I guess. I mean, not on purpose, he thought I was on the bus, but . . . Oh, it doesn't matter." I wasn't doing an awesome job of explaining myself, and I knew it. "Listen, he'll be coming back for me. Any minute, maybe. And we're not doing anything illegal at all, I promise, but we're kind of on the move and in a hurry. It's just, like, usually not great when the police start asking us questions, so I was hoping to kind of avoid that if possible. I know . . . that doesn't really sound like it makes sense, does it?"

Salvador looked at me for a second, a sad sort of small smile on his face. He traded a look with his mom.

"No," she said, her voice kinda quiet. "It makes sense."

Salvador looked over at the back of the gas station. "Good news is they think you're still in the bathroom. Bad news is the police are definitely on the way. And once they look in the bathroom, it's only a matter of time before they come sniffing around out here."

"I don't want you guys getting tangled up in this," I said.

Salvador's mom looked back at me, and the kindness I'd seen at the back of her eyes was right up at the front now.

"It's a little late for that," she said, but she reached back and patted my knee with a warm hand when she said it, so I knew she was saying it honest, not saying it mean.

"My dad *is* coming back." I stretched up and snuck a peek out the window. "He's gonna be coming in the other direction, south-bound," I said, pointing. "The other off-ramp must be over there, across the bridge. If you take me over there and drop me off, I can just flag him down when he pulls off the highway. You can't even see the ramp from this side of the highway, so it's perfect."

Salvador squinted across the highway.

"Yeah. We could probably make it that far."

"What do you mean?"

Salvador shook his head.

"Our car. It, uh . . . It's not running so good. That's why we're parked here. We barely made it off the highway and into this parking lot."

I took a closer look around the back seat and noticed for the first time the balled-up laundry, the food wrappers, the pillow squished against the far door.

"How long have you been here?"

He shrugged.

"Just since this morning."

This morning? They'd been living in this crappy parking lot for a whole day?

"What are you waiting for?"

Salvador grabbed a cell phone off the center console and held it up.

"We're waiting for my *tía* to call us back."

"When my dad gets back, we can help you!" I said excitedly. "We can give you money to fix your car! I promise!"

Salvador's face closed up.

"Did we ask for help?" he said, his voice suddenly cold.

"Well, no, but . . ."

"This car isn't fixable, but we got plenty of money for bus tickets," he said. "I bought *your* slushy, remember? We just need to get in touch with my aunt so we know what city to go to and she knows to pick us up. I never said we needed your help. *We're* the ones helping *you*."

His voice was low, but hard. I'd stepped in it, and I knew it.

His mom's hand went from my knee to his. She gave him a raised-eyebrow look.

"Easy, *mijo*," she said. Then she said something to him in Spanish, something tender but firm. He nodded and looked away.

"No, you're totally right," I said. "I'm sorry. Thank you for helping me. You, like, totally saved my butt in there." I opened my door a crack. "Okay, I can make a run for it. Across the overpass. Thanks again, *so* much, for—"

"No," Salvador's mom interrupted me with a shake of her head. "Close the door. You'd have to run straight across the parking lot. There's no trees or nothing. We'll get you over there."

"You don't have to . . ."

"I know we don't have to," she said. "But we're going to. End of story. I'm not going to sit here and watch a girl get grabbed by some cops."

I looked at Salvador. He shrugged and smiled a little.

"No use arguing with her," he said. "Trust me. Oh, and here's this." He handed me the slushy over the seat. "I took a sip, and I'm sorry."

"It's okay," I said. "You can have all you want."

"No. I mean that I'm sorry that I took a sip. It's disgusting." I saw the hint of a smile playing at the corners of his mouth.

I took the cup from his hand and flashed him a quick grin.

"Yeah," I said, "I know."

Salvador's mom turned the key and the car cranked to life, more or less. Mostly less. There was some grinding and a wisp of smoke from under the hood and a sharp stink that smelled an awful lot like something burning. But the engine did rattle up to a stubborn rumbling grumble and stay there, which I guess sometimes is all that counts.

"Get down," Salvador reminded me, and I ducked down back under the window as the car stumbled into motion and we rolled out of the parking lot.

The drive was short, but we never really got up to what you'd call cruising speed. There was a fair amount of shuddering and jerking and quite a bit more grinding and the burning smell got significantly stronger. By the time we'd limped over the overpass and clunked down the other side to the off-ramp, I was feeling pretty bad for the car and thinking we'd really asked way too much from it. It was probably only a quarter mile from start to finish but, shoot, when a horse has only got three legs, I think you really ought to just let it hang out in the barn.

I heard the crunch of gravel as we pulled off the road. There was a final screech from under the hood and a more substantial poof of white smoke when Salvador's mom dropped it into neutral and killed the engine (and, for the record, I don't think the phrase "killed the engine" has ever been more appropriately applied).

"What did you say was wrong with this car?" I asked, peeking up to check our location.

Salvador shook his head.

"Everything, man. 'Bout a hundred miles back a shop hooked us up and did what they could, but even that dude wouldn't guarantee we'd make it to the state line. Said there's so many things wrong with this old piece of junk that fixing it all would cost more than it's worth." He reached forward and petted the dusty dashboard. "But, hey, she's gotten us around for years. I'm gonna hate leaving her behind." He sighed, his fingers still tracing little paths on the dash. "Stupid, I know," he said, shooting me a look and rolling his eyes.

"No. I totally get it."

Salvador gave me a shy little smile. He peered up the highway off-ramp. Pairs of headlights came and went on the highway beyond.

"What kind of car does your dad drive?" his mom asked. "Could be hard to know it's him in the dark."

"Nah," I said with a snort. "I'll know it's him. We're driving a—"

But my Yager description was cut off by Salvador's mom's quick gasp and hissed curse: "*Policía!*"

I followed her pointing finger and saw the police cruiser pulling off the highway on the other side of the bridge, exiting toward the gas station we'd just left. It would be only a matter of minutes now before they found the bathroom empty and came looking for me.

"All right," I said, cracking the door. "Y'all can head back over there. I'll hide in the ditch here and wait for my dad. Thank you *so* much again for everything."

Salvador spoke some words to his mom in Spanish and she said some back, shaking her head emphatically.

"Stay here," she said to me. "I wouldn't want someone leaving my Salvador in a ditch by the side of the road, and I'm not doing that with you."

"And we're not going back over there as long as the cops are there, either," Salvador added under his breath.

"Why?" I asked, which I knew was totally rude and nosy as soon as I said it.

Salvador's face went cold again, but this time his eyes slid away from mine instead of glaring.

"None of your business," he said, which was true, but then he added more quietly, "I just hope they don't come looking over here."

Then, my ears picked up a sweet sound, a sound I knew well and recognized in one happy heartbeat.

Now, most people wouldn't think that the sound of a 2003 diesel engine roaring up a highway off-ramp is a sweet sound, but then again most folks think it's gross to put guacamole on pizza, so who cares what most folks think? Guacamole on pizza is *amazing*, and so is the sound of your home rolling back to you.

Then, there it was. Or, there *they* were.

Yager, in all its ragged beauty, came roaring up out of the darkness, and I tell you it was something to see. Her headlights were on, and for some reason the red and yellow hazard lights were flashing, too. I could see Lester behind the wheel, and even thought I could just make out the gray shape of Ivan hunkered on the dash.

Rodeo, though? Rodeo was kneeling up on the roof, hair and beard whipping in the wind, holding tight to a safety rail with one hand and holding his other hand to his forehead like a sea captain looking for land, eyes locked on the gas station across the highway. He was flashing from shadow to brightness to shadow to brightness from the blinking hazard lights around him, his skin painted in warm reds and yellows like a campfire.

Rodeo, crown prince of freaks, had never looked more freakish.

That man is hopeless. He is wild and broken and reckless and beautiful and hanging on by a thread, but it's a heckuva thread and he's holding it tight with both hands and his heart. He was coming for me.

My smile was so wide my face hurt.

That man is my hero. Most of the time.

"What the heck is—?" Salvador started to say, but I was already jumping out of the car and running into the road, waving my arms over my head and doing some sort of combination of laughing and crying.

CHAPTER
FOURTEEN

I suppose jumping out in front of a speeding bus in the dark ain't the smartest move in the world, and it did take Lester an uncomfortable amount of time to see me and bring Yager to a skidding halt, but he did manage to stop her a full two feet before hitting me, so I don't see why he gave me such grief about it later.

Lester cut the engine and ran for the door at the same time that Rodeo whooped and jumped from the roof to the hood and then to the asphalt and then barreled into me, squeezing me in a rib-crushing hug that was darn near painful, but I didn't wiggle or fight, I just worked my own arms free so I could wrap them around him and return the favor. We stood there in Yager's headlight beams, right there in the middle of the highway off-ramp, holding on to each other in the darkness and not letting go.

"Oh, honeybear," he murmured, kissing me hard on the top of my head. "I'm so sorry, I'm so sorry, I'm so sorry, I'm so sorry, I'm so sorry, I'm so—"

"Shut up," I said, then pulled back to look him in the face. "It's not your fault, Rodeo." Lester was standing a little off to the side, smiling and shaking his head.

"You gave us a scare, girl," he said.

"I'm sorry."

Lester wrinkled his brow and looked back and forth between me and Rodeo.

"We leave you at a gas station and *you're* apologizing to *us*? Y'all are a trip."

He stepped forward and held his fist out and I reached out to bump it with my own.

"Glad you're all right," Lester said quietly, then shook his head again. "Can't believe we left without you."

I shrugged as best I could with Rodeo's arms still wrapped around me.

"It was no big deal. But I'm glad you morons caught on so quick."

"We didn't," Lester said, then pointed at the bus's windshield. "It was that cat of yours. Started going nuts the minute we pulled out, pacing and scratching at the windows and howling. Made a big ol' fuss. Rodeo kept hollering at you to get your cat under control and when you kept ignoring him, he went back to check on you. So, don't thank us. Thank that noisy feline right there."

Ivan was sitting on the dash, pressed against the glass, eyes on me. He opened his mouth in a *meow* that rang right through the windshield.

I pulled loose from Rodeo and stepped forward to tap the window by Ivan's face. He rubbed against the windshield where my fingers were touching it.

"Thank you, Ivan," I said, and my voice cracked just a little. He was purring so strong I could hear it through the glass. I had already loved that cat with a fierceness, but right then . . . whew.

That Ivan. The first time he ever used his voice, he used it to speak up for me.

It's something to have someone who misses you when you're gone. And it's something to have someone who fights to get you back.

I turned back toward Rodeo and saw Salvador and his mom behind him, standing by their car.

"Oh, hey," I said, then grabbed Rodeo's hand and dragged him over toward Salvador and his mom. "Introductions!" Rodeo was still in a bit of an emotional daze, and Salvador's mom was giving Rodeo and Yager a look that was doubtful at best, but we *were* still parked in the middle of the road, so I didn't have a lot of time for a warm-up.

"Salvador, this here is Rodeo. Rodeo, this is Salvador. And this is . . ." I trailed off, hand held out toward Salvador's mom, realizing I probably shouldn't just call her "Salvador's mom."

"Esperanza," his mom offered with a smile. "Esperanza Vega." My mouth dropped open.

"Esperanza," I whispered. "Like from the book! *Esperanza Rising*!"

Ms. Vega just kinda smiled and shrugged, but I was blown away. That was one of my favorite books ever, and here she was . . . It was a sign, for sure. I got goose bumps. I shook my head and got back to the business at hand.

"And this is Esperanza Vega. She's Salvador's mom. They looked out for me while I was waiting for you."

Rodeo held his hand out and then so did Salvador's mom and

they shook. Ms. Vega looked up into Rodeo's eyes and I saw that magic work and saw her soften up just a bit.

"Thank you, ma'am," Rodeo said in his bone-deep genuine way, and Ms. Vega smiled and said, "My pleasure," and then Rodeo shook Salvador's hand and they had pretty much the same exchange and then the idea hit me and I pulled Salvador off to the side, off into the shadows of the ditch.

"You should come with us," I said, and Salvador opened his mouth to protest but I beat him to it. "It's not help," I said, holding up my hands. "I know you don't need it. It's repaying a debt. You saved my butt, and I owe you one. I know you don't wanna mess with those cops over there and it's only a matter of minutes before they come over here snooping around and no offense, but I don't think this car's gonna make much of a runaway vehicle. Y'all are heading that way, right?" I pointed up the highway in the direction Rodeo and Lester had just come roaring back from. Salvador sniffed and nodded. "Well, so are we. It just makes sense, man. Once your aunt calls, we can drop you off at the nearest bus station. Come on. It's the least I can do. Please?"

As Salvador's eyes darted around in thought, I went through it in my own head, too. I couldn't take my eyes off the prize—which was still waiting for me buried under a tree a couple thousand miles away—but having the Vegas on board for a day or two wouldn't interfere with that at all, as far as I could see. It was a win-win, and I'm all for win-wins.

Ever since I'd gotten Ivan, I'd been seeing the world a little differently. He was like that first sip of cold water when you didn't even know you were thirsty, and now I didn't wanna stop drinking. I'd made that decision for me, and I'd also made the secret choice to head home, no matter Rodeo's no-goes and hang-ups. I'd spent a long time mostly worried about Rodeo and what he wanted. Maybe it was time to start worrying about someone else.

I liked Salvador. It'd be fun to have a friend on board. *I* wanted it. And what I want matters, too, right? I nodded to myself.

Salvador looked at me, then away up the highway, then over at our bus.

"Don't you have to, like, ask your dad?"

"Don't worry about that. I'll talk to Rodeo, you talk to your mom."

So that was it. Salvador shook his head, but he walked over and pulled his mom to the side and started talking with her while I walked over to Rodeo.

"Hey," I said. "We got room for two more." I didn't ask it, just said it.

"Two more what?"

"Two more passengers," I said, and pointed a thumb at the huddling Vegas. "They're going our way and their car is broke down." Rodeo opened his mouth just like Salvador had, but I was on a roll and getting good at not giving other folks a chance to kill my momentum. "I know what you're gonna say, but save it. We owe 'em, Rodeo. I was alone. And they saved me. From the *cops*."

Rodeo's head jerked back.

"Wait a minute, what? What did you do? We were gone for, like, fifteen minutes!"

I waved his words away and shook my head.

"That's not important right now. What is important is us returning the favor and giving 'em a lift. It's only right and you know it." I blew out a breath. "Okay. Now go ahead and say whatever you were gonna say."

Rodeo took a step closer to me. A little smile played at his lips.

"What I was gonna say, sugarbug, is that after this whole she-bang, I'd do just about anything you ask me to." Then he smiled wide, and I smiled right back. "Of course they can hop in if they want to. They brought my honeybird back to me. They can have the whole doggone bus if they want it."

I heard a throat clearing behind me and saw Salvador waiting, his mom standing beside him.

"We, uh, good?" he asked.

I looked at Rodeo and he nodded, still smiling.

"Oh, yeah," he said. "Absolutely."

"You gonna ask them the questions?" I asked.

Rodeo shrugged.

"What the heck. But we should make it quick." He took a step toward Ms. Vega and Salvador and squared up to 'em. "So, lady and gentleman, we got three questions we ask new travelers. You ready?"

"Uh, I guess?" Salvador said.

"All right. First, what's your favorite book?"

"Serious?" Salvador asked.

"Serious. Favorite book."

Salvador thought for a second.

"Well, last year in school I read *Ghost*, by Jason Reynolds. That one was pretty great, I guess."

"Yes!" I shouted. "That book is amazing!"

"Okay, sounds like you passed that one," Rodeo said. "How about you, ma'am?"

Ms. Vega twisted her mouth for a second in thought and then answered, "*La muerte de Artemio Cruz*," and then added, "by Carlos Fuentes."

"Fuentes." Rodeo nodded. "Nice. Next question: What's your favorite place in the whole world?"

This time Ms. Vega answered first.

"A kitchen, cooking with my family. Any kitchen. As long as my family is there."

Rodeo shook his head and looked down at his feet and then smiled up at Ms. Vega.

"Great answer. *Great* answer. And you, Salvador?"

Salvador sniffed.

"I don't know."

Rodeo shrugged one shoulder.

"Give it a shot."

"We been lots of places, me and *Mamá*," Salvador said. He looked at his mom, who was standing there in the day's-end darkness looking back at him, and his face softened. I saw it.

It's funny how sometimes when a face goes gentle, it ends up looking stronger somehow.

There was powerful love there, between Salvador and his mom. A love that spoke for itself.

He looked back at Rodeo and shrugged.

"I guess my favorite place is just wherever she is."

Rodeo nodded. A slow nod. He looked Salvador in the eye, then looked at me, then looked back at Salvador. He held out his hand and Salvador took it and they shook.

"No more questions," Rodeo said. "The ride's yours if you want it. We owe you."

"What was the last question?" Salvador asked, cocking his head.

"What's your favorite sandwich."

Salvador snorted.

"For reals? Aren't you gonna, like, ask us if we're criminals or something?"

Rodeo laughed.

"You never asked if *we* were criminals," he said.

"True. But I kinda want to."

Rodeo guffawed at that.

"Fair enough, man. Well, we're not criminals, and I get the feeling you ain't, either, and that's good enough for me if it's good enough for you. You need a hand with your suitcases and stuff?"

"Sure."

As we all walked over to the Vegas' car and started grabbing their stuff, Rodeo asked, "So, just curious, what *is* your favorite sandwich?"

Salvador thought for a second and then asked back, "You ever eaten a *torta* from a taco truck?"

"Oh, brother, are you *kidding* me?" Rodeo slapped Salvador on the shoulder. "You and me are gonna get along just fine, man."

Their stuff was loaded and Lester fired Yager back up and

we were ready to roll when all of a sudden Salvador jumped up and shouted "Wait!" and flew out the door. He crouched down for a minute by their dusty old car and when he climbed back up the steps, he was holding a dented hubcap in his hands.

He looked around at us, sitting there staring at him.

"Wanted something to remember her by" is all he said.

I looked at Rodeo and he was looking at Salvador and he had a wide-open expression on his face, and then he looked at me and I looked away quick, but I tell you I really dug Salvador at that moment. That kid already had some things figured out.

And that, right there, is how Salvador and Esperanza Vega joined our adventure.

FIFTEEN

$\int$o here's what I learned about Esperanza and Salvador Vega.

They were pilgrims on a quest, just like me and Rodeo.

Salvador didn't seem to like talking about family stuff too much, so it was tough prying details out of him. They'd left their home in Orlando a few days before. His mom and his aunt had worked together, but they'd both lost their jobs somehow. His aunt knew someone who said she might be able to get them both jobs in some little town outside St. Louis, Missouri. She had left a few days before them, and they followed her once they'd gotten everything figured out and packed up their stuff. His aunt had told them to just head north toward St. Louis and she'd work out the details on the job and let them know where she was . . . but then their car had broken down at the same time that his aunt had mysteriously stopped answering her phone.

That's when me and my watermelon slushy entered the story.

"How'd they lose their jobs?" I asked.

"None of your business," Salvador said after a second. He didn't say it all rude or mean or anything, but there was a definite don't-push-it edge to his voice, so I shrugged and rolled with it.

"Fair enough," I said. "So . . . you really have no idea where you're going?" It was about an hour after Rodeo and Lester had swooped back and picked us all up. The bus was dark, lit only by the drifting headlights of other cars on the highway. Ivan was sitting on the couch between me and Salvador, and we were taking turns petting him.

Salvador shrugged.

"Well, we don't *not* know where we're going. We're going to St. Louis. Kind of. Missouri, at least."

"You *don't not know* where you're going?" I repeated, raising my eyebrows. "Missouri's a big state, man."

"My aunt's gonna tell us where to go," Salvador muttered, scowling. "Her friend's cousin had some connections at a hotel or something, but she didn't know exactly where. That's all. She's gonna call and tell us once she finds out, and then we'll go there. That's it. No problem."

"All right, all right," I said, putting up my hands in surrender. "No problem here. Rodeo and I haven't known where we're going for, like, five years, so I got no room to judge. At least you're heading *somewhere*. Theoretically, anyway."

Salvador had his backpack sitting next to him, and an ID tag hanging off one of the straps caught my eye. It said, "Property of Salvador Peterson."

"Why's that say Peterson?" I asked. "Isn't your last name Vega?"

Salvador's jaw clenched.

"Peterson is my *dad*'s last name." He said the word "dad" like it was a curse word. "I don't go by that anymore."

"Oh. How come?"

Salvador chewed on his upper lip, his eyes narrowed. His nostrils were flared. I wasn't an idiot. I'd had enough experience with no-goes to know I'd just bumped into one.

"Never mind," I said quick. "None of my business, right?"

"Right." He looked up toward the front of the bus and pointed at the driver's seat with his chin.

"So why do you call him Rodeo? Why don't you call him Dad?"

"Because that's what he wants to be called."

"Okay. But he *is* your dad, right?"

"Shhhh," I said, dropping my voice to a hush. "Keep it down. He'll hear you."

Salvador's eyebrows lowered.

"Who cares?"

"*I* do. He gets upset. It's hard for him."

The look of confusion on Salvador's face was clear as day, even in a dark bus.

"All right. Yes, he's got another name he don't use, and, no, I don't ever call him Dad, and both those things have the same reason behind them." I took a second, thinking how best to explain. Life's a tricky tangle to unwind sometimes, and Rodeo's a heckuva knot to throw into it.

"So, I used to have two sisters and a mom."

"Used to?"

"Yeah. They died, like, five years ago." Out of the corner of my eye, I saw Salvador's mouth drop open but I kept on talking, saving him from having to try and say something thoughtful and sympathetic. "It was real tough on Rodeo. Darn near killed him, I think. He was . . . He was . . ." My words left me for a minute, remembering. How Rodeo had been, back then, back after it happened. How everything had been. I shook my head. Going back there in my head wouldn't do any good. "Once he kinda got his feet back under him, he couldn't stand to stay there, where we lived. Too many memories, I guess. So we sold the house and all our stuff and bought this bus and we been on the road ever since. No looking back. One big adventure." I tried to put plenty of pep in my voice at the end, but somehow it came out wrong and flat, like a week-old balloon. So I propped it up with a smile, showing my teeth in the headlight glare.

Salvador was just looking at me, all serious.

"It's good," I reassured him. "What happened, happened. There ain't no need for us to dwell in all that sadness. So we don't talk about it, or them, and then we don't have to be sad, and then Rodeo can be okay. That's my job. It's good."

There was quiet then. Between Salvador and the road and Ivan and the night and me.

Salvador broke the quiet, but he broke it gently, with a voice that was low, like a warm mug in cold hands.

"But why don't you call him Dad, then?"

"It's all part of that no-looking-back deal, you see. If I call him Dad, it just reminds him. Of them, I mean. My sisters. And he doesn't like that. So, when we hit the road, we left all that 'Dad' stuff behind. Picked ourselves new names. He became Rodeo, I became Coyote. We did it all legal and everything. Changed our last name, too, to something that showed our new lives: Sunrise. A fresh start."

"Wait. So your actual name is Coyote Sunrise?"

I grinned. "Yep."

"And your dad's name is *Rodeo Sunrise*?"

I pursed my lips and nodded.

"Huh," Salvador said doubtfully, then shrugged. "Kinda fits, actually. But . . . how do you pay for stuff? I mean, if your dad's not, like, working or whatever?"

"Money's not a problem. There was a settlement. Because of the accident, I mean. We got money from the company whose truck . . . well, whose truck caused the accident."

We sat in quiet for a while. A few minutes, even. And then Salvador broke the silence with another question.

"What were their names?"

"Whose?"

"Your sisters."

I looked up at him, saw his waiting eyes. He had nice eyes, Salvador did. Quiet eyes. I know it's weird to call eyes "quiet," since I've never seen a *loud* eyeball, but it's the truth. Salvador's eyes were quiet, and something about that quietness kinda gave you the courage to talk to them.

I glanced toward the front, making sure Rodeo wasn't listening. I had a feeling like when you're holding something too hot in your hands and you gotta set it down. I leaned forward so my mouth was so close to Salvador's ear that I could smell his deodorant. It had a kind of distracting pine-tree smell to it.

"Ava," I whispered, "and Rose."

The names were like candy in my mouth for just a second. Sure, it turned sour soon enough, but for a few breaths the sweetness made it hard for me to talk.

I leaned back into my own spot.

"Those are pretty names," Salvador said, and I just nodded.

Then he asked, "What's your real name? The one you had before?"

I opened my mouth, snapped it shut, then opened it again. Salvador just waited calmly, which was actually kinda infuriating.

I worked real hard to smile at him, and when I answered him my voice was as light as anything.

"None of your business," I said.

He smiled back a little, smiled at how I'd used his own words against him, but it wasn't much of a smile.

"Fair enough," he said, and I gave him the same smile back. He shook his head. "Man. We're a mess."

"Who?" I asked.

"All of us," he said with a little laugh. "Me and my mom are heading off to somewhere we don't even know, for a job we aren't even sure exists. And you and your dad are doing whatever this is, driving around and, like, *pretending* that—"

"We're not pretending anything," I cut in, my voice cold. "And we're not a mess. We're okay, Rodeo and me. Better than okay. Better than anybody. We're *solid*, solid as the Rockies."

Doubt was drawn all across Salvador's face.

"Whatever. What do you call this?" He gestured around us at the bus.

"We call it . . . We call it . . . *living*. Freedom. We call it taking care of each other. And moving forward." Salvador stared at me, his face still unconvinced, his eyes still maddeningly quiet.

"It works for us," I said.

"Does it?" he asked. "I mean, maybe it works for *him*. But does it work for you . . . *Coyote*?"

He said my name the way people do when they curl their fingers in the air like sarcastic quotation marks. He said my name like it was a joke, like a punch line, like an elbow to the ribs.

My throat hurt. My stomach churned.

I am not a mess. I am not a joke. I am not fragile. I am not broken.

I stood up, bent down, and picked up Ivan, a limp body and a weak *squeak* his only protest at being disturbed mid-nap.

"I'm going to bed," I said to anyone who happened to be listening, and I walked back with my cat and I pulled the curtain to my room closed behind me and I slept just fine, thank you.

CHAPTER
SIXTEEN

*N*ow, here's the thing with grudges: I don't have much experience with 'em, so I'm probably not all that good at holding them. But I do my best.

So when I got up the next morning and stumbled out through my bedroom curtain, I was all set for a day of spurning and ignoring stupid Salvador and his quiet eyes and his pine-tree armpits. I mean, I'm never that much of a morning person, but that particular A.M. I made double-sure I had that chip lodged firmly on my shoulder before I left my room.

Yager was lit up golden in the morning light and Lester was stretched out snoring on the couch. Rodeo's feet were sticking out from under his blanket pile. I shook my head at their sleeping selves. What's the point of having two drivers if they both go to sleep as soon as I nod off?

Salvador's mom was sitting in the same seat she'd been in the night before, looking out the window. I didn't see Salvador, but then I jumped a little when something stirred right next to me and I saw Salvador, lying propped up against the side of the bus and blinking at me sleepily, with Ivan curled up sound asleep on his lap.

Salvador, sleeping in *my* home, with *my* cat? Ivan, sleeping with stupid Salvador, instead of with me? They both had a lot of nerve.

"Good morning," I said, and while those words are technically nice words I said them so cold you coulda stirred 'em into a glass of milk and made ice cream, but then Salvador answered in a husky whisper without a moment's hesitation, looking all serious right up at me, "I'm sorry."

Now, I'd never had someone answer a "good morning" with an "I'm sorry" before, and I'll admit it threw me off. I was still a little dreamy-brained, and I thought maybe either he had heard me wrong or I had heard him wrong, so I said, "I *said*, 'Good morning.'"

Salvador nodded.

"I heard you. I just wanted 'I'm sorry' to be the first words I said to you today."

I blinked at him.

"I was, like, a jerk last night. I don't know why I . . . do that sometimes. Trying to act tough or something, I don't know, like I don't care or whatever, but it's not . . . I mean . . ." Salvador trailed off and scowled, then started over fresh, still whispering every word. "I know I made you mad and I know it was my fault and I haven't been able to sleep. I didn't wanna, like, disturb your privacy or whatever, so I been waiting out here for you to come out so I could tell you I was sorry."

I took a breath, desperately trying to find that chip I'd put on my shoulder.

"Sure looks like you were able to sleep."

"Well, maybe a little," he murmured, rubbing his eyes.

"Why are you whispering?" I asked.

He pointed at my traitorous cat, passed out on his legs.

"Ivan's sleeping," he said in that annoying way he had of making it seem like the answer was obvious.

I *supposed* I could maybe forgive Salvador, seeing how contrite he was and how thoughtful he was being toward my one and only Ivan. I *supposed* my shoulder was pretty much chip-free about the time he whispered my cat's name. But I also supposed he didn't have to know that just yet. Nothing wrong with letting someone know that a little "I'm sorry" don't get them totally out of the woods that easy.

"I gotta pee," I said, starting to walk past him with my chin held high.

"Wait," Salvador hissed. "So, are we cool? Do you forgive me . . . Coyote?"

The way he included that "Coyote" there? That was smooth. He coulda just said, "Do you forgive me," but he added that "Coyote" and he said it soft but he said it right. He didn't say it like a punch line; he said it like it was a real name. Like it was a good name. And when he said it like that, he wasn't just saying my name; he was saying with his eyes and his voice, "This is your name and this is how I should've said it and this is how I'll always say it from now on."

"Well," I said to him, and I may even have let a little smile creep in. "Let's just say I don't *not* forgive you, Salvador Vega."

And then I walked away and left him sitting there with my cat, because it was time to wake up Rodeo and get some more miles under our belts. Plus, I wasn't joking, I really did have to seriously pee.

CHAPTER
SEVENTEEN

Sometimes, when you're on the road for a long time, and the highway is humming along underneath you and the sun is shining sideways through the windows and the world is blurring by through the glass, something magical happens. No. "Magical" ain't the right word. "Magical" feels glittery and fake and cute. This feeling, the one I'm talking about, is almost the opposite of that. It's solid, and deep down, and a forever kind of smooth, like river rocks. This feeling I'm talking about is this: It's a rising up, like you're taking flight and leaving the road behind, like you're in a moment that somehow lifts up free from the rest of your life. In that moment, wherever you just were and wherever you're about to be don't matter one little bit; just for a few breaths, you're everywhere and nowhere, and you can feel your soul touching something big, some kind of truth that's hidden most of the time. It's like the first time you ride a bike: All at once, out of nowhere, the wobbling world settles down to a thrumming harmony, there's a balance that goes down to your bones, a kind of balance you never knew was there until it came alive all around and inside you; the falling stops and the flying starts and everything just *hums*, everything just *rings true*. It's like that, this feeling I'm talking about.

I know, I know—come on, Coyote. I sound like Rodeo. It doesn't make any sense. Unless you've ever felt it, I mean. Because once you feel it, you know it ain't any kind of nonsense at all.

Well, anyway. I had one of those moments the first morning that Salvador and his mom were with us.

It was like this:

It was that sleepy early-morning time and we were mostly feeling quiet. It was warm but not hot, and we had some windows cracked so there was a breeze flowing around us. Lester was up driving. Salvador and me were on opposite ends of the couch, me reading and him just looking out the window. Ms. Vega was sitting in the Throne across from us, and Rodeo was sitting on the floor, leaning back against his bed, plucking lazily at his guitar.

He wasn't playing a song, really, just picking and strumming through some chords, but then a song started pushing through and he slid right into it and I knew which one it was. It was one of my favorites, and when Rodeo started murmuring the words, I couldn't help myself and I started to sing along. We were both soft at first but then our voices found each other and we got louder, opening our throats a bit to let the song out. Rodeo's eyes caught mine and we traded smiles as we sang. Out of the corner of my eye, I could see Salvador and his mom looking at us and I could have been self-conscious, I guess, but heck, it was *my* living room even if it was moving at seventy miles an hour, so why shouldn't I sing in it?

> *"When the light is on my side*
> *Love reveals itself to me—*
> *Then I can, yes, I can,*
> *I can be set free."*

It's sort of a slow song but one you really kind of have to shout, and as we headed into the next verse we did, tilting our heads back and hollering it out.

"Yeah, sing it!" Lester called back from the front. I smiled bigger and really started belting it out. I heard a rhythm sneaking in under our voices and realized that Ms. Vega was clapping along, not just on the beat like most folks do, but funkier . . . hitting offbeats, throwing in some accents and exclamations, adding a whole new flavor to the song. Rodeo cheered her and gave her a big smile and I saw that Salvador's knee was bobbing along to the music, his chin rocking a bit.

I fished under the couch where we always kept one of our tambourines, just in case, and tossed it to him. He caught it but then froze and looked at me wide-eyed, all awkward all of a sudden.

"Play!" I encouraged him, then crowed out the end of the second verse:

> *"When you're tired, and you're torn,*
> *Humankind seems filled with misery—*
> *Then you can, yes, you can,*
> *You can be set free."*

Salvador still wasn't playing, and I laughed and shook my head at him. How the heck can you be shy about playing the tambourine? Lord, all you have to do is bang it on your knee.

Rodeo jumped into a clumsy guitar solo and Salvador said to me, "Who is this?" and I said, "This is us!" back to him, all smiles and grooving on that rising-up feeling and he said, "No, like, who sang this song?" and I answered him, "Langhorne Slim!" and he said, "Who?" and I said, "It don't matter, it's us singing it now, come on and play!" and I leaned over and slapped the tambourine he was still holding like it was a dang bomb and he swallowed but then he started playing, just hitting it against his leg on the beat, about as lazy as you can play a tambourine, but it was better than nothing and that happy jingle-jangle was just what the song needed and his mom started clapping louder and Rodeo and I launched into the final verse.

Ivan, no doubt roused from a nap by all our carrying on, came yawning out through my bedroom curtain and then stopped and took in the scene. He didn't look all that impressed. He weaved his way through the concert, tail held tall and straight, and hopped up into my lap. He looked up at me, his eyes that crazy crystalline blue, and I scratched him just right behind his ears.

I love that Ivan had five laps to choose from, and he chose mine.

My heart was full right there. I sang that song with Rodeo right over the top of that clapping jingle-jangle rhythm and the world swirled around me and Lester was drumming on the steering wheel and keeping us flying through it and the one and only Ivan was warm on my lap and then it happened, that feeling, the lifting-up-from-the-world feeling. I was sitting in the middle of the music with all those singing souls and it felt like forever, it felt like always, it felt like a little piece of the biggest thing in the world. It felt like family. My whole heart was tingling.

And then, of course, the song ended. Come on, Coyote, of course it did. The clapping stopped. The tambourine disappeared. And I fell back to earth, back down into my bones, and I felt that it was only a cat on my lap, felt the empty space on the couch beside me, and maybe I don't know why, but I felt something like tears sting their way into my eyes and I looked away from everyone else, looked off out into what was just kind of an empty highway world.

There's so much sadness in the world.

CHAPTER
EIGHTEEN

"*G*ood lord, it is *hot*," Rodeo said, taking one hand off the steering wheel to wipe his forehead.

"It's Georgia in August, man," Lester said with a chuckle. "What did you expect?"

Rodeo wasn't joking. It *was* hot, and having all the windows in the world down didn't help that much. Salvador and his mom were still back half-sleeping on the couch, and Lester and me were sitting up front by Rodeo, squinting into the sunshine and sweating through our clothes.

"Yeah, brother, but it's, like, melt-the-ChapStick-in-your-pocket hot, and it's barely nine o'clock in the morning. That ain't right."

I laughed along with Lester, but I wasn't really thinking about the heat or worrying about ChapStick. I stared straight ahead and tuned out their conversation. My mind was all maps and miles and minutes. I'd done a little casual conversational digging, trying to see how much driving we'd done while I'd been sleeping the night before. It was tricky, getting info without Rodeo catching on that anything was up. But I knew that me getting to where I needed to be depended on Rodeo not knowing we were going there.

From what I could tell, once I'd gone to bed Rodeo had driven for a couple hours, and then Lester had done the same, and then he'd gotten too tired and pulled over and parked until the morning. They'd both taken their sweet time sleeping in, so by the time I'd gotten up around seven thirty, I figured we'd already been parked for a few hours. They'd gotten us out of Florida and into Georgia, though, so at least we were making progress. We were getting closer and closer to that memory box. I got tingly and all scratchy-throated just thinking about it.

"Coyote?"

Lester's voice shook me out of my thoughts. I realized he was looking at me, waiting for me to answer a question. I'd been too lost in maps and memories to hear.

"Sorry, what?"

Lester laughed.

"Girl, you were a million miles away there."

Actually, by my calculations I was more like twenty-five hundred miles away, but I just smiled and shrugged and let it slide.

"I said, is it really worth it? Driving all the way across the country to get it? I mean, how bad can you want it?"

My mouth went dry. My breath stopped in my lungs. I saw Rodeo glance away from the road to look at me.

"Want what?" I croaked. All I could picture was that memory box buried under those trees. All I could think to answer was, "Yes! Yes, it's worth it. I want it so bad, it hurts."

Lester wrinkled his forehead at me.

"The sandwich," he said. "That's why you're on this trip, right? For some magical pork chop sandwich?"

I blinked. Forced my mouth into a smile. Lester and Rodeo'd been talking about my fictitious Dead Dream. That's all. I tried to slow down my racing heart.

"Oh, yeah. Sorry. I'm still tired, I guess." I noticed Rodeo giving me another curious look. "But, yeah. It's totally worth it. The pork chop sandwich, I mean. It's amazing."

"Must be," Lester said, clicking his tongue and shaking his head.

"Oh, they're solid grub," Rodeo jumped in. "All loaded with pickles and onions and mustard. Side of fries. That's good eating."

"I could go for that," Lester said. "I'm *starving.*"

Rodeo shot him a thoughtful look.

"Yeah? It is about breakfast time." Rodeo eyeballed me. "We're crossing a river a few miles ahead, little bird. What do you think— Dine 'n' Dip?"

I was stuck. I most definitely did *not* want to pull over to swim or eat or anything else. I wanted to get as far as we could as fast as we could, and we'd only been driving about an hour and needed to make up some lost time. But I couldn't think of any excuse not to stop. I was *always* down for a Dine 'n' Dip. Rodeo'd be suspicious for sure if I passed it up now.

"You betcha," I said, and flashed him a double thumbs-up to hide any frustrated hesitation that might've snuck into my voice.

"All righty." Rodeo grinned and held up his palm and I slapped it in a high five. "Alert the troops, monkey pie."

I crossed the aisle to stand on the seat by the door. There was an old brass bell, a little bigger than a soup can, bolted to the ceiling. Rodeo had picked it up at a secondhand store a couple years back. It was pretty tarnished and dented-up, but it did the job when an announcement needed to be made or a hippie woken up. We called it the Holy Hell Bell on account of if you really put your arm into it, that old bell made a holy hell of a racket.

I grabbed the bell's knocker and whipped it back and forth, making an almighty clanging. Lester laughed out loud, and back on the couch I saw Salvador jump up like a snake had crawled up his pant leg. Ivan, sunning himself in the tomatoes, just put back his ears and glared at me.

"Grab your suits, folks!" I hollered over the din. "Five minutes 'til a Dine 'n' Dip!"

The river wasn't much—I coulda thrown a rock right across it, if it was the right rock—but it was shaded by trees and cool enough without being cold and there were grassy spots on the bank to sit and eat at, so all in all it was a perfect river for a Dine 'n' Dip.

Lester, Ms. Vega, and Rodeo took a seat in the shade and started in on the sandwiches we'd made from grub from our cooler. Salvador and me headed straight for the water. I'd changed into my swimming suit and he was wearing an old pair of cut-off jean shorts and we were both *ready* to cool off in that water.

The river was cool and coffee-with-plenty-of-milk-colored and the bottom of it squished up between my bare toes. Salvador and me stood by ourselves, hip-deep in the muddy water.

I don't know if Salvador was peeing or not, but I know I was. Some folks probably say they never pee in the water when they're swimming on a summer day, but some folks are definitely liars. I'm sorry, but if you're already standing in a river and you're getting *out* to go pee, you're doing it wrong.

And for the record, I'm pretty sure Salvador *was* peeing. He was awful quiet and looked a little preoccupied for those first twenty seconds or so. I was upstream, so I didn't care either way.

For a while we did that hug-yourself-and-breathe-through-clenched-teeth thing you do when you're getting used to the water, even though it wasn't all that cold. We grinned at each other, shivering. And then, at some point, we both got awkward.

I mean, I was wearing just my swimsuit, which was a two-piece. And he was standing there with no shirt on. I don't care who you are, it changes the tone of a conversation if you can see each other's belly button.

"So," Salvador said, and I did some sort of weird laugh and said, "Yeah," and that's about as far as we got for a bit.

But me? I don't do awkward. Life's too short.

"Race you to the other side," I said, looking at the far shore.

Salvador looked doubtfully at the water in front of us.

"I don't know if I wanna go under," he said. "It doesn't look, like, super clean."

"Chicken," I said.

"I'm not a chicken."

"Well, either you're afraid of the water or you're afraid of losing. Either way . . ."

Salvador scowled.

"Ready," I said, and he looked at me and shook his head.

"Set."

"No," he said, all stubborn, but I saw him moving his feet and readying his body.

"Go!" I shouted as I dove, and out of the corner of my eye I saw him wait only, like, half a second before diving in beside me.

Salvador was a little older than me. He was taller, with longer arms, and yeah, sure—even I'd have to admit that he *maybe* had stronger muscles than me.

I ain't saying that as an excuse. I'm saying it as a *brag*. 'Cause I beat that boy to the other side of the river by so much that my hair was practically dry by the time he came thrashing up to me.

I was sitting there in the shallows, smiling and breathing easy.

Salvador splashed up beside me and flipped over on his back, gasping up at the sun.

"You," he said between breaths, "are really fast."

"Yeah." I grinned. "Being a strong swimmer is something Rodeo's always been big on. We even stayed in a town for four weeks once so I could take advanced lessons."

"Cheater. You didn't warn me you were so fast."

"You didn't tell me you were so slow," I said, and Salvador fake-scowled and splashed me and I splashed him back and we both snorted and then closed our eyes and looked up at the sun to dry our faces. There were clouds rolling in, dark ones, but the day was still mostly hot and the sun still mostly bright. The awkwardness was gone, just like I'd planned. Putting a boy in his place is a great way to take the tension out of a situation.

Across the way, Lester, Ms. Vega, and Rodeo were chatting, chewing on their breakfast.

"So," Salvador said, "why you guys heading north?"

"I already told you. For that pork chop sandwich in Montana." Salvador sniffed.

"Uh-huh. Right. Now, what's the real reason you're heading north?"

I eyed Salvador for a second. He looked back at me, waiting. He was a little too smart for my own good.

"Getting something," I said vaguely. I don't know why I wasn't eager to talk about the memory box with Salvador. Maybe I was just kinda digging our summer swimming hole vibe and didn't wanna get all heavy by bringing my stuff into it. Salvador wasn't letting go that easy, though.

"What kind of something?"

I blew out a breath, fluttering my lips.

"I'll show you mine if you show me yours."

"What?" Salvador's face flushed deep red in, like, a second. He was a much faster blusher than swimmer.

"Geez. I mean, I'll tell you where we're going if you tell me why your mom and aunt lost their jobs."

Salvador's face closed up hard and lost its blush.

"That's personal."

"Likewise."

Salvador narrowed his eyes at me and I narrowed mine right back.

"Fine," he said.

"You go first."

Salvador rolled his eyes but said, "My mom didn't lose her job. We left for . . . other reasons." He was looking away from me, his body tight and tense.

"Okay," I said carefully. "Like . . . ?"

Salvador blinked. A lot. And fast. When he turned to me, he turned so fast I almost flinched, and his eyes were red and watery.

"I'm only telling you this because I was a jerk last night," he said, and I kinda nodded, and then he looked away from me and said, "We left because of my dad."

That's all he said. Just said it and left it sitting there. But I didn't jump in with a question or nothing, 'cause I could tell he wasn't done talking. He just needed a sec. So I gave it to him.

"My dad's a jerk," he said finally. "He's always been a jerk." He shook his head. "Well, I mean, not *always*. Like, sometimes he's cool. Fun and funny and stuff. But he's got this temper. And when he's mean, he's *mean*. And when he's mad, he's *mad*. And when he's mad, sometimes he . . ." Salvador trailed off, his voice kinda low and broken. I kinda thought I knew where he was going and my eyes were stinging already. Then, Salvador finished the sentence. "Sometimes he . . . hits."

I swallowed. Blinked a couple times.

"He hits you?"

Salvador, still looking away, shrugged. "Mostly my mom."

That "mostly." Boy. That word just hung there. Now I knew why Salvador stopped using his dad's last name.

Up in the riverside trees behind us, a bird chirped out some sort of cheerful song that just didn't fit the moment. Salvador scooped a rock up off the muddy bottom and chucked it out into the river.

"My aunt's been trying to get Mom to leave him forever. 'Cause of all that stuff. And we tried, a couple times. But it's hard. 'Cause he's, like, so sorry after. Or acts like he is. Until the next time." He dug up another rock, sent it skipping across the surface. "But . . . I don't know. Maybe we just finally realized that there'll always be a next time. So we left. And here we are."

We sat in silence for a second, the muddy water flowing around and between us.

"I'm sorry he hit you," I said.

"I don't care about him hitting me," Salvador snapped, his eyes flashing back to me, full of fire. "I mean, whatever. I care about him hitting *her*. I hate that he did that. I hate that I couldn't stop him. I hate that I couldn't take care of her."

"It's not your fault, Salvador. It isn't your job to take care of her."

He gave me a funny look, then snorted.

"Yeah. You're one to talk."

I opened my mouth to reply, but nothing came out.

He looked away from me, out across the water to where our separate parents sat, eating in the shade.

"I think it *is* our job to take care of each other," he said. Then he shrugged. "I mean, we're all we've got."

That Salvador. He's a smart one, maybe.

I looked at him out of the corner of my eye. Sitting there in the water. Scowling and squinting, looking all tough. And also kinda looking not hardly tough at all. Looking kinda small and scared and sad. Come on, Coyote—like I didn't know you could be scared and sad and tough all at the same time, like I didn't know you could be a million different things all at the same time.

There's so much sadness in the world. Really, there is.

I pushed up off the bottom so the water floated me down an inch until I bumped into Salvador's shoulder. He looked at me, looking at him. He shook his head.

"No. Nope. Don't do that."

"What?" I said.

"Don't give me that look."

"What look?"

"Nah. I see it. You got that . . . that . . . *sympathy* look on. I know that look. I *hate* that look. We're not pitiful. We're strong."

I swallowed and wiped the look off my face, even though I didn't know I'd been making it 'til he told me. 'Cause I knew that look, too. And I hated it, too.

"Okay," I said. "Yeah. I get that look all the time. Everywhere we go. And I'm with you. It's the worst."

Salvador nodded and scratched at his cheek and looked out across the water.

"Let's make a deal, Salvador. Right here. I promise to never feel sorry for you, if you promise to never feel sorry for me." I held my dripping hand out to him.

His eyebrows flicked up and a little smile tickled the corners of his mouth.

"Yeah?"

"Yeah." I pushed my hand closer to him. "No sympathy."

He looked at my hand for a second, then reached out and took it. His hand was as wet as mine but warm, and he squeezed softly.

"No sympathy," he echoed.

We held each other's hand for a minute, until I think we both kinda realized that we were holding each other's hand and then we dropped them and looked off in different directions.

"You worry about him coming after you? Your dad, I mean?" I asked.

"Nah. I don't think he was ever all that excited about being a husband. Or a dad. He knew we were leaving, didn't even try to stop us. I think he's glad we left." Salvador's voice got awful tight there at the end and he looked away and cleared his throat, and I didn't say nothing, just let him have that moment.

"Okay," he said after a few seconds. "Your turn to tell. What are you really going to Montana for?"

Now, I'm not sure how much of my whole deal I'd been *planning* on sharing with Salvador. But I sure as heck knew that after all the hard truth he'd passed my way, Salvador deserved the truth, the whole truth, and nothing but the truth.

I took a big ol' here-I-go breath and then dove in.

"Well, we ain't really going to Montana," I began, and then I laid it all out. I told Salvador all about the park and the memory box and the call from my grandma and he listened close and quiet, nodding and squinching up his eyebrows. He was a good listener, that Salvador. Some folks listen without really listening, but Salvador ain't one of 'em. I kept it short, but everything I said he took in and put someplace inside himself. When I was done, he nodded slow to himself.

"Well. That's . . . That's, like, legit. I mean, it's important. No joke. I hope you get there in time."

"Me, too. And, remember: You can't breathe a word of this around Rodeo. If he finds out where we're really headed, he'll turn that bus around faster than . . . well, I don't know what. It'll be fast, though."

Salvador nodded seriously, then looked over at Rodeo.

"How long you gonna keep it a secret?"

I sighed. "As long as I can. Maybe a little longer, even."

Across the way, the grown-ups were finishing up their eating and starting to stir around a bit.

"Probably better get back," I said, and Salvador said, "Yeah, probably," and we stood up and took a couple steps deeper toward the middle, but then Salvador stopped and faced me and looked me in the eye and said, "Hey," and for one mortifying moment I thought he was gonna give me a hug or something, but then he just held his fist out and smiled a little and said, "You're cool, Coyote," and I bumped his fist and returned the smile and said, "You're cool, too, Salvador Vega."

I looked back at the river.

"Shoot," I said.

"What?"

"I'm already breaking our deal."

"Huh?"

"I mean, I *do* feel sorry for you."

"What for?"

"For how bad I'm gonna beat you swimming back across this river," I said, but I was already snickering before I finished the sentence and he shook his head and laughed and said, "Shut up, Coyote," and splashed water at me and that was that.

CHAPTER
NINETEEN

So, here's a memory. It's one of those weird memories that feels magic and unreal, like a song you wake up singing. It feels sweet and gritty like brown sugar in my mind. Maybe because it starts with me sleeping. Or maybe because it really was magic. I don't know. But here it is.

We were pulled over. Somewhere in Nevada, I think. Rodeo had driven the night before until the desert around us was silver with light from the full moon and the sky was crowded with stars. We were on a little two-lane highway, not a big ol' interstate freeway. Rodeo had his window open, so cool desert air flowed all around us. The radio was off. When there were no cars coming the other way, which was most of the time, he turned off Yager's headlights and we rolled through the night, nothing but moonlight showing the way.

That's how I fell asleep: moonlight all around, the desert air playing with my hair, Rodeo humming quiet to himself.

It was cool.

But that ain't the memory.

I woke up to Rodeo whispering my name, soft and excited. I'd fallen asleep up front, not back in my room, and I was curled up against the window. The bus was still, silent, and there was pinkish-yellow light seeping in through the windows.

I blinked, rubbed my eyes, tried to figure out where the heck I was.

Rodeo was kneeling on the seat in front of me, his own face still puffy with sleep but his eyes bright and looking out the window.

"Coyote," he whispered again, "look."

I straightened up and looked out the window that had been my pillow.

We were pulled over on a dirt road. I guess Rodeo had parked there to sleep once his eyelids got too heavy to drive.

The desert was waking up around us, the sunrise just starting to warm up over a red-rock mesa in the distance.

At first I didn't see her. My eyeballs were dry and crusty and she blended in so well. But then her big ears twitched, circling around after some sound, and there she was.

A coyote. Slender like a deer. Mottled brown and gray fur that looked coarse and soft at the same time, somehow. Long, skinny snout pointed our way. Eyes that were sharp, that were smart, that were wild, that were looking right at us. But not just at the bus . . . She was looking right in the window to where we were sitting, looking back.

"Your namesake," Rodeo whispered.

She was only, like, fifteen feet away, just standing there among the sagebrush. Her bushy tail held low, ribs rising and falling with her breathing, ears twitching and turning. Just standing there looking at me and Rodeo.

"Whoa," I said, smiling.

Rodeo was smiling, too, his eyes crinkled up with it.

"Good morning," he murmured, either to me or to the coyote, or maybe to both of us.

Then the coyote's head turned back toward the desert behind her. She lowered her head and yipped, one little bark.

And out of the shadows of the sagebrush tumbled two little brown bodies.

Pups.

They scampered up to her and stopped, one between her legs and one by her chest. They were all ears and legs, just as clumsy and cute as could be. They sniffed at her quick and then stopped, looking to where she was looking. Looking at us.

A mama. A mama and two babies. Daughters, maybe. Appearing out of a sunrise dream to visit us.

I looked up at Rodeo, excited.

But Rodeo's smile faded. He raised a hand, slow and kinda shaky, and pressed his fingers to the window, reaching out toward that mom and her two little ones. His eyes were full and wet.

I didn't say nothing. I looked at them coyotes, too. And I was trying my best to breathe and swallow.

I don't know how long we all stayed like that, us and the coyotes. Looking at each other, sitting quiet. Whether it was a few minutes or a few seconds, though, that time felt full, stuffed thick with life and feeling, splitting at the threads with breathing and thinking.

The sun finally poked its head over that mesa, and its sharp white light pierced the dawn's softness.

The mama coyote raised her nose, sniffing at the sky. Then

she lowered her head and looked at us and whined, just once. It wasn't a sad whine, or a hurt whine, or a scared whine. I don't know what it was. But I know it was for us.

Rodeo took a trembly breath.

"Once upon a time," he said, his voice hoarse and quiet. "Once upon a time."

And then, just like that, they were gone. The mama gave us one last look and then trotted off, as quick and graceful as you can imagine. Her babies followed, jogging along behind her. In a heartbeat they were gone, melted back into the desert or whatever dream they'd come out of.

Me and Rodeo sat looking at where they'd been, looking at the emptiness of the desert the mama and her babies had left behind. Rodeo's hand was still on the window, his eyes still full.

He sighed.

He leaned his head against the cool glass. I heard him sniff, once.

And then he went back to sleep. I heard his breathing get slow and regular.

I think maybe he was hoping that if he fell back asleep fast enough, he could catch up to that mama and her babies. That he could dream about them. Get a little more time with them. It's a nice thought.

I don't know if he did or not.

So there's that. I ain't never leaving that one behind, that memory.

It's a good one, I think.

I think.

CHAPTER
TWENTY

It was only, like, twenty minutes after the Dine 'n' Dip, as we were rolling down the road again and I had a belly full of breakfast, when the call came in.

I was sitting at one end of the couch, and Salvador was sitting on a box in front of me. Me and him were in the middle of a fairly epic match of Uno, piling up the ratty cards on a suitcase on the floor between us. Ivan was lying half on my lap, nudging my hand any time I had the nerve to stop scratching him.

I'd just hit Salvador with a vicious Draw Four when the moment was interrupted by a jarring, urgent ringtone.

Our heads snapped up, but no one moved for a second until Salvador came to his senses and jumped up and tugged the phone out of his pocket and looked at the display.

"It's my *tía*!" He punched the "Answer" button and dove right into an excited, rapid-fire conversation in Spanish. His eyes were shining, and he was wiggling like a puppy as he nodded and answered and questioned. The sun was coming in sideways through the bus windows, warming up his skin to a bright richness and sparkling his eager eyes. That kid was lit up, inside and out.

A weird, lumpy sick feeling settled down in my stomach as

I sat there watching Salvador talk to his aunt. It was a strange, sad kind of nervous and I didn't like it, and I looked away from Salvador and down at the cat purring in my lap, the cat that was happy and mine and not going anywhere.

Salvador ran up to his mom at the front of the bus and handed her the phone and then bounced back my way, swaying with the motion of the bus and standing there like he was too excited to sit down.

I slid Ivan off me, ignoring his surly side-eye, and stood up next to Salvador.

"So what's up?" I asked in a whisper.

"We're back in business," he said. "She lost her phone and our number was *in* her phone, which is why she wasn't answering or calling back. But she got a new phone and finally got our number through my *tío* who lives in Houston."

"Okay," I said. "Awesome. So . . . now we have an address to drop you off at?"

"Uh . . . I don't know yet. She was . . . kinda weird about that. She's talking to my mom about it now." His face clouded over and I followed him back up to the front to listen to his mom's half of the conversation, which was all a Spanish mystery to me. Salvador's scowl deepened as he listened, though. Lester, sitting in the seat behind Rodeo, was watching Ms. Vega close. Rodeo was tossing glances Ms. Vega's way, too. We could all tell something was up.

Finally, Ms. Vega hung up the phone. She looked out the window and said something to herself under her breath. She closed her eyes and shook her head.

"*Mamá?*" Salvador murmured.

She looked at him, but didn't say anything.

"Everything all right there, Ms. Vega?" Rodeo asked, his voice soft.

Ms. Vega swallowed. She lifted her chin. I saw her do it, saw her reach down inside herself and find strength. She was all kinds of strong, that Ms. Esperanza Vega.

When she spoke, there was no quiver to her voice.

"No," she said, soft but clear. "Everything is not all right."

TWENTY-ONE

Salvador sat down beside his mom. The bus rumbled along, no one talking, everyone waiting for Ms. Vega's news.

"Your *tía* doesn't have jobs for us," she said to Salvador. "And she's not in St. Louis."

"What?" Salvador asked.

Ms. Vega shook her head and her eyes narrowed.

"It's that *Chris*." She said the name like a curse word. "I told her he was no good." Then she spat another word, this time in Spanish, and I'm not gonna repeat it here because I'm not sure what it means, but based on how she said it and how Salvador's eyebrows went up when she said it, I'm, like, a hundred percent sure it *is* a curse word.

Salvador looked over at the rest of us.

"Chris is, uh, my aunt's boyfriend. He was the one who said he knew someone who'd hire her and Mom."

"So . . . where is she?" I asked.

Ms. Vega took a deep breath, then said, "Petoskey," and for a second I thought it was another Spanish curse word, but then she added, "She's in Petoskey, Michigan."

"Michigan?" Salvador blurted.

Ms. Vega nodded.

"*Sí.* That's where Chris says he can find us jobs *now.*" She rolled her eyes. Then she closed them and shook her head, her lips pursed tight. Salvador put an arm around her shoulders.

"Ms. Vega," Rodeo said, "don't you worry one second about this. Michigan's a beautiful state. One of my favorites. It's no big deal at all for us to swing up and drop you off up there."

My mouth went dry.

"What?" I exclaimed. "We can't go to Michigan!"

All the heads turned to me. I hadn't totally planned on shouting that out. It just kinda flew out of me in the moment. I stammered for something to say to fill the silence left by my words.

"Um. I mean. Isn't that, like, um, out of our way?" Yeah. Yikes. That was even worse. I knew I sounded like a total jerk. Even Lester was looking at me with a girl-are-you-serious-right-now look. But I was desperately trying to picture a map of our straight-shot route across the U.S. and desperately trying to figure how a zigzag detour to Michigan would look on it and desperately trying to remember how many hours I had left before I lost that memory box forever.

"Out of our way?" Rodeo said. *"Coyote."* Ouch. He said my name in a way I'm not sure I'd ever heard before, or at least not in a long, long time. Surprised. Disappointed. Sad. My face burned red. I was glad he was driving, glad I didn't have to look into his eyes when he said my name that way.

Salvador was looking at me. I could see his mind racing. He knew my secret.

"No," he said quick. "You guys don't have to take us. It's too far. We can take a bus, like we were gonna do."

— 153 —

That Salvador. He's a good one.

But Rodeo shook his head.

"No way, brother. You're already *on* a bus, remember? We ain't gonna abandon you folks in some dirty ol' bus station when you're already on a perfectly good bus right here. A little side trip okay with you, Lester?"

"Fine by me, man."

Rodeo made eye contact with me in the rearview mirror.

"Coyote?" he asked, his voice careful and testing. "Any reason we shouldn't take our friends here to where they need to be?"

I don't know how long it took me to answer. Honestly, it was probably, like, three seconds. It felt like a heckuva lot more, though. 'Cause in those three seconds, about a thousand thoughts shot through my mind. The memory box, sure. And the map and the ticking hands of the clock, yeah. And the fact that I had a secret to keep, and that if I said, "Well, actually we *do* need to abandon these folks in a dirty ol' bus station because I've been lying to you the whole time and we're actually heading back to the one place in the world where you don't want to go," my whole quest would be dead in the water anyway. But I also remembered Ms. Vega unlocking her car in a gas station parking lot to let me in to hide before she even knew me. And Salvador, with his listening eyes and his secret sharing and his first-thing-in-the-morning apologies.

Keeping my secret and getting that box was something I had to do. But maybe so was helping Salvador and his mom. Come on, Coyote—there wasn't no "maybe" about it.

"Of course not," I answered. I stretched a big grin onto my face and hoped it was big enough to hide the butterflies that were flat-out rioting in my stomach. I pointed with both hands out the windshield toward the horizon. "Michigan it is!"

Rodeo looked at me a second in the mirror, then smiled and nodded.

"Chart us a new course, Lester!" he called. "We got a family to reunite."

I could only fake a smile for about another four or five seconds, so when Lester started tapping on his phone, I got up quick and headed back to my room. I was all sweaty and nauseous and I needed to see a map ASAP.

I'd just flopped down onto my bed and opened the atlas when Salvador hissed, *"Coyote! Can I come in?"* through my curtain door.

"Yeah," I answered, and before his body was through the curtain he was already talking a couple miles a minute.

"Coyote I'm *so* sorry listen you don't have to take us there I know you need to get home and if I tell my mom what's going on I know she'll make Rodeo drop us off and—"

"Shut up a sec," I interrupted, not looking up from the map under my fingers. I traced the line from where we were in Tennessee up through Michigan and over to Washington, comparing it with my eyes to the straight line we had been traveling. "I think we can do this." I started to measure the distance with my fingers when something dropped onto the map, making me jump.

"Here. Use this." It was Salvador's phone. He already had the little map thing open and everything. "Just punch in where you wanna go."

I snatched it up and got to tapping.

"Okay," I narrated while I worked. "So, we're almost to Chattanooga, Tennessee, right now. From here to Poplin Springs—that's home—is . . . thirty-seven hours. If we add Petoskey into the middle of it, the drive time goes up to . . . huh." I blinked. Checked it again. Then I beamed up at Salvador.

"What?" he demanded. "How long?"

"Just forty-five hours. That's only eight hours longer. We can *totally* do this." Relief washed over me like a sunrise. Lord. I'd almost blown my secret, endangered my mission, and abandoned my friend—for nothing.

"Are you sure? I thought your timeline was, like, pretty tight." Salvador's forehead was all crinkled up in concern.

"It is. But we had a few hours of wiggle room."

Salvador still looked doubtful. I stood up to look him in the eye.

"This is important. You and your mom getting to your aunt safe, I mean. It's worth it, man. More than worth it. We'll get you there." I held my fist out toward him. He looked at it a second, eyes unsure, then back up at me.

"You're a good friend, Coyote," he said quietly. Then he bumped my fist and flashed me a shy kinda smile and turned and walked out of my room.

I let his words tingle in my heart for just a second. "Friend" wasn't a word I'd heard all that often. It *is* one of those words that once you hear it, you wanna hear it a lot more.

But I didn't have much time for tingling. I chewed on my lip, thinking.

I hadn't had many extra hours to start with, and I'd just given away eight of 'em. For this whole thing to work, we were gonna have to do a lot more driving and a little less sleeping.

Which meant it was time for me to have a heart-to-heart with Lester Washington.

TWENTY-TWO

"You want me to what?" Lester's voice was flat, his face set in a distinctly are-you-kidding-me kind of expression.

We were stopped for gas somewhere in Kentucky later that same afternoon. Rodeo had gone inside to use the bathroom and Lester was out pumping the fuel, and I knew it was my chance, so I took it.

"I want you to drive all night. Oh, and don't tell my dad that I asked you to. That's it."

"That's it, huh?" Lester cocked an eyebrow. "I'm gonna need a little more information, if you don't mind."

I eyed the convenience store door, checking for Rodeo. I'd noticed that Rodeo grabbed his book before he went in, so I figured I had a few minutes.

"I'm, uh . . . Well, I'm just kind of in a hurry. An *important* hurry. So I wanna cover as many miles as fast as we can."

"Uh-huh," Lester said. He crossed his arms and leaned against the bus. "Lay it on me, kid. This isn't about some pork chop sandwich, is it?"

I sucked on my teeth for a second. Squinted one eye against the afternoon glare and looked at Lester. He was good people, no doubt about it. And I needed his help—no doubt about that, either. But if I took a risk and told him everything and then he blabbed it to Rodeo, I'd be sunk.

I blew a strand of my hair out of my face.

"You promise not to tell Rodeo?" I asked, and without a pause Lester shook his head and said, "Nope," but when he saw my look of dismayed betrayal, he lightened up a bit.

"Okay, okay," he said. "Is whatever's going on illegal?"

"No, sir."

"Is it dangerous? You gonna get hurt?"

"No, sir."

It was Lester's turn to suck on *his* teeth. He considered me for a few seconds, an eyebrow arched.

"Ticktock, ticktock, Lester," I said.

"Okay. *If* I decide it's not illegal and *if* I decide it's not dangerous and *if* I decide I'm not worried about you, I promise not to tell your daddy. That's the best I can do."

I clicked my tongue. That was about three more *if*s than I was comfortable with, but I didn't have a ton of options. I took a lung-filling breath and spat it all out at once, starting with "You know how I told you about my mom and my sisters?" and ending thirty seconds later near the bottom of my lungs with "And so I gotta get back there by Wednesday morning, otherwise it's gone forever and I just couldn't live with that. The end."

During my spiel Lester's face had gone from an amused what-is-this-weirdo-girl-up-to expression to something more serious. When I was done, he just looked at me a second. Then he nodded a small sort of nod, more to himself than to me.

"And you really can't tell your daddy all that?"

"Not yet," I said with a shake of my head. "We haven't been back in five years, and if he had his way, we'd never go back. It's just too sad for him. And I get that. But losing that box is too sad for me. So I gotta get as close as I can before he finds out."

"And then?"

I shrugged.

"I'll blow up that bridge when I come to it, I guess."

Lester stepped in closer so I could see the little brown flecks in his green eyes.

"Coyote, I will not lie to your daddy. If he asks me, I'm telling him the truth." I waited, breathless, for what he was gonna say next. "But other than that, I'll do everything I can to get you home in time."

I couldn't help it. I threw my arms around ol' Lester in a big hug.

"Thank you, thank you, thank you," I said, and he kinda laughed and patted my back awkwardly and said, "All right, all right," and then the gas pump *clunk*ed off and I let him go and he screwed the gas cap back on Yager.

"I better go take a nap," he said. "I got a long night ahead of me."

I grinned at him.

"Darn right you do." I felt a million pounds lighter, with Lester and Salvador helping me carry that secret around instead of having to do it all by myself.

Sometimes trusting someone is about the scariest thing you can do. But you know what? It's a lot less scary than being all alone.

CHAPTER
TWENTY-THREE

It was dark, and I squinted when the headlights from an oncoming car flashed into the bus. We'd found a good place for a quick dinner that was only a few miles off the highway and were now just about ready to make our way back to that humming interstate. We were supposedly in Ohio, at least according to all the signs and maps. No offense to Ohio, but it's one of those states where sometimes it's kinda hard to tell whether you're there or not. Rodeo was settling the bill and hitting the bathroom and the rest of us were hanging out in Yager, ready to get back on the road. Lester, bless his soul, was saddled up in the driver's seat after telling Rodeo, "You know, I feel like driving for a while tonight."

Salvador and I were sitting back on the couch, letting our stuffed bellies settle.

"So," Salvador asked me, "I think you should give *your* answers now."

"My answers to what?" I asked him.

"To the questions. The ones you asked us before you let us on."

"Why should I answer those?"

"Well, *we* all did. You know our favorite books and places and sandwiches. And I don't know yours."

"All right, Mr. Salvador. Fine. Favorite sandwich is definitely a BLT. It ain't fancy, but it's perfect. If you put plenty of mayo on the bread and plenty of pepper on the tomatoes, it doesn't get any better."

Salvador curved a doubtful eyebrow at me.

"Okay. I mean, I'd throw away the lettuce and the tomato and just eat the bacon, but whatever."

"Well, then, you're an idiot, Salvador Vega. It's the balance that makes it great."

"I don't want *balance* on a sandwich, weirdo. I want cheese."

"You're not allowed to argue with the answers. You asked me *my* favorite sandwich, not yours. Don't mansplain my own sandwich to me. Or, *boy*splain, I guess."

"What's 'mansplaining'?"

"Mansplaining is when a man explains something to a woman like she's an idiot when really *he's* the idiot. It's a thing. I read about it in the *Times*." Rodeo makes me read the *New York Times* front to back anytime we see it for sale, so I'm generally super informed about most of the important things going on in the world. It's a blessing and a curse. There are a lot of awful things going on in the world.

"Fine," Salvador conceded. "BLT it is."

"Okay, best book is easy, too. *The One and Only Ivan*, hands down. Fantastic."

"I haven't read that one."

"Well, then, you're gonna. Nonnegotiable. I've got the book, I've got a reading light . . . You can start tonight."

"Maybe. Now, last question."

"Favorite place," I mused, looking off into the night. Funny, as many times as we'd asked other folks that question over the years, I'd never really thought about my own answer to it.

Several places floated right to the top of my mind. Sampson Park, of course, the very place I was headed. Just picturing that place brought back all sorts of memories. Memories of laughter, of chasing, of seasons, of warm hands holding mine. But I couldn't say that one. I couldn't make my very favorite place be a place I hadn't been to in five years, a place that was about to get bulldozed into oblivion. Too sad.

I thought of my grandma's house, with its cozy library and huge, comfy couch and bunk bed in the basement. Well, it *used* to have a bunk bed in the basement. I guessed maybe it didn't anymore—no need for it. I thought of my own bedroom in our old house, the room I'd shared with Rose, the room that had a fish tank and our scribbled pictures taped to the wall and the giant stuffed bear in the corner. No. I couldn't pick any place that I wasn't allowed to ever go to again. Also just . . . too sad.

It was a tough question. With me and Rodeo, places weren't places we loved. They were places we just passed through and left in our rearview mirror. Like people.

I looked up at the ceiling, thinking. And then I smiled. 'Cause I was looking at my answer.

"I'm not gonna tell you," I said, and when Salvador opened his mouth to argue I held up a finger and continued, "I'm gonna *show* you. Remember when you very first saw Rodeo?"

At that moment, the man himself came bounding up the bus stairs and patted Lester on the shoulder in the driver's seat and flopped down into one of the seats. I jumped up and said, "Rodeo!

Permission for a ride in the Attic." I pointed a thumb at Salvador. "With a wingman."

Rodeo squinted out the window. I knew he was checking to make sure we were within his very strict Attic rules.

"It's dark," I said. "Pitch. And we got, like, five quiet miles to the highway, all on back roads."

Rodeo pursed his lips, then shrugged, then flicked his chin at Salvador.

"Check with his mom. Tell him all the rules. Be safe."

"Got it."

I filled Salvador in on what was going on and his eyes lit up and he begged his mom and eventually got a yes, and next thing you knew I was pulling down the rope ladder from its hooks by the hatch to the roof. It was back by the curtain to my room, and we'd painted clouds on the ceiling all around it so that when we opened it during the day it looked like sunlight shining on a cloudy day.

"Keep it below thirty-five, Lester," I heard Rodeo saying from the front as I clambered up the swinging rungs. A few clicks of the latches and then I swung the hatch open and pulled myself up onto Yager's roof.

A second later Salvador was beside me, looking around at the little rooftop world.

I mean, there wasn't *that* much to see. It was pretty much just the yellow metal roof of a bus. But there was a metal railing that Rodeo had installed all around the edge, proving he had at least a little more sense than he let on sometimes. And it was all lit up by stars and silver moonlight seeping down from the sky.

"This is cool," Salvador breathed, crawling to the edge to peek down at the ground.

"Yeah. This is the Attic. We eat up here sometimes, or hang out. Sometimes we even drag our blankets up and sleep out here."

Beneath us, Yager's motor rumbled into action and Salvador's eyes went wide.

"Come on," I said, and he followed me at a careful crawl up to the front of the bus. I lay down on my stomach with my fingers on the front rail, and Salvador settled in beside me.

"Are we, uh . . . Are we really gonna ride up here?"

He was acting all tough, but I smiled 'cause I could hear the nervousness in his voice.

"Sure. But we never go fast and it's only on little roads with no traffic and it's not scary at all, you'll see. The rules are easy: No standing up. Knock three times on the roof if you want to stop. That's it. All right?"

Salvador breathed through his nose and nodded fast, like yeah-sure-obviously-I-ride-on-the-top-of-buses-all-the-time-what's-the-big-deal.

He still looked scared. So I decided to share one more thing with him, besides my favorite place in the whole world. I leaned in close so our faces were almost touching and I said, "You can shout secrets."

"Huh?"

"Once we're moving. With the engine roaring and the wind and everything, you can shout your secrets. Just shout 'em out at the world, or up at the moon, or into the wind. And no one will hear them."

Salvador swallowed.

"Why would you do that?"

"Because . . . Because it feels good. To say stuff you normally can't. To shout the truth. Sometimes I just shout . . . *names*."

"Whose names?" he asked, but he asked it quiet and serious and in a way that kinda told me he already knew the answer.

"Their names," I whispered. "Up here, I can say them. Up here, I can *shout* them."

Salvador nodded.

"So," I said, looking away from his eyes, which looked like they were very close to feeling sorry for me, which would be a broken promise, "feel free to shout a secret, if you want to. No one'll hear."

"*You'll* hear, Coyote."

I looked back at him and grinned.

"Yeah. But I won't tell."

He smiled back. And then we started moving.

Slow at first, but faster by the second. We turned out of the little diner parking lot and onto the two-lane road and then we really started moving and the wind pushed our hair back and blew tears into our eyes and Salvador tightened his grip on the rail and lowered his body even farther.

Thirty-five miles an hour don't seem like much when you're *in* a bus. But I'm telling you, it feels like something else altogether when you're *on* a bus.

I turned my head to Salvador, and he was smiling big, his teeth shining white in the moonlight.

"You gonna do it?" I hollered.

"You first!"

All right. All right.

That secret-shouting thing, that was personal. I'd never shared it. So, yeah. I was a little nervous. Come on, Coyote—I was shaking.

I'd never really had a friend before, maybe, and I'd never shared my favorite place with anyone before, maybe, but both those new things felt like *good* new things, so I figured maybe I had room in my life for even a little more courage.

I wriggled up onto my knees, still holding the rail with both hands. The wind whipped through my hair and I narrowed my eyes against the rushing air.

I looked up from the glare of the headlights to the softer light of the stars up above. And I thought of my big sister, the sister who helped me learn to write my name and who let me crawl into her bed when I was scared at night. I breathed it all in—the wind, the stars, the memory—in one big breath and then I threw my head back and let it out.

"Ava!" I shouted. "Ava!"

I closed my eyes and thought of my little sister, the sister who loved blowing the puffy heads off dandelions but always messed up and called them dandy*flowers*, the girl who cried whenever *I* got in trouble, even if she was the one who'd told on me—and I sucked in another breath and then let it out, too.

"Rose!" I hollered into the darkness, into the world, into my memories. "Rose!"

I didn't have to even try to remember my mom, didn't have to work to bring up a memory of her. She was always there, smiling, waiting. I could feel her fingers on my forehead, brushing my hair out of my eyes and tucking it behind my ears.

"Mom!" I yelled, pushing past the break in my voice. "I love you, Mom!"

My chin dropped to my chest and I knelt there, my eyes closed and my lungs heaving.

There was a stirring beside me and I knew Salvador was pulling himself up onto his knees.

He knelt next to me for a second, and then his shout rang out over the wind.

"I act tough," he yelled, "but I'm afraid almost all the time!"

Whoa. That was a good one. A big one. Salvador wasn't playing around with this secret-shouting thing.

I opened my eyes just as Salvador turned to look at me. His eyes were big, his mouth open, his T-shirt whipping around his body. There were tears in his eyes. But that could've just been the wind.

I had tears in my eyes, too. But that could've just been the wind, too.

We both looked so darn serious, shouting on our knees into the night on top of a moving bus.

Every once in a while in life you kind of zoom out and see what you must look like from outside your body.

We looked ridiculous.

I mean, we looked *awesome*, but . . . also ridiculous.

I laughed. A big, guffawing sort of laugh.

Salvador's eyebrows dropped for a second, but I think he realized pretty quick that I wasn't laughing at him or his secret.

Then he laughed, too. A real wide-mouthed, shoulder-shaking sort of laugh. He leaned over, bumping me in the shoulder. I bumped him back. We both faced back toward the front.

"I miss my family!" I shouted at the road up ahead.

"Sometimes I cry at night when my mom is asleep!" Salvador screamed.

Our shoulders were pressed together.

"I want to go home!" I hollered.

"I miss my friends!" Salvador shouted.

"I don't *have* any friends!"

Oops. My mouth snapped shut. I hadn't planned on sharing *that* particular secret. I may have gotten a little carried away.

Salvador's head turned toward me, but I kept my eyes straight ahead.

He looked at me for just a second. Then he looked forward again.

And then he shouted, "I really want Coyote to be my friend!"

My throat went tight and my stomach went all topsy-turvy. I blinked extra hard.

Salvador waited, then looked into my face. I had a hard time meeting his eyes.

"So?" he shouted right into my face like I couldn't hear him, and then he added "Will you?" and I laughed and then I screamed right back into his face, "Well, I won't *not* be your friend!" and he laughed, too, and then he yelled into my face, "Good enough!" and we both laughed and dropped back onto our stomachs and then somehow without saying anything we both rolled over onto our backs and lay there, looking up at the starry sky.

"Thank you," Salvador said in a not-shouting voice, his eyes still on the sky, and I wasn't even sure what he was thanking me for, but I wasn't raised in a barn so I just said, "You're welcome," but then that felt weird so I also said, "Thank *you*," and he said, "No problem."

He's all right, that Salvador.

More than all right, maybe.

But the next day, I had to say goodbye to him forever.

CHAPTER
TWENTY-FOUR

*P*etoskey, Michigan, came just too darn soon.

Petoskey, Michigan, wasn't just a city or a dot on a map or even a waiting *tía*; Petoskey, Michigan, was a goodbye.

Nothing personal against the good people of Petoskey, but by the time I got to Petoskey I *hated* Petoskey.

I thought I'd never fall asleep the night before, but next thing I knew I was blinking my eyes awake and the sun was rising. I could just feel in the air that we were deep in Michigan, and I hated it. I yawned and then scowled at the sunlight.

Ivan was lying next to me, blinking his sleepy blue eyes at me.

"Well. No sense in dragging this out, amigo. Time to tear off the Band-Aid, I guess."

Ivan just yawned at me, so I got up and walked out through my curtain.

Lester was heroically still up behind the wheel and Rodeo was snoring in his blanket pile and Ms. Vega was asleep on the couch. Salvador was awake, though, sitting in the chair across from the couch, reading the dog-eared copy of *The One and Only Ivan* I'd given him the night before. He looked up at me when I walked out and then away real quick, so I knew he kinda felt the same way I did, maybe.

I clenched my jaw and walked up to him.

"Hey," I said, and he said "Hey" back, and I leaned down to look at the pine trees whizzing by the window that looked distinctly like Michigander pine trees and I said, "Where are we, exactly?" and Salvador shrugged and then said, "Lester said we're, like, an hour away—about half an hour ago," and I said, "Oh, cool." A few seconds passed and then I said, "Hey. I don't do goodbyes, all right? You're cool, and we're kinda friends, and we're dropping you off, and that's fine. When we get there, could you just grab your stuff and hop on down? I don't wanna say goodbye. It's easier that way. Okay?" This was a lesson I'd learned the hard way, from all the times I'd almost made friends with some kid in a campground or hotel or city park or public library and then we'd left 'em behind. I know goodbyes, and the best goodbyes are the ones you don't say out loud.

Salvador blinked at me.

"Okay."

And I started to walk away toward the front of the bus but Salvador said, "Wait," and then he handed me a folded piece of paper. I took it and walked away and plopped into a seat by Lester and opened it up and all it had written on it were the words "Your Friend Salvador" and a phone number.

I held the paper in my hand and looked out the window, some weird version of a smile on my face.

I'll give it to Salvador: He was totally good about honoring requests from kinda friends. The drop went just like I'd asked. There was a phone call with his aunt to find out where she was and then Salvador and his mom bustled around, gathering up all their stuff. At one point Salvador came up to me with my copy of *The One and Only Ivan* and I said "Keep it," but other than that I kept my eyes on the pages of the book I was reading. And then we were there.

We met his aunt at a restaurant next to the hotel she was staying in. We pulled into the parking lot and Salvador and his mom got all excited when they saw her, through the window, sitting in a booth. I kept reading, my hand scratching at Ivan's furry back.

There were *some* goodbyes, but none for me. Rodeo and Lester wished them well and helped them unload their suitcases and stuff, and there were probably some hugs and whatnot, but I wasn't really paying attention.

Rodeo and Lester climbed back aboard and the door shut, and I accidentally looked up a little and saw, through the restaurant windows, Salvador's aunt jump up when he and Ms. Vega walked into the restaurant and there was some more hugging and what looked like a lot of excited talking.

Reuniting with family must be nice.

I put my nose back in my book.

Rodeo eased down into the driver's seat and looked at me for a second before asking, "How you doing, sugarplum?" and I just said, "Get this pile of junk moving, old man" without even looking up from my book but out of the corner of my eye I saw him nod and then the engine fired up and we were off.

I did sneak one more peek, though. Just one quick glance out the window, since I had to clear my throat anyway.

Ms. Vega was talking with her sister; they were holding both of each other's hands and looking right into each other's eyes, talking close and nodding. The way sisters do.

Salvador was standing next to them. He was standing there in the restaurant holding that dirty old hubcap under one arm. He was looking at me, and his other arm was raised in a wave.

My book was way more interesting than saying goodbye to any dumb boy holding a stupid hubcap.

Come on, Coyote—it sucked. It really, really sucked. Not the book. The saying goodbye to the stupid boy. *That* sucked. I blinked and I flared my nostrils and I clenched my teeth and I reminded myself that it was all right, that I was all right, that everything was all right.

"Hey there, sweet daisy," Rodeo called out as we rumbled back toward the street. "Give me a once-upon-a-time."

I closed my book and took one big ol' heart-cleaning, mind-clearing breath and threw something like a smile onto my face. That was the thing to do, I knew. That was how we rolled. I guessed.

"Once upon a time," I began, "there was a . . . a *horse*."

"Ooh, I love horse stories. Hit me, kid."

I could see that Lester was watching me from the seat across the aisle. I didn't feel like being watched. I set my book down and leaned my forehead against the window.

"Well, she was a *fierce* horse. Always swore that no person would ever ride her. She galloped across the prairie alone, mane and tail whipping in the wind. She was free." I swallowed, looking hard for some sparkle to put into my voice. I couldn't quite find it.

"All right," Rodeo coaxed, "and then . . . ?"

I breathed in, breathed out. The bus felt so empty around me I couldn't hardly concentrate at all.

"And then. And then, one night, she was running along, and . . . and an owl flew along beside her. And he looked down at her. She was racing her shadow in the moonlight."

"Oh, yeah. Killer image, Coyote."

"And the owl said . . . *um* . . . he said . . . well, he *asked* her . . ."

"What'd he ask her?"

I looked up at Rodeo. He was drumming his fingers on the steering wheel, bobbing his head, moving in his seat a little. There was a little smile on his face. He was always like that when we got moving again.

I stared at him.

I'd made a friend. And we'd just left him behind. We'd *just* left him behind. Now I was all alone again. Rodeo knew all that. He knew every bit of it. And he was sitting up there smiling and bouncing in his seat and bopping his head to the music.

"What'd he ask her?" he said again.

"Are you *happy*?" I asked him. My voice was raspy when I said it, kinda whispery and hoarse. I don't know why.

Rodeo stopped drumming and bouncing. He looked back at me, his forehead crinkled.

"Why'd he ask her that?" he said.

I opened my mouth. But before I could answer, Lester interrupted.

"Hey! Hold up, man. Something's up."

I followed Lester's pointing finger and saw him.

Salvador, running after us across the parking lot. Still holding that stupid hubcap in one hand. He was sprinting and waving his free arm at us.

Rodeo pumped the brakes and we eased to a stop and Salvador came huffing up to us.

My heart was doing something crazy in my chest, but I ignored it and jumped up and was standing on the steps when Rodeo swung open the door.

Salvador was standing there, chest heaving.

"Hey," he said between gasps, and I couldn't read his face. It looked kinda mad but not at me, and kinda excited but not necessarily in a super happy way, so I said, "Uh, what's up?"

He squinted at me sideways and said, "Can we, uh, get a ride?"

My heart dropped because without even realizing it, something like hope had sprung up inside me when Salvador had come running, but it died again with that stupid question. I'd thought he was coming back, but all he needed was a ride to their hotel or something.

"Oh. Sure. Where to?"

Salvador shook his head.

"You're not gonna believe it," he said, and I said, "Okaaaaay. Where?" and he shook his head and looked away and then looked back at me and he kinda squint-smiled with one side of his mouth and said, "Um . . . you ever heard of Yakima, Washington?"

I'd like to say I was all cool about it.

But, nah. Not really. Come on, Coyote—not even close.

I whooped so hard it hurt my throat a little and I jumped down to give that Salvador a big ol' hello-again-and-welcome-back hug that darn near knocked him down.

Turns out I was wrong about Petoskey, Michigan. I kinda love it.

And it turns out I was wrong about goodbyes, too.

The best kind of goodbye is the kind where you don't actually have to leave the person behind.

CHAPTER
TWENTY-FIVE

And just like that, our bus was back to being full.

For the first time ever, Rodeo skipped the three questions for our new rider, I'm guessing because she was really just joining folks who were already on and so that was, like, a loophole or something. Salvador and Ms. Vega and Ms. Vega's sister, Concepción, all piled up onto Yager with their suitcases and duffels and hubcap. While Ms. Vega explained what was going on to Rodeo and Lester, I dragged Salvador back to my room so he could give me his version.

We sat down at the edge of my mattress and he laid it all out for me.

"Okay, so this is, like, a total train wreck," he said.

"What happened to the job for your mom?"

"There never *was* a job," Salvador spit, his face tight with anger. "*Chris* told my *tía* there was a job, but turns out *Chris* was full of crap, which is no surprise to anyone except my *tía* because *Chris* has always been full of crap. So they get up here and my *tía* keeps asking about where the job is and *Chris* keeps lying and stalling and then she wakes up this morning and there's some dumb note from him saying he's sorry but he's just, like, not ready for all the responsibility of a relationship or whatever and he's *gone*, like totally gone, with his car and his stuff and most of their money."

"You serious?"

His eyes flashed at me.

"Does it sound like I'm joking?" he snapped, and I pulled my head back, but he clicked his tongue and turned his eyes down a little and said right away, "I'm sorry. I'm just, like, super pissed."

"No, no, I get it. That's crappy." I reached back and scooped up Ivan from where he was curled up at the end of the bed and handed him to Salvador. Ivan shot me an ears-back look, but he's chill so he went with it.

Salvador sat with Ivan in his lap and scratched his head, and Ivan leaned into it and started purring and I saw Salvador's shoulders relax just a tad. Cat therapy works. I sat for a minute, letting Ivan work his magic. Then I pushed on.

"So, um . . . Yakima?"

"Oh. Well, that's an *actual* job. Not through *Chris*, either. My *tía* used to work with a lady and they were "tight" and when all this started to go down my *tía* called her. She's working at a hotel in Yakima. Actually, her and her husband, like, own it? Anyway, she says she's got jobs for my mom and my *tía*, one hundred percent for sure. We just gotta get there. I'm sorry we keep messing up your plans."

I spread my hands and grinned.

"Are you kidding? This is *perfect*! Now we have an excuse to go all the way to Washington!"

I kinda expected Salvador to smile back and maybe give me a high five or something, but he just nodded and looked down at his hands and I remembered the secrets he'd shouted and realized that this whole thing probably wasn't as much fun for him as it was for me. I took my smile down a notch and said, "Salvador, I'm really sorry all this is happening to you and your mom," and he shot me a suspicious look and said, "Sorry? You're not breaking our promise, are you?" and I said, "Of course not," and he nodded and said, "Good," and then we both agreed it was probably time for a game of Uno.

Rodeo is always saying how the universe seeks balance. Just like with a lot of things Rodeo says, I'm not entirely sure what he means, but I do know that only a few hours after the bad news about Chris and the jobs and everything, the universe gave us another passenger, and she was most definitely on the positive side of the scale.

Her name was Val, and this is how she ended up with us.

We'd driven all the long day through the upper peninsula of Michigan. Salvador's aunt volunteered for a three-hour driving shift, which I thought was awful nice. I spent most of it sitting up behind her with Ms. Vega, chatting and laughing. They were close, those two. They told me all sorts of funny stories about when they were growing up. There was quite an incident involving ketchup squirted on a white *quinceañera* dress, and something about their mom walking in on Salvador's mom with a boy. They wouldn't give me all the details on that one, but the embarrassed blood running to Esperanza's face pretty much told me what I needed to know. It was nice, spending time with sisters who knew each other and loved each other. Plus, Concepción had a laugh like I'd never heard, loud and sudden and rowdy. I couldn't help but laugh along when she did, even if I didn't get the joke.

Anyway, sometime late that evening, when we were out of Michigan, through Wisconsin, and into Minnesota and it was already starting to get dark and some folks were settling into sleeping positions, we stopped at a gas station to give Yager a fresh tank. I was a desperate kind of starving and headed into the little store and got me one of those spicy hot dogs they always have spinning on those rolling stove things. I love 'em. Give me one of those and a cold bottle of Squirt (which I also bought, of course) and I'm in heaven. I honestly ain't sure exactly what Squirt is supposed to taste like, but I do know that what it *does* taste like is absolute refreshing perfection.

I was already one bite into the dog and heading back out to Yager when I saw her.

Well, really, I heard her.

She was sitting on the pavement up against the store, and she sniffled. Just a little sniffle, but it caught my ear and I stopped in my tracks and then backed up a step to stand in front of her.

She was wearing ripped-up jeans and a black hoodie and she had a nose ring, which I've always thought are kind of awesome. When I stopped, she looked up at me and I saw her eyes were all red-rimmed.

"You all right?" I asked.

Her eyebrows dropped and her eyes narrowed like she was getting ready to answer all tough, but then the toughness in her eyes gave way to wetness. She rolled her eyes and I saw them fill up before she looked away from me.

"No," she answered, and her voice broke when she said it.

"What's the matter? You thumbin'?"

She blinked at me.

"What's that mean?" Her voice was hoarse.

"You know. Hitchhiking. Looking for a ride somewhere."

Her eyes filled up again.

"Yeah. I guess."

"Well, where you headed?"

She shrugged again, then coughed out a dry laugh with no funny in it whatsoever.

"Away."

"You running away?"

She snorted.

"Not exactly. More like kicked out."

"Kicked out? Of your home? How come?"

She looked at me a second, sizing me up, then shook her head.

"You wouldn't understand."

I took a swig of my Squirt.

"Try me."

She sniffed, scratched at her neck, then said, "My parents just found something out, and they don't . . . *approve* of who I am. Of *what* I am, I guess."

"Well, what are you?"

The girl swallowed a couple times, then said in a broken voice, "I'm gay."

I didn't say anything. That didn't seem like any kind of reason at all to kick a perfectly nice person out of her house.

But when someone's hurting, you gotta do *something*. Always kindness, like Rodeo says.

So I set my bottle of Squirt down on the curb and took my spicy dog in both hands and carefully ripped it into two pieces, right in the middle. I held half of it out to her.

"Wanna share?" I asked.

She shot a cautious look at the half hot dog between us, then took it.

"Careful," I warned as I sat down beside her. "It's spicy. There's jalapeños cooked right into it."

She took a bite and I asked, "What's your name?"

She answered around her mouthful of hot dog.

"Valerie." Then she swallowed and added, "Val."

"My name is Coyote. Nice to meet you." I held out a hand and she shook it.

The girl sniffled and then took another bite and while she got to chewing, I got to thinking.

Now, obviously I was thinking of giving this girl a ride. I don't care who you are, if you see some girl crying at a gas station at night, you can't help but feel like you oughta help 'em if you can. Just look at that nosy lady who called the cops on me when Rodeo left me behind the night I met Salvador. There is such things as good help and bad help, though, and I was more interested in seeing if I could give Val the good kind. Plus, that bit about Val's parents really got my fur up like Ivan's when he sees a dog. My very favorite aunt—my mom's sister, Jen—is gay, and her wife, Sofia, is my very favorite aunt-in-law, and the thought of someone hating on them just 'cause of who they love made me want to put on boxing gloves.

Also obviously, though, I couldn't do anything more to mess with my timeline. But if this Val girl didn't care where she was going, it wouldn't slow us down one bit to help her out and let her on board. Heck, if she had her license, she could even help drive and get us there sooner, maybe.

But thirdly obviously, Rodeo has rules about taking in runaways. Anyone who's under eighteen is a no-go, for lots of good reasons having to do with the law and whatnot.

There were a lot of "obviouslies" bouncing around in my head during that first conversation with Val.

"How old are you?" I asked.

She looked me up and down.

"Nineteen," she said.

"Nineteen? Huh. You look young. Still living with your parents?"

"I'm going to school. Or I *was*, anyway. Community college."

I looked around the parking lot. It was a busy interstate truck stop, with plenty of folks coming and going. Not all of them were the kind of folks you'd want to leave someone crying with, if you know what I mean. I looked at Val, sitting there on the cement with tear-puffed eyes and no home to go to.

There's so much sadness in the world.

I took a second and rinsed the spicy out of my mouth with Squirt.

"Well, you wanna come with us?"

Val narrowed her eyes.

"Who?"

"Me and Rodeo. We're in that bus over there. We got a few other passengers, too. We're heading west, toward Washington State by way of Boise, Idaho. We could drop you off anywhere you wanna go."

Val eyed the bus.

"You're not, like, *weirdos* or something, are you? You're not dangerous?"

"Oh, we're definitely weirdos. But we ain't the dangerous kind."

She snorted. Then she tilted her head.

"I actually *was* kind of thinking of heading to Seattle. I got a cousin there who's pretty cool."

"Well, that's perfect! Meant to be."

Val chewed her lip for a second. Then she closed her eyes, opened them, and stood up.

"Okay. I guess."

"Great. First I gotta ask you some questions, though."

One minute and three questions later, Val was following me up Yager's dirty steps. Rodeo had taken over the wheel, and he pursed his lips at Val.

"Who's this?"

"A new fellow passenger, Rodeo." I did my best to sound confident and enthusiastic.

Rodeo blew a long breath out through his nose.

"This bus," he said, keeping his voice low so Val couldn't hear, "is a home for two people." He held up two fingers to make his point. "You. And me. And we now have"—he looked around the bus, his lips moving as he counted—"*seven* people on board. *Seven*, honeybear. And a cat."

"Yeah," I said, holding up my hands, "but it's built to carry fifty-six, right?" which I could tell from the look on Rodeo's face the moment I said it was actually *not* a good angle for me to take.

"I already asked her the three questions," I said.

"Really."

"Yes, sir."

"What's her favorite place?" he asked, and I could tell he was testing me and I resented that, for sure.

"Her grandma's kitchen," I said with some brass in my voice to let him know I didn't appreciate him thinking I was lying about asking her. "On a Sunday morning."

Rodeo pursed his lips.

"It's a good answer," I said.

Rodeo stewed a moment longer, then nodded.

"Yeah," he said, "it is." But then he shook his head and looked out at the nighttime parking lot of fluorescent lights and gas station litter.

I didn't say anything. I knew we was teetering right on the edge of his kindness and I didn't wanna push him out of it. Plus, I knew him. I knew my dad. You give him the chance, his kindness wins every time.

And, sure enough.

Rodeo turned in his seat. He turned and looked into Val's eyes.

He looked into them slow and quiet and gentle. And he smiled a smile that was small but still showed the white of his teeth.

And he said, right into Val's eyes, "Howdy. What's your name?"

She cleared her throat.

"Val. Sir."

"How old are you, Val?"

"Nineteen. Twenty in May."

Rodeo nodded.

"All right. You can call me Rodeo. There's food in the cupboard there if you're hungry."

And Rodeo turned back to the windshield and turned the key and good ol' Yager rumbled to life.

I pulled Val up behind me and she gave me a look, eyebrows all crinkled up.

"What the heck was that?" she whispered.

I put a hand on her shoulder.

"That was you getting a ride. Pick out a seat, Val. Make yourself at home."

TWENTY-SIX

Val and Salvador and me got along like blueberries in a muffin.

That first night we must've played a dozen games of Uno before we gave in to sleep.

Val was funny. She was quick with jokes and had a way of saying them that got me every time. But she was also a listener. Her eyes were always wide and looking into the eyes of whoever was talking, and she nodded along or shook her head or rolled her eyes to match what they were saying. Plus, she called Ivan "one of the handsomest cats I've ever seen," so she scored a lot of points with that. She was a good one, that Val.

We talked about all sorts of stuff. Dreams and hopes and whatnot. Even Salvador felt comfortable sharing stuff around her, which is saying something. I told her everything; I told her about my mom and sisters and the accident and everything, and about why we were on this trip in the first place, though of course I was careful to talk quiet and make sure she knew not to gab about all that stuff in front of Rodeo. She teared up when I told her all that, which made me kinda uncomfortable, but she also reached across and held my hands tight in hers, which I liked an awful lot.

I learned a lot about Val that night. She was a poet and was hoping to someday move to New York City. She'd thought she wanted to be an actor, but last year had decided she wanted to do something in publishing and work on writing her own books someday. She thought anyone who puts ice cream on apple pie is crazy. Her favorite singer was some lady named Fiona Apple, and if you made her laugh hard enough she did this snort thing that was hilarious and adorable.

I also learned something about Salvador that night. Something surprising. Something good. We got to talking, somehow, about regrets. Things we wished had gone different, things we coulda or shoulda done different. It was *exactly* the kind of topic that was a no-go for Rodeo, so I was into it.

"Megan" is what Val said. "She was so *cool*. I don't mean, like, the popular cool, I mean the *real* cool. I had, like, the *biggest* crush on her. Forever. And we were tight. But I never had the guts to tell her. And now . . . Shoot. Now I'll probably never see her again."

"That sucks," I said, and Salvador nodded his agreement.

"What's yours?" she asked me.

I looked for a second at the headlight-speckled blackness out the bus windows.

"Well. I guess my regret is kind of a work in progress. I regret waiting this long to go back for that box. Waiting until it might be too late. If I make it in time, well . . . no regrets, I guess. But if I don't . . . If I lose that box forever . . ." My words choked off. Val and Salvador both had the decency to sit for a beat of silence, giving me a chance to finish. I *was* finished, though. Some things you just can't quite put into words, and not speaking them is the only and best way to say them.

"Well, we better make it, then," Salvador said. "Right?"

"Hells yeah," Val agreed. "No regrets, sister."

Now, I knew that Val meant that "sister" part in just a casual sort of way, like how guys call each other "bro." I knew that. But still. I wasn't sure at first whether or not I liked her calling me "sister," but that was only for about a second and then, just like that, I decided that I did like it. I liked it a heckuva lot.

I smiled at 'em both. Then I tilted my head toward Salvador. "How about you?"

He shook his head.

"Nah."

"What do you mean, 'nah'? *We* both shared. You can't hold out on us, Salvador."

Salvador shot me a look, but I was having none of that.

"Seriously," I said. "That ain't fair. And you know it. Give us a regret, man."

"Okay, okay." He sighed. "Here, hold on a sec." Salvador got up and went and rustled through the pile of suitcases and stuff that his aunt had brought on board with her. He found what he was looking for and came back and set it down on the little table that held our Uno cards.

My jaw dropped.

"Is that what I think it is?" I asked.

Salvador nodded. He unclipped the latches on the hard black case, swung the top open, and pulled out a shiny, deep-brown violin.

"You know how to play that?" I said in a whisper.

"Yeah," he answered, kinda quiet and shy.

"You any good?"

He shrugged. But I could read that shrug. That was definitely a you're-darned-right-I'm-good-but-I'm-not-gonna-like-brag-about-it-or-anything kind of shrug. I grinned in the darkness. That Salvador. A secret badass violin player.

"Cool," Val said. "So . . . what's the regret?"

Salvador ran his fingers over the violin's strings, not hard enough to make a sound, but gentle enough so you could tell he loved that thing.

"My *mamá*. She's never got to hear me perform. I mean, she's, like, heard me practice and stuff. I'm in this—or, I guess I *was* in—this youth orchestra thing. First-chair violin. Youngest ever. But she always had to work when we had a concert or whatever. We had a big one coming up, too. I was, like, a featured soloist and everything. And, man, I got that sucker *down*. I *own* that solo. And she'd already worked out to have the time off. She was gonna get to finally see me, up there on a stage, with the lights on and the audience and everything. But then . . . then all *this* happened, and we had to leave, and now . . ." He sighed and shook his head. "But, you know, whatever. It's not like the end of the world or anything."

The way Salvador said that, the way his voice sounded all defeated and hopeless, made it sound like it kind of *was* the end of the world.

"Crap," I said. "Man, that *totally* sucks."

"Suck city, no joke," Val agreed, and she hit him on the shoulder in a friendly sort of way and then leaned back on the couch. "So . . . play us something."

"Nah," he said, softly putting the violin back into its case.

"Come on!"

"No," he said, and he said it firm enough that we knew not to push it. "I'm not in the mood. It just . . . bums me out, okay?"

Salvador snapped the latches closed with a loud double click.

"I'm wiped out," he said. "I'm gonna hit the sack."

"Yeah," Val said with a sad kind of sigh. "Me, too."

And that was that. I guess that's how regrets are . . . they're anchors, not balloons. And we were sunk.

I sat there in the swaying bus, looking out at the highway headlights.

I watched as Salvador walked up and scooted into the seat next to his mom. I watched how she put her arm around him and leaned to kiss him on his cheek and then how he leaned his head down to rest it on her shoulder. Her shoulders had sort of been slumped in defeat most of the time since I'd met her. She cried at night. I heard her once. When Salvador was asleep. Just little sniffles and some ragged breathing, but I heard it. Saw her dabbing her face. I didn't tell him about it, of course. It was almost funny, thinking about that secret he'd shouted on our Attic ride. Almost funny that they both secretly cried at night when they knew the other one was sleeping. But not really funny at all, really. I thought about how brave they both were, and how tough. I thought about what they'd been through, with his dad and everything. And her courage, in leaving behind their whole life and everything. And then finding out there would be no job in St. Louis, and then her abandoned sister in Michigan, and now heading out to someplace they'd never been for a job they only hoped was waiting for them. Life just kept hitting 'em, and they just kept on going.

They could use a win, those two. They deserved one. The world owed it to 'em, I thought.

An idea slowly sparked to life in my head as the miles flew by. An idea I kind of fell in love with the more I thought about it.

Ivan purred in my lap, looking up into my eyes. I scratched my fingernails down his spine.

"I think we can do this, Ivan," I whispered. I smiled at him and he blinked in agreement.

I was *thinking*.

Okay, maybe more like *planning*.

CHAPTER

TWENTY-SEVEN

It took some planning, this little plan of mine, along with some persuading of Rodeo, though not too much because this scheme was kind of right up his alley. It took more than a few whispered conversations between me and Lester and me and Rodeo and probably Lester and Rodeo, too. There was quite a bit of phone searching and location researching and timeline checking. I did the math and counted the hours and added up the miles three times, four times, five times. It was Monday night. We could pull off our plan Tuesday morning. The day before I had to get home. With Lester driving at night, we had twelve extra hours. Twelve. I could give up thirty minutes to help out a friend. It made my stomach kinda squeeze with anxiety, but I could do it.

We had to do all our whispering and planning that night, while Salvador was sleeping. But by the time we rolled into Billings, Montana, we had the pieces in place. We'd still need a lot of luck and we all knew there were plenty of things that could go wrong, but we were gonna give it a shot.

It all started at breakfast. We pulled off into a diner Lester had picked out on his phone earlier. We all shuffled off the bus and went inside and ordered our food and camped out at a bunch of tables.

No one noticed when Rodeo slipped right back outside again and ducked around the corner.

We all ate and chatted and used the bathroom and Lester and I did our best to dawdle and drag our feet and convince everyone else to do the same. Minutes passed and most of us were done eating, and Lester and I started trading nervous glances.

Then, finally, when folks were just starting to get restless, Rodeo ambled back in through the doors, walking easy as you please but breathing a little hard if you looked close.

I shot him a well-how-did-it-go kind of look. With one of his magic eyes he gave me a quick little wink. And I had to shove a forkful of eggs into my mouth to hide my smile. The plan was a go.

We all piled back onto the bus and then Rodeo fired up Yager and we were off. We didn't head toward the highway, though. We drove right out the back of the parking lot, across an alley, and into a different, bigger parking lot.

Rodeo rumbled Yager up to the rear of a big red-brick building. There was a dumpster and loading ramp and some unmarked double doors, and that's about it. No signs, no other cars, no nothing. Rodeo cranked on the parking brake and killed the engine and Lester hopped off and ducked through the double doors at a jog. Everyone else just sat there, looking at the empty parking lot and then at Rodeo.

"What are we doing?" Salvador asked.

Rodeo just did a big dramatic yawn-stretch thing like he hadn't heard the question.

I figured Lester had enough of a head start by that point, so I stood up and walked to the front of the bus. I gave the Holy Hell Bell a couple of good clangs and then looked back at everyone and cleared my throat.

"Ladies and gentlemen," I began. "We been covering a lot of miles, and not taking a lot of breaks. So, Rodeo and Lester and I have planned a little something. For your, uh, enjoyment."

"Some entertainment," Rodeo added, spreading his hands wide, "to revive your morale and inspire harmony."

"Come on," I said, and led the troop off the bus and toward the double doors. They were propped open with a brick and I grinned, remembering me and Lester and Rodeo's first planning session.

"If it's got a double door, I can probably get us in," Lester had said, and I'd asked, *"How?"* and Lester had answered, *"I've worked in plenty of bars and theaters and stuff. There's a trick I know that'll get you through just about any double doors, as long as they're kinda old and not chained shut. It's exactly* why *places do* chain *them shut,"* and I'd said, all excited, *"What's the trick?"* and Lester had pointed a finger at me and said, *"Uh-uh. I'm not telling* you," and then he looked at Rodeo and said, *"But I'll tell you."*

We walked into darkness. I paused, blinking the daylight out of my eyes, and Lester called out from somewhere ahead of me, "Keep on coming, you're clear," so I shuffled straight ahead and heard the rest of the crew making their way behind me.

The floor was cement, polished and smooth. Shadowy shapes emerged, things covered in cloth, ropes dangling from the ceiling.

I could hear Lester rustling around, holding up his end of the bargain.

"Okay, I'm going up to the controls," he whispered to me. "Sound's good to go. Just head through that curtain 'bout twenty feet ahead of you."

"Got it."

The cement gave way to a creaking wooden floor beneath my feet. I ducked under a dangling rope and felt ahead of me with my hands until my fingers met thick velvet. I kept on, feeling with my hands along the curtain until I got to the break in the middle where the two curtains met.

I waited a tick, letting the rest of the group bunch up behind me.

"All right, y'all," I said. "Right this way." And I held open the heavy curtains.

We were on a stage, looking out on a dark auditorium full of empty red fabric seats. There was a single microphone on a stand in front of us, at center stage.

"What in the . . . ," Concepción started to say, and then wherever Lester was he musta flicked the right switch because a single spotlight flashed on, training a bright circle of light on the microphone. I knew he was off somewhere in "the booth," as he'd called it, where he'd be able to make the lights and sound and stuff work. All his experience as a musician had really paid off for our little plan.

"Stairs are just to your left, folks," Rodeo said, his voice back to mellow and easy. "Head on down and get yourself a front-row seat." He sidled up close to me and whispered, "I put it over there by the piano." I nodded, knowing exactly what he was talking about.

Everyone else filed down the stairs off the stage and squeaked down into one of the seats.

It was a big place. Could probably fit a couple hundred people. At the back, behind the last row of seats, was a pair of double doors leading out to an entry area. Beyond that were some big glass doors to the front parking lot.

I stepped up to the microphone and squinted into the spotlight. I cleared my throat. Wrestled for a minute with the swarm of butterflies that came to life out of nowhere in my belly. Living on a bus for five years with a solitary hippie, I hadn't gotten much practice at public speaking.

"Hello," I finally managed, and flinched a little at how loud my voice boomed out from the microphone. "Welcome, fellow travelers, to the Billings Center for the Performing Arts. We've planned a little, uh, cultural treat for you. So, sit back and enjoy."

I could barely see the faces of the folks, the spotlight was so bright. They mostly just looked confused.

I gulped. This was the scary part. The part where it all might fall apart.

"Um. Salvador Vega, please come up onstage."

Even through the brightness, I saw Salvador's jaw drop and his eyebrows lower. Saw his mom turn her head to him in surprise.

Salvador didn't move.

"Salvador Vega," I repeated, my voice getting a little higher and a little shakier, "please come up onstage?"

Salvador didn't move.

I was crashing and burning. Epic fail.

But then I saw Ms. Vega nudge him with her elbow. Kinda hard, actually. I heard her murmur, "Go, *mijo*."

And I heard Val say in her voice that was sharp even when it was soft, "Go on, man."

And then he did.

He shook his head, and he clenched his jaw, and his hands were in fists, but he stood up and walked over to the stairs.

I went to the piano and saw it sitting there in the shadows where Rodeo had put it while the rest of us were chowing on breakfast. I clicked open the latches of the case. I pulled it out gently. I grabbed the bow. And I met Salvador at the top of the stairs.

I held the violin out to him.

"Coyote," he said, his voice quiet and shaky and also definitely not super friendly. His eyes were serious.

"I know," I said quick and soft. "This looks cute and all, but I know in a lot of ways it's really not cool. To spring this on you without asking. But there ain't no pressure. You had a regret. We're giving you a shot. If you don't want this, that's cool. I could do a tune on my uke, and Rodeo is just itching for an excuse to run out and grab his guitar. We can go instead. It's all good." I swallowed, then leaned into him a little closer. "So. I'm sorry for the ambush. But. If you want the chance to play that solo for your mom on a stage with lights and an audience . . . here it is." I pressed the violin into his hands. They took it, natural and familiar.

He looked down at the instrument. Then out at the audience, sitting in their seats. Then up at me.

"I'm gonna get you for this," he said. But he didn't hand me back the violin. And he didn't go back to his seat.

He swallowed. A swallow so big I could see it in the Adam's apple in that skinny neck of his. "What's the name of the song?" I asked.

"Huh?"

"The song you're playing. What's it called?"

"Oh. Uh, it's Violin Sonata Number Two. In G minor. By Handel."

"Okay." I turned and started back toward center stage, but Salvador grabbed my arm.

"Coyote, it's, like . . . *ten minutes* long."

I smiled at him.

"Well, we better get started, then."

I walked out to the microphone.

"Please welcome Salvador Vega, of Orlando, Florida, where he was *first* chair violin in the . . ." I trailed off and looked over at him, standing just out of the spotlight.

"Orlando Youth Orchestra," Salvador mumbled.

"Where he was first chair violin in the Orlando Youth Orchestra," I finished. "Today he'll be playing for you Violin Sonata Number Two, in G minor, by Handel." I spread my arms wide and bowed my head. There was an awkward second or two.

I raised my mouth back up to the mic.

"This is where you clap," I said, and then they did, and then

I walked out of the spotlight past Salvador, who was still looking pretty pale and still shooting me a fairly wicked glare. I bumped his shoulder as I passed and whispered, "No regrets, brother."

I walked down the stairs and took the first seat in the first row, way off to the side. Val was sitting in the middle with everyone else, but she got up and scurried over and sat next to me. She grinned and held a fist out toward me and I raised mine to bump it, then we both sat back to listen to the music.

Salvador stepped up to the mic. I ain't gonna lie—that boy looked *super* nervous. He tried to flash a smile at the crowd, but it didn't stick around long. He ran his bow along the strings a few times and adjusted the screws at the top of the violin neck, tuning it to sound just right. I was pretty impressed he could do all that by ear.

Then he notched the violin up against his neck and stepped up to the mic and held his bow on the strings and took a deep breath and was just about to play . . . and then he paused. And he leaned forward so his mouth was by the mic. And he fixed his eyes on one particular person there in the front row.

And he said, *"Es para ti, Mamá."*

Out of the corner of my eye, I saw Ms. Vega dabbing at her eyes.

Oh, that Salvador.

Then he started playing.

And the music poured out of that little wooden violin in his hands, and it swirled out through the air and microphone and the darkness, and it filled up the room and our ears.

It'd be easy to go all poetical and gush about how beautiful he played and how mesmerizing the music was and how we all sat there in awe of the amazingness of it all. And it'd be true, of course. He *did* play beautifully. And the song *was* mesmerizing. And we *did* all sit there in awe of the amazingness of it all. It's all true.

But those kinds of words are usually a waste of time. 'Cause there ain't no words or no poetry that could wrap up what it was like sitting there listening to that Salvador play that violin of his. It was *something*.

Rodeo says that anywhere outside can be a church, 'cause anytime you're in nature you can feel god.

Well. I guess me and him learned that day that you can feel god inside, too.

Salvador was wearing a raggedy tank top undershirt, holey blue jeans, and flip-flops. But I tell you, he wouldn't have looked one bit better if he was wearing a fancy tuxedo and thousand-dollar shoes. That Salvador looked like a hero up there. And he played like an angel. He was *something*.

Man. That kid could *play*. He didn't just play his heart out up there on that stage. He played *my* heart out, too.

Now, Salvador had said that the song was ten minutes long.

Something I'll be mad about until the day I die is that I only got to enjoy about four minutes of it.

Because about four minutes into it, Val looked over her shoulder. And her body jerked. Then she elbowed me, and I looked where she was looking.

Back past the last row of seats, out through the auditorium

doors. Right through the entryway, right to the glass front doors of the Billings Center for the Performing Arts.

Right to where a security guard was holding up one hand and peering through the glass door while he fumbled with a ring of keys in his other hand.

TWENTY-EIGHT

I froze, but only for a second. Then I moved.

I jumped up and started off toward the front door, running quiet and doubled over so I wouldn't distract Salvador or his audience. I heard shuffling and glanced back and saw Val following right behind me, and I was glad. I'd only known her for, like, twelve hours, but I could already tell she was the kind of person you wanted on your team.

We made it through the auditorium doors at about the same time that the guard managed to open the front doors and come striding in. I stepped forward to meet him, and Val real smart stopped to close the auditorium doors behind us, blocking us off from that beautiful music.

"What are you doing in here?" the guard demanded, walking toward us, his voice loud and suspicious.

"Shhh!" I said. "Quiet!"

Now, all I was trying to do was make the fella hush a bit so he didn't interrupt the magic happening back in the auditorium. But I said it harsh and kind of bossy, and I'll tell you what, even though it wasn't exactly a "plan," that bossiness really kind of got us off on the right foot.

Because that fella, he hushed. His mouth snapped shut and his eyes opened wider.

He was young. All pale and smooth-cheeked, maybe twenty or twenty-one. We were *not* dealing with some hard-as-nails, grizzled police detective.

Val, she figured out the score pretty quick. She came up beside me just as he repeated quieter and more polite, "What are you doing in here?" and she answered back lightning quick, "What are *you* doing in here?"

The guard blinked.

"I'm, uh, I'm—"

"You're interrupting, is what you're doing," Val interrupted. She jerked a thumb back over her shoulder. "We've got an important audition going on right now."

The guard licked his lips and his face screwed up in confusion.

"What kind of audition? There's nothing on the schedule, and nobody told me there'd be—"

"An *important* audition. I thought I said that the first time. My brother is auditioning to go to the Juilliard School in New York City. The judge flew all the way out here to hear him."

The guard gulped. He looked desperately at me, then back at Val. I'll give it to him, though: He was clearly out of his league with Val, but he didn't give up that easy.

"Do you, uh . . . Do you have permission to be here?"

"Do you think we'd be here if we didn't have permission?"

"So, you're saying this is, like, *cleared* and everything, by—"

"Yeah. Obviously. It was cleared by the director."

Now, I knew that Val was blowing a lot of smoke and taking a shot in the dark. But it didn't show one bit. Her voice was calm and confident and downright *mean*. She didn't make it seem like *she* was about to get in trouble. She made it seem like *he* was about to get in trouble.

It was awesome.

Still, it was a risky move. My armpits prickled hot and my mouth went dry. The dude squinted dubiously at Val. Then he spoke.

"Mrs. Marshall cleared this? She gave the okay?"

"Uh, *yeah*. She's in there right now," Val said, jerking her head toward the closed doors behind us. "You can hang out and talk to her after the audition if you want, but I wouldn't interrupt right now, if I were you. You know how she can be."

It was another risk. Another shot in the dark.

But the dude nodded.

"Oh, yeah. I sure do," he murmured.

Val was shooting into the dark left and right, but she was hitting the target every time.

Then, just like that, Val went nice.

"Listen," she said, her voice softening and sweetening, "I'm sorry they didn't let you know about this. It was kind of last minute. But please don't mess this up for him. It's his one chance."

The guard's whole body eased up. He took a couple calming breaths and wiped at his forehead real quick. He was so visibly relieved that he was now somehow mysteriously on Val's good side. I almost smiled.

"So that's your bus parked out back, then?" he asked.

Val blinked.

"Of course," she said after a second. "We're from the . . . the Montana Music Conservatory. It's a private school. Very, uh, prestigious."

"Y'all are students from a school?" he asked, somewhat doubtfully. His eyes went from Val's nose ring to my scuzzy cargo shorts and bare feet.

Val just laughed, a big, easy head-back laugh. She even reached out and shoved the guard's shoulder playfully.

"Uh, *yeah*. Who else drives around in a school bus?"

The dude sniffed and his eyebrows flickered up. He smiled, then laughed along with Val and shook his head.

"Yeah, yeah," he chuckled. "Well, *that's* true."

I kinda wanted to jump in and suggest that in fact there might be any number of interesting, trustworthy people besides students who drive around in school buses, but I figured it wasn't the time or place for that point to be made.

"All right, well, I'm sorry I barged in like that," he said.

"You were just doing your job," Val assured him, holding up her hands, smiling wide.

The guard backed up to the front door and opened it behind him.

"I hope your brother makes it," he said, smiling at Val.

"Oh, *thank* you," she said.

But then the guard stopped halfway out the door. His eyebrows scrunched down.

"But . . . if the audition is so important, why is he dressed like that? I saw him. He's wearing jeans and an old w—"

"Ex*cuse* me?" Val shot in, and her voice was right back to acid and flames and sharp knives.

The guard's eyes went wide again.

"I, uh, I just mean, he's wearing—"

"Ex*cuse* me?" Val repeated, her voice rising and adding a few more degrees of nasty.

"Well . . . well . . ."

"Ex*cuse* me?" She took a step toward him, her hands in fists and her head tilted to the side like she couldn't believe what she was hearing. I know I couldn't.

The guard gulped.

"N-n-nothing. Just . . . have a good day. Sorry."

And then he was out. And the door closed behind him and he stood there for a second, blinking at Val. And then he turned and got out of there, double-quick.

We watched him go, hustling back toward his security car.

"Hey, Val," I said out of the side of my mouth.

"Yeah?"

"I think you should seriously reconsider giving up on that acting dream of yours."

She snorted.

"Thanks."

"That was amazing. Especially at the end. I think he would've given you his keys if you'd asked."

Val grinned at me.

"That 'excuse me' trick is like magic. It works, like, seventy-five percent of the time. If you say 'excuse me' all mean and rude and then just keep saying it louder, people will just, like, *surrender*."

"I'm gonna remember that one."

Out the window, the guard was still sitting in his car. He hadn't pulled away yet.

"You know," I said, "he might still put it all together."

"Yeah."

"We should beat it."

"Yeah."

Me and Val walked in just as Salvador played out the last, ringing note. The front-row audience jumped to their feet in a standing ovation.

Salvador, up there in his blue jeans and old tank top, took a deep bow. Ms. Vega was wiping tears from her cheeks. So was Concepción. I made eye contact with Lester, who was clapping from behind the glass of the booth at the back of the auditorium, a huge smile on his face. I shot him we-got-a-semi-serious-situation-here eyes and motioned for him to come on, and he did.

Val and I hurried the crowd out the back as fast as we could without freaking anybody out or ruining the good-times vibe. Salvador was practically glowing. He and his mom were the last to leave. She ran up to him onstage and they stood there in the spotlight in a long, tight hug as everyone else filed quietly past them and out the back door.

There's so much happiness in the world.

As we rolled out of the parking lot, we were all quiet. I think we all still had Salvador's music echoing in our hearts and didn't wanna let it go just yet.

I was settling into my seat, Ivan on my lap and a book in my hand, when Salvador turned from where he was sitting with his mom in the seat in front of me. He looked into my face with those serious eyes of his and said, "Thank you," all quiet and solemn, and I said, "It was no big deal," and he shook his head and said, "Yeah, it was," and I said, "Salvador, you are *really* good," and he shrugged all modest but then smirked and said, "Well, yeah, of *course*," and we both smiled and then he added, "We are *definitely* getting you home in time, Coyote Sunrise," and then he turned back around and that was that.

It was a nice moment. It really was. Everything, at that moment, was going so well.

Of course, it all fell apart. Everything does, if you give it long enough. Secrets especially.

CHAPTER
TWENTY-NINE

We only got about another thirty minutes down the road. Rodeo was driving. He hadn't said a word since we'd gotten rolling again. I'd kinda noticed a tight stiffness in his body language, but I'd ignored it because I was feeling so good about the whole Salvador-and-his-mom violin thing. There was no ignoring it, though, when out of nowhere Rodeo hit the brakes and pulled over on the side of the highway in the middle of nowhere, Montana.

He turned off the engine. Pulled the keys out of the ignition. Turned toward where I was sitting in the second row of seats. Looked me right in my eyes. And then asked me:

"Where are we going, Coyote?"

The bus sat in silence. In my periphery, I could see Lester, sitting quiet and watching close. Salvador was still as a statue in front of me.

I swallowed.

"Butte, Montana," I said, "for a pork chop sand—"

"Coyote," Rodeo cut in, "where are we going? Don't you lie to me."

I almost gasped, those words of his took me so by surprise. We didn't talk harsh to each other like that, me and Rodeo. We weren't the lying types. Well, at least not out loud. At least not me. At least not until recently.

"I ain't lying," I lied. "We're going to Butte for pork chop sandwiches."

Rodeo blinked. He breathed in. He breathed out. He kept his eyes right on me. He shook his head.

"Yeah?" he asked, and his voice was some horrible combination of tired and sad and hurt and bitter and angry. "Then why have you been acting so weird ever since that call with your grandma? Why are you so anxious to get back on the road every time we stop? Why were you gonna leave Salvador and his mom at the side of the road? And why . . . why did Salvador just tell you he was gonna get you home in time? Why, Coyote?"

Salvador's head dropped when Rodeo said that. Lester blew out an oh-boy-here-we-go breath.

I opened my mouth. Closed it.

Time was up. And in a lot of ways, I was ready. More than ready. When Rodeo turned around and demanded that I tell him the truth, part of my heart said, "Oh no," but another part of my heart said, "Thank god, finally."

I raised my chin. I made myself look right into his eyes. And I told him the truth.

CHAPTER
THIRTY

"Rodeo," I said soft but firm, "we gotta go home."

His face closed up, and quick. You ain't never seen something go so cold and closed so fast in your life, I guarantee it. I saw him go back inside his eyes, pulling hard away from me and toward his distant insides.

"Coyote," he said, his voice small and tired, *almost* angry. "We *are* home."

"You know what I mean. We gotta go back. To Poplin Springs."

He shook his head, his eyes narrowing.

"That's a no-go, Coyote. You know that."

"Sorry, Rodeo. It's a 'go' this time. We have to go back."

He didn't actually shift or move, but I swear that man shrank right there, just folded into himself and got smaller. His eyes, those amazing eyes, looked hurt. Like I'd slapped him. And they looked wary, too, like he wasn't gonna let me slap him again.

"Is your grandma sick?" he asked, looking away from me.

I almost thought about lying for a second, saying, "Yeah, she's dying!" I think even Rodeo would've gotten to yes pretty quick for that. But I was kinda done with lying.

"No," I answered. "She's fine. It's Sampson Park."

He looked up at me again, cocking his head curiously.

"They're tearing it out. All of it. Digging it up and paving it over."

Rodeo shook his head. His shoulders relaxed a bit, but he still looked tight.

"Well, that's a shame, sugar pie. It's a pretty little park. But what's that got to do with us?"

This was the tough part. I was gonna have to go down a whole list of no-goes, say a whole lot of unsayable things, utter out loud some names we'd long ago silently agreed to never say aloud again. I was digging up graves with these words, waking up ghosts. Ripping off scabs.

"May twenty-first, five years ago," I said.

His eyes slid away from me again.

"Pardon?"

"May twenty-first. Five years ago, plus some. It was Ava's tenth birthday."

He flinched when I said it. When I said the name of my big sister. Ava with the long hair, Ava with the wide smile, Ava with the loud laugh, Ava with the tombstone with an angel on top.

Rodeo shook his head.

"Damn it, Coyo—"

"We went to the park. Me. Ava. Mom. Rose."

He squeezed his eyes shut hard when I said it, like I'd smashed his thumb with a hammer, when I said the name of my little sister. Rose, who loved her silly dances, Rose, who sang along way too loud to songs she didn't know, Rose, who pinched her neck when she was sleepy, Rose, who was buried beside Ava under a tombstone carved with birds.

"I'm sorry," I said quiet, a whisper. Then I kept going.

"You were still at work. We made a memory box, us four. We each picked out some things to put in it. Pictures we took. Pictures we drew. Notes, letters. Stuff we made. Locks of our hair. We put it in that old metal box we used to play cash register with. We took it to the park and we buried it. Off in the corner, under all those trees. And we rolled a big rock on top. We were gonna come back in ten years and dig it up, look at all the memories. We promised we would. *I* promised I would. But then—" I broke off, my voice lost in a sea of broken glass. But there wasn't time to stop, wasn't time to get lost. "But then five days later they were gone."

The last word hung there, saying everything but leaving so much out.

Rodeo sat with his head down, his eyes closed. He was rocking back and forth, just a little bit.

"And now, it's just me left. And they're tearing out that park. And they're gonna bulldoze those trees. But they're not getting that memory box. That's mine. And we're going back to get it. It's all I got."

Rodeo shook his head.

"No," he said. Then again, "No."

He stood up and his hands were in fists, but his eyes weren't fighting eyes, they were begging eyes.

"You *don't* got it. It's gone, Coyote. Gone. And you don't need it. There ain't no living to be done in the past. This is our living, Coyote, right here. This is our life. This is our home. It's all we have and that's just fine, 'cause it's all we need. We ain't going back. Not ever. We go *forward*."

Rodeo said that whole sorry speech like it meant something, he said it like it was the end of the conversation, but there weren't one single cell of my body or soul that moved a millimeter.

"I know you don't want to," I said, and my voice didn't have an ounce of give in it. It wasn't mean, but it wasn't holding hands and blowing kisses, either. "But we're going. We are, Rodeo. I don't care what you say. I ain't leaving that box to get lost forever. And if you won't take me, then I'll hitchhike. I swear I will."

"Let's call your grandma," Rodeo said. "Have her go get the box, keep it safe until—"

"No. No. It's not her box. It's not her memories. It's not her mom, and it's not her sisters, and it's not her promise. It's mine. *Mine*, Rodeo. I need that box. And I want to get it. I want to get that box like I promised I would. Like I promised *Mom* I would. And I'm gonna."

Rodeo shook his head hard and started to say something, but I didn't even let him get a word out.

"You don't have to come with me into town if you don't want to. You can stop at the city limits and I'll walk in. I don't care. But you are getting behind that wheel," I said, pointing at the driver's seat, "and you are driving me home. Or I'll stick my thumb out and make my own way there. But I'm going. And I hope you'll take me."

Lester cleared his throat. Lester, who was driving across the country to get what his heart wanted.

"Listen, man. I could stay with you. Get to Boise later. We could leave you one town away or whatever and I could take her in. This is important, brother."

Rodeo looked at him.

"You knew?"

Lester shrugged.

Then Salvador spoke up. Salvador, who was trying to keep his mom safe while she was trying to keep him safe.

"Come on. Sir. She needs this."

Rodeo looked at him, his eyes wet and blinking.

"Yeah," Val jumped in. "You gotta let her do this." Val, whose parents didn't want her to be who she was but was fighting for it anyway.

"Rodeo," Esperanza Vega said—Esperanza Vega, who knew a lot about the good and the bad in life and was doing everything she could to give her son more of the good and less of the bad— "you are a good man. So *be* a good man. For your daughter."

Those voices rang out, one by one. It was something. It was crazy. For a second, I felt like I had a family.

I stood up and stepped toward Rodeo. I stepped right up to him, so we were almost touching. He was just standing there, not looking at me.

"What are you always saying about people, about all these other people we see? That they're just passengers in life. That they're just coasting by, along for the ride. That people got to wake up and take their own destiny into their hands. Well, aren't I a person? You've made all these lists of no-goes, Rodeo, and I've respected them. Now, it's my turn. Not going back? Losing that box? That's a no-go, Rodeo. I'm calling it."

I leaned closer, bent my neck so I could look up into his eyes. His eyes were wounded, but he didn't look away. He held my eyes in his.

"Please, Rodeo," I said in the softest whisper I could manage that would still be heard.

We stood there, eye to eye, for a heartbeat or two.

"I don't know," he said at last, his voice scratchy. "I don't know if I can make it all the way. I don't know if I got this, little bird."

"That's okay, Rodeo. *I* got it. I got enough for both of us. Don't worry about getting me all the way there. Not yet. For now, you just gotta keep going. One mile at a time, right? You can do that, can't you, Rodeo? You can just keep going? For me? You love me, don't ya? Well, then, do this for me. Take me home. One last time. Because you love me."

Rodeo, he let out a breath, shaky and soft. He swallowed and stepped back, put his hand on the back of the seat. His eyes were down again, his eyebrows wrinkled in thought. I could see it, could see him wrestling with it in his heart.

He closed his eyes, then opened them again and looked up and into mine, even managed the ghost of a little smile, and he nodded. He nodded a yes at me and my heart started to sing, but I wanted more.

"I wanna hear you say it," I said soft, though I felt mean

saying it. Like I was kicking a beat dog. But I wasn't taking any chances.

He blinked, but he nodded again.

"I'll take you," he said, his voice scratchy and faint. "I'll take you back."

"Say you promise," I insisted, leery of loopholes even though Rodeo wasn't really the loophole type.

He raised his chin and looked at me straight on, head up and eyes clear.

"I promise you, Coyote. I'm taking you back."

I couldn't help it. A big ol' smile broke across my face, even though it wasn't exactly a happy sort of moment, really. It wasn't a gloating smile, just a glad one. I *really* didn't wanna hitchhike. There are some total weirdos out there.

Rodeo nodded once more, then rubbed his eyes and turned around and sat down in the driver's seat and brought Yager to life with a rumble.

I settled into the seat. Ivan jumped up beside me and I gave him a happy squeeze.

"Oh," I said, remembering. "And we gotta make it by tomorrow morning, so keep it moving."

His head snapped to me.

"Tomorrow morning? Honeybear, we're in Montana. I don't think we can—"

"It is about a seventeen-hour drive from Billings, Montana, to Poplin Springs, Washington, via Boise, Idaho," I said, looking at the clock above the windshield. If Rodeo didn't think I'd done my homework, he was sorely mistaken. "We have twenty-four hours to get there, give or take. We got this. But we better get rolling. Hit the gas, old man."

Rodeo gave me a long look. He shook his head, once.

And then he hit the gas.

CHAPTER

THIRTY-ONE

 would've guessed that Rodeo deciding to break five years' worth of stubbornness and take me back home would be the only major life-changing decision made on our bus that day, but I would've guessed wrong. Because about three hours down the road, Lester Washington had his own momentous, buckle-your-seat-belt change of heart.

Lester was driving. We were still in Montana. I was sitting in the seat behind him, reading and sweating and trying to take my mind off what I was gonna do the next day.

We'd stopped for gas and just barely gotten rolling again when he flicked on the turn signal and pulled Yager onto an exit ramp. No big deal—I knew that it was about time for our left turn toward Boise.

We pulled up to the top of the exit ramp, where there was a stoplight. A road went to the left, a road went to the right, and straight ahead was the on-ramp to get back onto the highway. The light was red, and Yager shuddered to a stop.

I looked back at my book, found my spot, kept on reading.

And reading. And reading.

At some point, I kinda realized that we'd been stopped at that red light for an awful long time.

Just as that was dawning on me, I heard the honking start.

I looked up. We were sitting there. Lester had his hands on the wheel. The light was green. And we weren't moving.

"It's green," I said, and looked back at my book. But there was no lurch, no rev.

"Lester! Light's green!" I said, and snapped my fingers.

Nothing. Well, almost nothing. His shoulders rose up and then dropped down in a big sigh.

The honking from behind us doubled.

I dropped my book and leaned forward on my knees so I could see his face.

He looked okay. I mean, he didn't look like he was having a stroke or a heart attack or anything, and he was breathing and awake. He looked serious, though. Jaw clenched. Eyes narrowed. Lips pursed.

"Hey," I said. "Lester. The light's green, man. I think the folks behind us are, uh, hoping you'll go. Soon."

"That way," Lester said, still looking straight ahead but pointing with one hand to the left, "is the way to Boise."

"Um . . . perfect," I said. Since, you know, that's where we were going and all.

We didn't move. Lester didn't twitch or add any other relevant details or anything.

"So . . . that's where we're going, right?"

Then Lester sighed again. And he dropped his hands off the steering wheel, which was not a great step forward. And he turned to look at me.

"I don't know, kid," he said.

"But that's where Tammy is," I said, and he said, "Exactly," and his eyes filled up with tears, and I said, "Oh," and then at that moment Rodeo came on up, roused from his bed pile by all the honking at our taillights and he said, "Hey, brother, what's going on?"

Lester didn't answer Rodeo, though. He was still looking me in the eyes.

"You got Salvador a stage so he could play that violin for his mom," he said.

"Um. Yeah."

"Because it was important to him," Lester went on, "so it was important to you."

"I guess so," I said, looking back toward the honking folks.

"That's what a friend does," Lester said.

"Um, okay. But . . . uh, do you wanna talk about this while we drive? Or, maybe, like, pulled over on the shoulder?"

"That's what she should do" is all he answered.

"Who?" I said, and Rodeo answered quiet, "Tammy," and I said, "Oh. Oh."

"That's what love is, right? Caring about what the other person cares about, because you care about them. And wanting them to be happy. Right?" Lester asked.

"I guess?"

"She should be helping me bust open double doors. Or she should be turning on the mic. Or, at least, she should be sitting in the front row." He looked away, shook his head, and looked back. "She shouldn't be the security guard, though. She shouldn't be the one kicking me out. In that whole crazy thing we did, that's the one part she shouldn't play."

He nodded. Sniffed. Put his hands back on the wheel.

I blew a breath out in relief. But then he dropped his hands again. Drat. I chewed my lip. The light went red again, but the honking didn't let up.

"But you know what? If Tammy *is* the security guard, if that's who she is, that's cool. That dude was just doing his job. Feeding his family. Keeping that joint safe. If she's the guard, then I shouldn't be breaking in. Right?"

"That's right," Rodeo murmured beside me.

Lester blew out a long, deep breath from the bottoms of his lungs. He looked back and forth between me and Rodeo.

"Salvador can't marry the guard," he whispered. "And the guard can't marry Salvador."

Rodeo was nodding and he said, "Totally, man," but I pulled my head back and said, "Wait . . . what?"

The light turned green. Lester nodded at me, his lips set firm with decision. He hit the gas, and Yager took off.

Straight forward. Across the road, right back toward the highway we'd just left. Not the one going to Boise.

"Wow, man," Rodeo said. "You sure?"

"Yeah. Yeah." The first "yeah" he said quiet and kinda doubtful, the second he said still quiet but with some sureness to it.

He pulled his phone out of his shirt pocket and handed it to me.

"Call Tammy. She's there in the Contacts."

I scrolled down through the names until I got to her. I pressed the little green phone icon and it started ringing, and I held it back out to Lester, but he shook his head and said, "No. I can't. I want you to talk to her."

"Excuse me?" I said, but I didn't say it mean like Val had, so it didn't work.

"I can't, girl. I need you to do it."

"You want me to break up with your girlfriend? Uh, no way."

"All you gotta do is—"

But whatever Lester was about to say was interrupted by Tammy's voice, coming out thin and scratchy from the phone in my hand between us.

"Hey, baby, what's up? You almost here?"

I looked at the phone. I looked at Lester.

He gave me begging eyes and mouthed the word "please."

I gave him how-dare-you eyes right back, but I held the phone up to my ear.

"Baby?" Tammy said.

I sighed.

"This isn't baby. It's, uh, Coyote."

"Who?"

"Not important. But Lester wanted me to call you."

"Okay. Everything all right?"

"Yeah. Well, kind of. I mean, for now. But maybe not in a minute?"

I wasn't, like, totally nailing my side of the conversation. In my defense, I'd never broken up with anyone before.

"What's going on? Is Lester there?"

"Yeah, yeah, but he's driving, so he can't talk."

"*Hey,*" Lester mercifully cut in at a whisper, "*tell her I love her.*"

I shot him a side-eye because it seemed like an odd place to start a breakup, but I was grateful to finally have some direction, so I went with it.

"He says he loves you."

"Okay. I love him, too."

"*She loves you, too,*" I whispered to Lester.

"*I'm not coming to Boise,*" he whispered back.

"But . . . he's not coming to Boise."

"What? Why not?"

"*What? Why not?*"

"*Because I love you.*"

"Because he loves you."

"Excuse me?"

"*Excuse her?*"

"*I love her. And we won't be happy together. We just won't be. So I'm not coming.*"

"He loves you. But you won't be happy together. So. He's not coming."

There was a pause at the other end that I would have to describe as long-ish and tense-ish.

"No." That's what she said, eventually. I opened my mouth. Shut it. I wasn't sure how to handle that. "No. He does *not* get to do this. Break up with me. Over the phone. Through some kid. No."

Lester looked over at me, waiting to hear her response.

I shrugged.

"She says no."

He twisted his lips.

"Tell her I love her."

I shook my head. *"You already said that. Give me something else."*

"Uh. Tell her I'm sorry."

"He's sorry."

"And I want her to be happy."

"And he wants you to be happy."

"Because I love her."

"Because he loves you."

"But I won't be happy without music. And she won't be happy with a musician."

"But he won't be happy without his music. And you won't be happy with a musician."

I heard heavy breathing through the phone. The crying kind of breathing.

"I know that. I know. But I love him. So much. For real." Her voice was broken and hurting and I felt guilty for all the bad things I'd thought about her.

"But she loves you. For reals. A lot."

Lester's eyes got all full of tears again, and I saw his lip shaking. I wasn't super sure he should be driving.

"I love her, too. That's why we gotta do this. We gotta love each other enough to say goodbye."

"He loves you, too. That's why you have to do this. You guys have to love each other enough to say goodbye."

Tammy sniffed.

"God. That's such a stupid line."

"Yeah," I agreed. "Sort of."

"But maybe kind of true, too."

"Yeah."

There was a long, shaky breath.

"God, this sucks."

"I know, Tammy. I'm sorry."

"I mean, I guess I knew it was coming. I just wouldn't admit it. 'Cause I love him so much. But, it's like . . . like sometimes you can love someone so much that you can look right past all the stuff that's not working, you know?"

I thought of Rodeo sitting in the seat across from me.

"Yeah. I totally do."

"What are you guys talking about?" Lester cut in, but I gave him a mind-your-own-business scowl and held a finger to my lips.

"Is he okay, though? Is he gonna be all right?"

"I think so. I mean, he's having a hard time with this. But he's doing okay, I think."

"Good."

"What are you talking about?" Lester spat out, his voice rising a bit.

"Quiet!" I hissed. *"I'm on the phone!"*

"Will you watch out for him? Make sure he's okay?"

"Of course. Are *you* gonna be okay, Tammy?"

"Oh, I guess. I'll do some crying, that's for sure. But, yeah. I got friends around. I just want him to be happy."

"He wants you to be happy, too."

"I know. He always did. Maybe he was too worried about me

being happy all this time, and not worried enough about himself."

"Yeah."

"You gotta look out for your own happiness, you know," Tammy said. "We all do. There's nothing wrong with that."

"*What. Is. Going. On?*" Lester's voice was getting loud to the point of being rude. I covered my ear with my other hand and turned away from him.

"You're right. You're so right, Tammy," I said with a sigh. "I'm just starting to figure that out for myself, actually."

"Good. It's important. Especially for us girls."

"Totally."

Tammy sighed, a big ol' heavy, lung-emptying sigh.

"Well. You tell him he can call me whenever he wants. I'll always be here for him."

"Okay. I will. The same goes for you, I'm sure."

"Thanks. Goodbye."

"Goodbye, Tammy. Take care."

And with that we hung up.

I looked back at Lester. He took his eyes off the road and gave me a "well?!" kind of look and started to open his mouth to say something.

"She says goodbye, Lester," I said, and handed him his phone. He took it, his mouth still hanging open.

I sat for a minute, thinking it through. Tammy had given me a lot to think about. Lord, life could be complicated. It was so hard to tell sometimes whether you were being the security guard, or the violin player, or the violin player's friend, or someone else altogether. Was Tammy being selfish in asking Lester to give up music, or was Lester being selfish in picking music over Tammy? Was Rodeo being selfish in not wanting to take me back . . . or was I being selfish in making him go back?

Out of nowhere, tears came stinging into my eyes. I just wanted everyone to be happy. Lester and Tammy and Salvador and his mom and his aunt and Val and me and Rodeo. It's hard, though, when everyone carries around a heart inside them that is so loud and so strong and so easily broken.

I stood up and headed back toward my bedroom.

I was tired.

And something else, too: I was almost home. And I was terrified.

CHAPTER
THIRTY-TWO

*N*ow, there are plenty of ways to wake up. There are good wake-ups, like when you drift out of sleep slow and easy and wake up curled up all warm with your cat. There's waking up on Christmas and waking up on your birthday and waking up to the smell of bacon cooking. All good wake-ups.

And then there are bad wake-ups. Rodeo waking up with Ivan clawing him bloody and me reaching for his neck comes to mind. And there's waking up vomiting. I did that once when I got food poisoning from eating a buffalo burger in Texas. Not great.

But I gotta say that the afternoon after I broke up with Tammy, I discovered a whole new level of bad wake-up.

As far as I know, there is no worse way to wake up than on a speeding, out-of-control bus full of people screaming and crying and begging for their lives.

I was sound asleep when it all started. I was snoozing along quite happily when someone screaming "Help us, Jesus!" kind of half woke me up and then a whole bunch of screams (some religious, some secular) all-the-way woke me up and by the time I could gasp and jerk upright, I could hear all kinds of hollering and blubbering and wailing and the bus was shaking under and around me. Then the bus lurched wildly to the side, nearly tossing me to the floor, and I tell you I just about peed the bed.

I jumped up and ran right out through my curtain to see that all hell had broken loose on board ol' Yager.

It was still bright in the afternoon, which was fortunate. So the whole terrifying scene was well-lit, if nothing else.

We were heading down a hill, and it was a steep downhill, too. All around us were big, pine-dotted brown hills. The trees were blurry on account of the fact that we were hurtling along at, oh, I don't know, two hundred miles an hour. Not really, of course, but in Yager anything over about sixty *feels* like two hundred. And we were definitely over sixty.

Concepción was at the wheel. Even from the back of the bus I could see her fingers in a tight death grip on the wheel, her shoulders hunched and rigid. She was doing the most consistent screaming: a high-pitched, screeching, repetitive sort of wail, like a siren.

Rodeo was crouched on the floor next to her, pointing at things and hollering and being not at all his normal laid-back self. Lester was up behind Rodeo and Concepción, and he was shouting and pointing and carrying on just like Rodeo was.

A gray blur came tearing toward me and I realized it was Ivan, ears back and eyes huge and fur standing up. I thought he was running to me, but he rocketed right through my legs and dove under my bed. Fair enough.

Before I could take in the rest of the scene, Yager did another dramatic sideways swerve that tumbled me to the floor with a breath-snatching *oof.* I shook my head and pushed myself up to my hands and knees, keeping my legs and hands spread wide for balance. Standing upright seemed like a foolish and short-term proposition, so I started crawling up toward the front of the bus, passing my fellow passengers in a tour of terror along the way.

First I passed Ms. Vega. She was bracing herself on the couch, her eyes closed and her lips moving in what I'm guessing was a prayer. She was far too busy pleading her case to the lord to notice me slinking past her.

Next came Val, sitting stiff and wide-eyed in the Throne. She was screaming, too—well, not so much screaming as wailing "Oh my god, oh my god, oh my god" with tears streaming down her cheeks. I crept past her and into the aisle between the seats.

Salvador was kinda surfing in the middle of the aisle, standing up but bent low, holding on to the seats on both sides, screaming his head off. Not words so much as *sounds*, though if they *had* been words I bet they would've been words I wouldn't want to repeat in front of my grandma.

Yager careened violently to the side again so hard it knocked me down to my elbows. Books avalanched off shelves, and I heard at least one tomato plant bust loose and crash to the floor.

"What's going on?!" I screamed as I pulled myself up to one knee and braced myself against the seat.

Salvador's head swiveled back to me. His eyes were like Ping-Pong balls.

"Coyote!" he shrieked, and he was way past trying to act tough at all. "Stay down!"

"What's going on?!"

And then Salvador told me.

Now, just like waking up, news can be good and news can be bad. Or, news can be flat-out terrible. Well, Salvador gave me some news that was definitely in that last category.

"The brakes went out! We're out of control!"

I hadn't eaten a buffalo burger in about two years, but I just about vomited when Salvador gave me that news. I eyed Rodeo way up at the front trying to help Concepción however he could.

I started crawling forward again, rocking with the movement of the bus. Salvador had his legs spread wide and I crawled right through them, hoping that he wasn't as close to peeing his pants as I was.

"What are you doing?" he asked.

I opened my mouth to answer, but nothing came out. So I kept crawling.

The truth is, I was freaking terrified. My stomach was somersaulting and my muscles were shaking and my lungs were heaving and my heart was drumming and my eyes were blurry and I . . . I wanted my dad. I just wanted my dad.

I ain't allowed to say that, though. That d-word, that's a no-go.

So I just kept my mouth shut and crawled up behind Rodeo.

He looked back over his shoulder and saw me coming up behind him.

"Hold on, honeybird!" he shouted. "And stay down!" He turned his eyes back to the front, and I did the same.

Almost wished I hadn't.

We were *flying* down that highway. We were passing cars left and right, which was where all the lurching and swerving was coming from. They had no way of knowing we had no brakes, so they didn't bother pulling to the side when we came up behind them and then Concepción would have to cut the wheel and careen around them, honking the whole way to try to warn 'em.

It musta been something for them, driving down the road minding their own business when out of nowhere a rattling old school bus full of screaming people roared by them like a drag racer.

Yeah. We got a few looks.

I wasn't worried about the looks, though. I was worried about the two semis in front of us, one in each lane, blocking our whole side of the highway. We were coming up on 'em fast.

"Guys?!" Concepción asked between shrieks. "Any ideas? What should I do?!"

"Lay on the horn!" Lester shouted, and even though Concepción had already been honking it, she switched to just holding it down in one long desperate *hooooooooooooonk*.

But the trucks either didn't hear us or couldn't adjust in time. They were exactly side by side, with only, like, a foot of space between them.

"How about the oncoming lane?" Rodeo hollered, and Concepción drifted across the yellow highway line, but then she yelped and cut back hard into our lane just in time to avoid a line of cars coming the other way.

"No good!" she screamed. "Too much traffic!"

The trucks were close now. In four seconds we were gonna smash into them.

"Help me, Jesus!" Concepción screamed skyward. Then she yanked the steering wheel the other way, to the right. We roared across one lane and my heart jumped up into my neck when I saw what she was doing. She steered Yager right onto the shoulder of the road, all the way over so that our right wheels were rumbling and crunching through the weeds and dirt, and we missed the back corner of the semi by what looked like, I swear to god, about half an inch.

Yager was really bouncing and shaking now and a fresh round of screaming and crying and praying erupted behind us.

Thanks to our unreasonable and horrifying speed, we didn't have to spend too much time driving on the shoulder, which I suppose was the silver lining to the whole nightmare.

Once we cleared the semi, Concepción veered us back onto the asphalt.

"There!" Rodeo cried, pointing out the front windshield. And we all saw it: in the distance, the highway flattening out, leveling out to a nice, long straightaway.

Salvation.

Between us and that, though, there was still at least a mile of road, plenty of traffic, and one decently sharp turn to the left.

"You got it," Lester breathed out, reaching to squeeze Concepción's shoulder. "You're doing great."

We weaved left, we weaved right, splitting the traffic and racing our way toward that blessed flat stretch up ahead.

We came up to the curve, all four lanes of highway bending off to the left. We were in the left lane and it was wide open in front of us. We were gonna make it. We just had to take the curve, pass a couple of cars, and then coast to a stop.

But then. Oh, there's almost always a "but then."

A car in front of us, one that was over in the right lane and not causing *any* problems, decided to pass the car in front of it. Which meant, of course, that it pulled over into the left lane. You know, the one that we were rocketing down.

Lester said a couple words I won't repeat, but with which I totally agreed.

Concepción cut to the right, going for her insane shoulder trick again. I mean, it had worked before, hadn't it?

But before, there hadn't been a van parked on the shoulder, up on a jack and missing a tire.

There were a few more bad words from the crowd up front, possibly even including me.

We cut back to the left, but both of our lanes were taken.

We all knew what she had to do.

I shouted, "Help us, Jesus!" so Concepción could focus on the driving.

We drifted into the next lane over. The one where cars were *supposed* to be heading the other way.

It was clear.

There was a red pickup coming our way, but it was a ways off. At our speed, it looked like we'd be able to pass the car and get back on the right side before we met that pickup.

"You got this, Concepción," Rodeo cheered.

We pulled up beside the car we were passing at the same time it was passing the car next to it.

Our hood passed its taillights, then its rear doors, then its driver, who was glancing down at his cell phone and didn't even notice us sneaking past him in our gigantic, bright yellow school bus.

Then our nose was past its hood, and it was sliding on back behind us. We had it.

But then we hit another "but then," of course.

That red pickup was getting closer.

"Get over," Rodeo said.

"I can't," Concepción said between clenched teeth.

"Get over," Lester said.

"I can't!" Concepción snarled. "We're not past him yet! We're not passing him at all!"

All three of our heads swiveled to see what she was seeing in her rearview mirror.

The car with the cell phone driver was not receding safely into the distance behind us. It was holding steady, right next to us.

"Is he *speeding up?*" I demanded.

"No!" Lester answered. "*We're* slowing down!"

It was true. We'd hit the bottom of the hill. The slope was fading away, and so was our madhouse speed.

"Hit the gas!" I screamed.

And, after all that stress about going too fast and wishing we could stop, Concepción floored the gas pedal.

Yager's engine revved high in protest, but it answered the call. We surged forward.

The cell phone car dropped back to our rear. The red pickup was cruising toward our front. Concepción gave the rearview mirror one last check, and then jerked the wheel hard to the right.

We barreled out of the path and back into our own lane and she kept going into the far right lane and took her foot off the gas and we rolled a little less fast and a little less fast and then there was a highway exit with a nice, long, steep uphill ramp. She took it and we rolled even slower up the slope, and when we were rolling along at, like, bicycle speed she pulled off onto the shoulder and then, *thank god*, we came to a sweet, sweet stop.

Concepción grabbed the gearshift and clicked us into park and yanked up on the parking brake. She turned the key and killed the engine.

We all sat or stood or crouched there for a few seconds, breathing and panting and slowing our hearts back down to a more survivable speed.

Rodeo straightened up. He blew out a big breath.

He turned back to the rest of us. I could still hear Ms. Vega praying, and Val sniffling.

His eyes went from person to person as the color slowly came back to his face. They settled on me and his eyebrows dropped, and he grabbed a blanket off a seat and handed it to me.

"Wrap this around yourself, little bird," he said quietly, and I realized that I'd come running out in such a hurry that I'd neglected to check my clothing situation. I was wearing nothing but a T-shirt and my underwear in front of Salvador and the whole world, which at any other time would have made me about six different kinds of mortified, but at that moment I was *alive* and just grateful to be so, so I just took the blanket and kinda tied it around my waist and didn't worry one bit about it. I glanced back at Salvador, but he was looking very conspicuously away from me and out the window, which I thought was very gentle-manly and honorable.

Rodeo wedged a shaken little half smile onto his face.

"Well," he said, "we're making good time. Anyone else need a bathroom break?"

CHAPTER
THIRTY-THREE

Rodeo crawled out from under Yager, his shirt and hands stained black with oil. He had a smear of dark grease across his forehead, too.

Me and Salvador and Val and Lester stood there on the shoulder of the road, waiting for the verdict. The sun was shining, the sky was blue, the air smelled of pine trees—and I was twisted in knots of worry. My heart was pounding a ticktock clock beat in my chest, counting down the seconds and the minutes and the hours I had left. We were, according to Lester's phone, about eight hours of nonstop driving away from Poplin Springs. It was two o'clock in the afternoon, the day before that park and my irreplaceable memories would be destroyed forever. Compared to where we'd started in Florida, home was right around the corner. But if our bus was stuck and staying that way, we might as well have been on the moon.

Rodeo didn't bother standing up. He sat there in the gravel, his back against Yager's tire, and wiped his hands with an old rag. He squinted up at me, then looked away.

"Well?" Lester asked.

Rodeo shook his head, looked back at me.

"Sorry, butterfly" is all he said. My eyes burned hot.

"Sorry, what?" Salvador demanded.

"Sorry, this is a big repair. Whole brake line snapped. I need parts. Parts we ain't likely to find around here," he added, waving a hand at the country around us.

"So . . . what are you saying?" Salvador asked, though I think he knew as well as the rest of us *exactly* what Rodeo was saying.

Rodeo huffed out a sigh.

"I'm saying . . . I'm saying we ain't gonna make it. Not in time. It'll be a couple days before this thing is moving again, and that's best case. I'm sorry, blueberry."

He said he was sorry. He *said* he was sorry. I wasn't so sure he really was, though.

My hands, which had been nervously tugging at my braid, dropped down defeated at my sides. My eyes burned and my throat got tight and my breathing came in big, broken gasps. No. No, no, no.

Lester *tsk*ed and shook his head and turned around.

Salvador, though, wasn't giving up.

"Can't you, like, patch it or something? Just for now?"

"Kid, there ain't no patching a brake line. And I'm not heading down any road without brakes I don't trust. Not after today."

"Well, couldn't Coyote, I don't know, take a bus or something?"

Rodeo shook his head.

"No, man. She ain't going without me. And I ain't going without Yager. She's our home, our life, everything we have is on her.

And what about Ivan? Nah. Sorry. We're both stuck here as long as Yager is stuck here."

I looked away. Because I knew.

Rodeo wasn't worried about Ivan. He wasn't worried about our stuff.

He was worried about himself.

I'm sure he wasn't lying about the brakes. Or about how long it'd take to fix them. But I knew he *was* lying about being sorry. He wasn't sorry one bit that we wouldn't make it home. Wasn't sorry one bit that he wouldn't have to dredge up those old memories he'd worked so hard to keep buried.

I ground my teeth together, hard.

He'd probably been hoping for an excuse, a chance to call it off. I bet he'd been praying for a way to not keep his promise to me.

But I couldn't let him have that excuse. Nope. No regrets, sister.

"I know what to do," I said. "I know how we can get it fixed."

"Wait a minute, honeybear, we can't just—" Rodeo started to say, but I spun in the gravel so he was at my back. I was done with him.

"Lester," I said, "get out your phone. Please."

I knew we had one chance to get old Yager fixed. Who in the world has school bus parts, and maybe even a mechanic who knows how to work on them? Well, a school district. Obviously.

We'd done it before, Rodeo and me. Needing a part or a little expertise, we'd called whatever school district we were closest to and chatted with their bus garage and, for the most part, found the folks there to be pretty darn helpful and kinda interested in seeing what we had going on with Yager.

I searched around on Lester's phone and found the phone number of the closest school district. I pressed "the Call button," and when I heard it ringing I handed it over to Rodeo. He was still sitting there all slack-boned, his face tired and neutral.

We waited while Rodeo squinted at the horizon, the phone pressed to his ear. After a bit he shook his head and hung it up.

"No answer," he said with a halfhearted shrug. "It's August. No one's gonna be working at the schools in August. It's hopeless, baby."

I was breathing fast through my nose, chewing on my bottom lip.

Rodeo looked up at me, his magical eyes not the slightest bit magical right then for me.

I turned around, stared off at the hills, my heart broken and my mind racing.

Hopeless. It's not a word I really cared for at that particular moment.

It did *feel* hopeless, there by the side of the highway with no help in sight.

But, here's the thing: Hope is a lot like parking lot cigarette butts—always there if you look hard enough.

My mind clicked. I spun back around. When I spoke, I spoke to Lester and Salvador.

"We don't need the schools," I said. "We just need the bus mechanic."

Lester just blinked at me. But Salvador's eyes lit up.

"The school district website!" he shouted, then he bent down and snatched the phone from Rodeo's limp hand. "Let's see if it has, like, someone's name. Then maybe we could call them at home or something."

Lester grinned.

"Brilliant."

Turned out it *was* brilliant. There on the district website, under "Our Staff," it had a long list of all the folks who worked there, with nice little smiling pictures next to the names. Down at the bottom, under "Support Staff," was a picture of a lady with big hair and bright red lipstick and a big smile, and the title "Transportation Maintenance Director," which Lester assured us was probably the title we were looking for. Her name was Tammy. I kid you not.

Tammy's last name was Smet, so Lester searched for Tammy Smets in Anaconda, Montana (which was where we were, more or less), and he found a number.

"It's ringing," he said, and Rodeo reached up for the phone. But Lester just gave him a look. A serious look. A quiet look. And he said, kinda soft, "No, man. I'll talk to her." Rodeo just scratched his nose and looked away.

We all stood there waiting breathlessly for a minute and then Lester said, "Hello? Is this Tammy Smet?" and me and Salvador exchanged quick little nervous-happy let's-see-how-this-goes smiles and then Lester said, "Well, my name is Lester and you don't know me, but I got a little question for you. Well, a big question," and then he turned and walked off a bit, away from the road and toward the trees, and we couldn't hear what he was saying anymore, but he said a lot.

I saw him talking into his phone, up there, in the shadow of the Idaho pines. He talked with his mouth, with his eyes, with his face, with his hands, with his heart. He paced and he nodded and he shook his head and sometimes he talked high and sometimes he talked low.

I watched him, a lump in my throat. 'Cause he was doing all that talking for me.

I loved that man, watching him talking for me by the side of the road. And I knew he loved me, too. Because that's what love is. Caring about what the other person cares about because you care about them. And want them to be happy. Right?

I don't know what he said. But he must've said it good, because a few minutes or a few lifetimes later, he came walking over to us and he put his hand over the phone and said, "What kind of bus is this?" and I answered, "This is a 2003 International 3800 school bus," and it might seem odd that I'd have that memorized, but it ain't, because most kids have their addresses memorized, right? Yager's license plate is Washington State JFS1150, by the way.

Lester did some more talking and then he handed the phone down to Rodeo, who was still sitting in the dirt.

"She needs to talk to you," he said, and Rodeo just looked at the phone for a second, but then he took it and he answered a few questions about brake parts and part numbers and stuff and then he said, "Uh-huh. Okay. Yep." And then he said the best thing of all: "All right. I'll see you in a little bit, then."

And I guess he probably hung up, but I didn't see it because I was too busy high-fiving Salvador and hugging Lester and doing a dance right there on the exit-ramp shoulder.

I didn't hug Rodeo. I didn't high-five him, either.

Tammy Smet showed up about an hour later in a big, rumbling diesel pickup truck. She had a toolbox and some work gloves and a whole bunch of parts and I'd just about never seen a prettier sight than her getting out of that truck and saying, "Howdy."

Lester shook her hand and Rodeo shook her hand and then she got to me. She looked me in the eye and asked, "You the girl?"

I shrugged.

"I'm *a* girl, ma'am. Don't know if I'm *the* girl."

"You're the one he told me about, though?"

"Yeah, probably."

She looked into my eyes a second longer, then pulled something out of her shirt pocket. It was a picture. A picture of a lady who looked an awful lot like Tammy. Friendly eyes. A big, warm smile.

"That's my sister," Tammy said. Then she added, "Charlene," and she added it soft.

"She looks nice."

"She was."

I looked up at Tammy and she looked down at me and then she said, "Let's get this ol' girl back on the road."

I smiled big and she smiled back. She started toward her truck, then stopped and turned to Rodeo.

"Uh, we will need to talk about *money*, though."

Now, Tammy was good people. But obviously she couldn't go around giving away expensive bus parts that the school district had paid for to any stranger that passed through town.

"Of course," Rodeo said when she told him how much the parts would cost. "We'll pay you for all parts and labor, no problem."

"Well," Tammy said, "the parts you *will* need to pay money for. The labor, though, is something else."

"What kind of something?"

"Lester over there tells me y'all are heading toward Poplin Springs."

"Yeah. That's right."

"And that's on the way to Silver Bar, right?"

Rodeo squinted.

"I suppose so," he answered all cautiously.

"Well, that's just perfect!" Tammy beamed.

"How so, sister?"

"It just so happens that I got an item that I been trying to get to Silver Bar. But I been so busy, I haven't had the chance. And then along you come, heading that way, needing a favor."

Rodeo sniffed.

"I don't need a favor. I can pay you for all parts and labor."

"Fine. You don't need a favor. And I don't really need your money. But you *do* need a new brake line. And I *do* need something taken to where you're going. And that's what I call just perfect." Tammy smiled, and there was a tough little glint in her eye. She was good people, that Tammy, but she also knew how to get what she wanted. Nothing wrong with that.

Rodeo shot me a what-did-you-get-us-into look and cocked an eyebrow at Tammy.

"This, uh, item. It is . . . legal to transport?"

Tammy's eyes darted away for a second.

"Yeah," she said, but she sounded awful vague when she said it. "Well, it ain't necessarily *il*legal."

Rodeo spit out a sunflower seed shell.

"Uh-huh. What is it?"

Tammy grinned her biggest grin yet.

Four hours later, we were back on the road.

The brakes were fixed and working like a charm. We could stop whenever we wanted, which is really what you're shooting for when it comes to brakes.

Salvador and Val were back on the couch, playing Uno. Ms. Vega and Concepción were chatting in one of the bus seats. Lester was trying to get some sleep on Rodeo's blanket pile. Ivan was conked out back in my bed.

Rodeo was driving, and he was doing a nasty combination of fuming and sulking, so I was doing my best to leave him alone while also keeping an eye on him.

We were moving. We'd lost about five hours altogether and the sun was almost setting, and I knew that getting there was gonna be a close call, but it sure looked like I was gonna make it. Home. I was gonna make it *home*. I was bouncing and tapping my feet; my heart and my stomach were fighting a war. My heart was trying to clap and sing a hallelujah song, but my stomach was pacing back and forth, wondering what in the heck I'd gotten us into. I felt like you do when you're sitting at the very tip-top of a roller coaster: You're happy, you're excited . . . but you're also holding your breath for what's coming next.

But thanks to Tammy, I did have something else to help occupy my racing mind.

I was sitting in the first row of bus seats, right behind Rodeo. I was perched at the edge of the seat, way over by the aisle. I was sitting there so I could have my arm around Gladys, to keep her calm while we drove.

I guess I should mention: Gladys was a two-hundred-pound Finnish Landrace goat with long white hair and an impressive pair of elegant horns, and she needed a ride to Silver Bar, Washington.

THIRTY-FOUR

*G*ladys, like Val and Salvador and Lester and Esperanza and Concepción, was a great addition to our troupe.

Gladys belonged to Tammy's daughter, Jessica, who had recently moved to Silver Bar. Gladys, who had been raised and bottle-fed by Jessica, was not a big fan of the move. She'd been moping around for weeks, Tammy had told us with a sad shake of her head. So there was to be a reunion between Gladys and Jessica. We and our bus were the means for that reunion to be possible.

The whole thing was very sweet and exciting. Well, *I* thought the whole thing was very sweet and exciting. Rodeo and I didn't see eye-to-eye on that particular issue.

"We can't have some damned goat in our home making a mess of our floor!" Rodeo had insisted. He'd darn near raised his voice, so I'd known he was serious.

"Oh, Gladys is house-trained," Tammy had assured us.

"*Gladys?*" Rodeo had exclaimed, momentarily distracted. He got back on track pretty quick, though. "You can't house-train a goat."

Tammy's eyebrows lowered and she cleared her throat.

"Maybe *you* can't house-train a goat. But apparently *I* can." And then she added, a little less confidently, "But, uh, you should probably pull over every couple hours and walk her around a bit. Just in case."

I liked Tammy.

Rodeo and Tammy stared at each other for a minute.

"This is ridiculous," Rodeo said.

Tammy softened her tone.

"Look. I *really* need to get Gladys to Silver Bar. She misses her mama. A goat is a loyal animal. She won't be any problem, I promise. Well, maybe not *promise*, exactly, but I *bet*, anyway. Think of her like a dog. She's been a housegoat her whole life."

"Housegoat?" Rodeo sputtered, but Tammy kept going.

"Those are my terms, buddy. Come on. This is a win-win. A win-win-win-win, if you count Gladys and Jessica. I'd really appreciate it. I'm helping *you*. Please. Help me out here."

Oh, that Tammy. I don't know if she was really that good at reading people or she just got lucky, but that was the perfect way to end an argument with Rodeo. He ain't good at being bullied. But he's exceptionally good at helping folks who need it. Always kindness. More or less.

Rodeo looked deflated. He was beat, and him and me both knew it. He now had a promise to keep *and* a kindness to offer and maybe he coulda fought one of 'em, but he was defenseless against both of 'em together.

He pointed a finger at me, but it was more of a surrendering finger than an angry finger.

"You're cleaning up any messes that goat makes," he'd said, and that was that.

Gladys had bright green eyes that always looked like they were laughing, and a braying bleat that cracked me up every time. She was a real people-goat, too, always wanting to be right by my side no matter where I was. I tried to get her to hop up on the seat next to me and I swear she was just about to, but then Rodeo put a kibosh on that.

Ivan was surprisingly low-key about the whole thing. He gave her a fair amount of owl-eyed staring when she first scrambled on board and his introductory sniffs were cautious at best, but within a few minutes they'd done some cordial mutual nose-sniffing, and within twenty miles he seemed to have forgotten that Gladys hadn't always been a part of our pack. He's some kind of cat, that Ivan.

Gladys *did* manage to eat basically an entire tomato plant before Salvador stopped her, but I think that's understandable behavior even for a well-behaved housegoat. All in all, bringing Gladys on board was a real upgrade for our group experience.

Around bedtime on that last night, I was sitting back on the couch reading by what was left of the sun's light shining through the bus windows. Ivan was snoozing on my lap. Gladys was curled up by my feet, blinking slow and sleepy. I suppose it was a pretty odd and specific scene.

Salvador was at the other end of the couch, just about ready to finish *The One and Only Ivan*. He was loving it. Obviously.

Lester walked back and sat down in the Throne. He shot a look at Rodeo up driving, then leaned forward with his elbows on his knees and asked me in a low voice, "Is he gonna be okay?"

I knew what he was talking about. Ever since the secret, and especially since we'd gotten the brakes fixed, Rodeo had been quieter and quieter. His eyes didn't have their sparkle. His answers were short.

"Sure," I said. "I mean, he'll be okay. He ain't happy about it, but he'll be okay." I think I was saying it to reassure myself as much as Lester. "He's been avoiding this for five years," I went on. "It's really hard for him. But he knows how much it means to me. It'll be okay."

"You really haven't been back in five years? At all?" Salvador asked.

I shook my head.

"Not even close."

"How you feeling?" Lester's voice was soft, his eyes deep into mine.

"Good. Well . . . kinda scared, I guess. And sad. Rodeo is right . . . it *is* sad to think about it. To think about them." I took in a breath, let it out. "But it's worth it. I think remembering them and being sad about it is way better than forgetting about them."

Salvador nodded and Lester murmured, "That's right."

I thought I was done talking, but then without planning it I said, "I miss them." I blinked fast and looked down. I rubbed at my eyes with the backs of my hands. "I keep remembering this one thing. There's this hill we used to sled on in the winter. Close to our house. We'd drag our sleds up there, and sometimes for fun, we'd all squeeze onto our one long sled. Mom at the back 'cause she was the biggest. Rose at the front 'cause she was the smallest. Ava and me in the middle. We had to kind of hug each other to stay on the sled and our legs were all tangled up and it was stupid and hilarious and . . ." I broke off. In my mind, I could hear us all laughing, feel the arms around me, see the sunlight glaring off the white snow. "And fun. So . . . happy. But then . . . the accident was so sudden. And me and Rodeo left so soon." I squinched my eyes shut tight. "And sometimes it feels like that moment is just on pause. Like once I get home, our life will start right back up again. I'll be back on that sled. And *they'll* be with me." I shook my head. "But I know that's not true. Out here, on the road, it's been easy to feel like they're just back there. Waiting. But once we get there—I mean, they *won't* be. I know that." I tried to swallow the strangling lump out of my throat. I looked up at Lester, then Salvador, blurry through my tears. "I really, really need that box. I do. But I'm just . . . I'm just afraid. Afraid of how gone they'll feel once I have it."

Lester's eyes were shiny. He was biting his bottom lip.

Neither one of them said nothing. But Salvador reached over. And he held on to my hand. And he squeezed it.

"This is gonna be hard. It's gonna be really hard." My voice started with a tremble, but I dug down to my heartbeat and ironed it out. "Like losing 'em all over again. But maybe I have to lose 'em all over again to get 'em back. And I *have* to get 'em back. I have to. No matter what."

It was a good moment, I suppose. A strong moment, and true. In a movie, there'd be an orchestra playing in the background. Good stuff.

I had no way of knowing, though, that it was the moment right before everything unraveled.

CHAPTER
THIRTY-FIVE

It was the middle of the night. Or at least it felt that way. Rodeo had driven all the long evening, turning down offers of help from Lester and Concepción and Ms. Vega. "Nah," he'd said each time they'd asked, "I'm good." But he wasn't. Not at all.

After a late potty break I noticed that Gladys was looking a little sleepy, so I wandered back to my room with her and lay down on the bed and she lay down on the floor next to me and kinda curled her legs up under herself and laid her chin on the bed, which was freaking adorable.

Ivan seemed to be picking up on my human emotional turmoil, and he stuck close by me, following me around in the bus, watching me out the windows when I was outside pottying Gladys, jumping right up on me when I lay down.

Everyone was quiet and resting or reading or looking out the window or dozing. Lester was back to snoring in Rodeo's blanket pile.

I dozed off, too, apparently. Not sure for how long. But when I woke up, I noticed two things: It felt like I'd been asleep for hours, and the bus wasn't moving.

I sat up. Gladys jerked upright with me and bleated. A sleepy little what's-going-on-and-what-time-is-it kind of bleat. I pressed my face to the window.

We were parked at a gas station. In the middle of nowhere, it looked like. There were no other houses or businesses or nothing. I jumped up and threw back my curtain door.

Then, I noticed two more things: There was no one in the driver's seat, and it was quiet.

Interstate highways, the big four- or six- or even eight-lane kind we were traveling on, make a kind of noise. All the time. It's the noise of hundreds of sets of tires humming on asphalt. If you're anywhere within about a quarter mile of one, or even farther sometimes, you can hear it. That sound had been the background noise to my life, and I noticed when it was gone.

Well, it was gone.

Out the windows, I saw darkness. I saw some trees. I saw a measly little two-lane road. I saw no exit ramps. I saw no big green highway signs. I saw no headlights.

I walked quick to the front of the bus, past all the sleepers, my stomach tightening and twisting. Lester sat up when I passed him and asked, "Where are we?" through a yawn, but I didn't answer. I didn't know where we were. But I knew where we *weren't*.

The only sound was Gladys *clip-clop*ping behind me.

The front of the bus was deserted. The keys were gone. The lights were off. The door was closed.

I jerked the door open and jumped down off the bus and closed the door in Gladys's face and hurried into the gas station.

There was one guy behind the counter, and he looked very bored and very tired. He was watching a little TV on the counter. He turned his head when the bell above the door jangled as I walked in.

"You're up awful late," he said in a friendly-enough voice.

"What time is it?"

He peered at a clock up on the wall.

"Almost four in the morning. Past your bedtime, I bet."

"Where are we?" I asked.

But at that moment, Lester came barging through the door behind me, clothes all sleep-wrinkled and his eyes puffy and blinking. "Coyote, where are we?"

I turned to the clerk with questioning, urgent eyebrows. He gave me a confused look back.

"You're in Wallowa. Well, just outside Wallowa, really."

I held my hand out to Lester and barked, "Phone!"

He fished it out of his pocket and handed it over and I got to tapping and then I got to swearing.

"What?" Lester asked.

"Wallowa," I answered, holding up the phone so he could see it. "Wallowa, Oregon. This town is *not* on the way to Poplin Springs." Lester's mouth dropped open when he saw the map I was holding up. "Not even close. We're, like, four hours off the route. In the wrong direction."

My head shot to the clerk.

"Where's Rodeo?" I asked him.

"Rodeo?" the guy answered with a baffled look. I didn't have time for his ignorance.

"Rodeo?" I hollered, heading toward the back of the store. "Rodeo?"

I pushed open the door to the men's room.

"Rodeo?" No answer. I kicked open the door to the only stall. Empty.

I stomped back out into the store.

"Where is he? Where's Rodeo?"

The clerk was standing up now, clearly pretty alarmed by the girl walking around his store and ransacking the men's room.

"Rodeo? You mean the bearded fella?"

"Yes! Where. Is. He."

"He bought a sixer of beer and headed out the back door. Is he your dad or something?"

"Something," I answered, and ran out through the back door with tears in my eyes and my hands in fists and my heart breaking and beating and breaking and beating.

CHAPTER
THIRTY-SIX

*I*t wasn't hard to find Rodeo.

The moon was bright. Darn near full. There was a little path winding out from the back of the parking lot and down through some trees.

I walked along the path, through the trees, under the moonlight, and down to a little river.

It wasn't big, but it was pretty there in the silver light.

Out a ways in the water was a little sandbar island. On that island was a log, washed up and setting there. And on that log was Rodeo, sitting with his back to me. I stepped out of my flip-flops.

The water wasn't that cold, and it wasn't that deep. Didn't even come up to my knees. It was August, after all. I barely noticed it.

The island sand was soft under my bare feet. It would've felt good.

I came around to stand in front of him. He didn't even look at me. Just lifted the bottle to his lips and took a long, gulping drink.

"Rodeo."

Nothing.

"Rodeo!"

Finally, his eyes slid to me.

"What?"

I hesitated. I was good at Rodeo. I knew, usually, how to push him. How to pull him. How to play him. But this . . . this was different. This was bad.

"I . . . I don't like when you drink, Rodeo."

Rodeo's eyes filled up.

"Yeah? Well, me neither, little bird." He leaned his head back, took another drink. "But here we are."

I just stood there, looking down at him, my mind stumbling, my blood pounding.

He looked up at me.

"We ain't going," he said.

"Yes, we are," I answered.

"Nope. I ain't going back. And neither are you. I ain't jumping into quicksand, sugarplum, and I ain't letting you jump in, either. We're staying safe, you and me, together."

"No, Rodeo, I have to—"

"No. It's a no-go, period. I'm sorry. But this ends now. Before you get hurt."

I took one breath. Then another. Hard breaths. Breaths that stuck in my throat and stung my nose. Breaths that fought with sobs for room in my lungs.

It was time. Time to put it all out there.

No regrets, sister.

"Too late," I said, and Rodeo squinted up at me and said, "What?" and I said, "*Before I get hurt?!* It's too late for that, Rodeo. Way too late. I'm already hurt. I been hurt. I been hurting for five years. By *you*. You're hurting me *right now*. So don't sit there and tell me this is about us not getting hurt. It ain't. It's about *you*, which is all it's ever been about."

Rodeo's mouth was hanging open.

"No, little plum, *no*. Listen, we don't need this, we don't need to . . ."

"*I* need this. *I* do. I can't keep doing what we've been doing anymore. I can't. I need to do this. And I . . . And I . . . And I need *you*, Daddy." Even in the moonlight, I saw him go pale when I said that word I hadn't been allowed to say in five years. So I said it again. "I need you, Daddy."

The sobs won, then. They pushed the breathing out. And all the moonlight looked like diamonds through my tears.

Rodeo rocked back. He looked away from me, hard. Not just with his eyes. With his whole head, off into the darkness.

"Hey," he said, his voice trembly. "Hey, now, you know you can't call me—"

"Why? Why, Daddy?"

I felt like a little girl, calling him Daddy. But I didn't care, not at all. I already felt like a little girl anyway, with my voice all broken and tears running hot down my face. And I didn't care, not at all. My feelings were so big they were choking me and squeezing the air out of my lungs and pushing the tears out of my eyes and I couldn't breathe or see and all I could do was feel, feel, feel.

I *wanted* to feel like a little girl. I wanted to. I wanted to feel like a little girl who has a daddy who wraps his arms around her and makes everything okay. I wanted to feel like a little girl who has a daddy, period.

"You know why, Coyote. You know why, partner." His voice was hollow, tender, begging.

"I'm not your partner," I gasped out through my crying. "I'm your daughter. *One* of your daughters."

"Stop it, Coyote," he said sharp. But the words were sharp with fear, not anger. "That's enough, now. We are deep in no-go territory here."

"I. Don't. Care. Why can't you be my dad? It's what you're supposed to be. It's what I'm supposed to call you."

Rodeo's chin dropped to his chest. "You know why. Because when you call me that, I . . . I *hear* them. I can hear *their* voices saying it when you say it."

Lord, he sounded so sad. But that was all right. 'Cause I was sad, too.

"Then you're lucky," I said. "You're so darned lucky and you don't even know it. Because I *never* hear them. I used to. Right after. I'd hear them. Ava. Rose. Mom." I saw each name hit him like a slap, but I didn't slow down. "I'd hear them when I woke up. I'd hear them in the middle of the night. I'd hear some kid talking in the next aisle in the grocery store, and I'd swear for a second it was one of them. But I don't anymore, Daddy. I don't ever hear them. I barely even remember what their voices sounded like. And I hate it. And you're trying to keep them *quiet*? I'd give anything to hear them again."

Rodeo shook his head. "That ain't no way to live, sugarbear, living in the past like that. We need to live for right now, for right now today, for—"

"No. I'm done with all that garbage. I been listening to your excuses for five years, and I'm done with that.

"'Remember' ain't a past-tense word. It's a *right-now* word. The kind of person I wanna be, right now today, is the kind of person that remembers my mama and my sisters, right now today. And tomorrow. And every day. I'm not gonna go one more day without them, not one more minute, not one more second. I can't. I'm not saying I *missed* them. I'm saying I *miss* them. Right now, today. And I'm not saying I *loved* them. I *love* them. Right now. Today."

My dad blinked up at me. He was crying. It just about killed me. But. Oh well.

My job wasn't to take care of him. Not anymore.

My job was to take care of me.

Then he said it. He said it so quiet I barely heard it. Said it so small that his lips hardly moved. But he said it.

"Me, too."

My breath caught in my throat. I gasped. A little gasp. But a gasp, still.

I lowered my voice. Made it soft. I had three words to say, and I said 'em hushed like a prayer.

"Say my name."

There was a pause.

"Coyote."

"No. That ain't my name. Say it. Say my name, Dad."

He opened his mouth. Closed it. Shook his head.

I wanted to hug him. I wanted to kneel down in the sand and take his hands in mine. I wanted to use my T-shirt to dry the tears off his face.

But I did not. Nope. I stood there. I stood there strong.

So he stood up. Stepped toward me. Wrapped me in a hug. Said, "Come on, little bird," in his broken voice.

But I didn't hug him back.

I reached quick into his back pocket. And I pulled out Yager's keys. I stepped back and gave Rodeo a shove, soft and small but a shove all the same, and he kind of dropped back down onto the log, his eyes looking unbelieving at the keys I held.

"Lester can drive," I said. "I'll come back and pick you up after. But I don't have time to wait. I'm going."

He shook his head.

"Don't leave me, Coyote."

"I don't want to. But you gotta say my name. 'Cause if you can't say my name, that means I don't matter to you. And if I don't matter to you, then . . . Well, I don't know." My voice cracked, froze, caught its balance, and stumbled on. "I . . . I know you don't need me, Dad. But I need you. I need a dad. Even if you don't need a daughter."

His jaw dropped open. He took three big breaths right in a row.

"Oh," he said, and then "Oh," and then he dropped the bottle he was holding. And he fell forward onto his knees.

"Honey," he said, "how could you . . . how could you think that I don't . . . *need* you? You are all I've got. You are all I care about in this whole world."

I couldn't see anything now. I blinked, but it didn't do any good.

"Then prove it. Say my name. My real name. Please."

He reached up. He grabbed my hands. And he said it:

"Ella." He choked a little, but then he cleared his throat and said it again. "Ella. I love you, *Ella*. I love *you*, Ella."

And he hugged me. He hugged me tight around my waist and I stood there getting hugged by my dad, crying.

"Let me tell you something," he said. "You know that third question? The sandwich question? You know why I ask that one?"

"Heck no," I said.

"It ain't about their answer. I don't care what they say. I don't even listen. I don't even look at 'em when they answer it. I look at *you*, Ella. I watch you, watching them. And I can tell by the way you look at 'em whether or not we should let 'em on board. That's all."

He let go and leaned back so he could look me in the face.

"You're my compass. You're what tells me which way to go whenever I'm lost. Which is darn near all the time. That third question don't mean nothing, sweet girl. *You're* the third question. And you're the answer, too."

I looked down at him.

"Dad," I said.

And he said, "What?"

And I said, "I need to go home. And I need to go there with you."

And he said, "Okay."

And then he said, "I'm so sorry."

And then I said, "I don't need you to be sorry sitting here. I need you to be sorry sitting on that bus."

And then he said, "Let's go."

And that was that.

CHAPTER
THIRTY-SEVEN

We had time to make up. Time, and miles.

With Rodeo's little four-hour detour—eight hours, round trip—our timeline was out the window. It was a six-hour drive to Poplin Springs, and it was a little after four in the morning. The soonest we could get there was ten A.M., well after the bulldozers would start up. If we were lucky, that is, and didn't have any flat tires or busted brakes or blown carburetors or anything like that. It was a race, pure and simple. It was just a matter of hoping we got there before, and not after. The upside was that now we were going right through Yakima, where about half our group was getting off. I mean, technically that's an upside.

We raced. Through the early morning and through a pretty decent chunk of the Pacific Northwest, we raced. Up hills and down hills and over rivers and around mountains, we rumbled along. Sometimes some of us slept. Most of the time most of us didn't. We stopped and did a couple of crazy gas fill-ups working as a team, with Rodeo filling the tank while the rest of us ran in for snacks or cleaned the windshield or hit the bathroom or walked Gladys. Everything was done at a run so we could hit the road again lickety-split. We tried turning on the radio a couple times, but no song ever seemed to fit quite right, so we mostly rode in silence.

The sun came up. Towns little and big blurred by. I spent half my time sorta not sleeping and half my time looking at the clock and half my time checking how many more miles we had to go.

We got to Yakima a couple hours after sunrise. Concepción had called ahead, so her friend was up and waiting, and her and Ms. Vega and Salvador hauled all their stuff off Yager and onto the sidewalk.

My feelings about goodbyes hadn't changed, though, so I didn't stick around. I couldn't. I was exhausted. I was scared. I was sad. I couldn't hardly sit still or see straight. There was no way I could throw a hey-there-my-best-and-only-friend-I-guess-this-is-goodbye-forever on top of it. I was feeling about seven different kinds of alone, and I really didn't wanna make it eight. So I took Gladys and walked her up the street a bit for a potty break, which she apparently desperately needed. I'd never known a goat could hold so much. I waited until the sidewalk was empty so I knew the Vegas had all gone into the house and out of my life forever, and then Gladys and me walked back to Yager and up the steps and I made it a few steps toward the back before I froze solid in my tracks.

"What are you doing here?" I asked, and Salvador answered, "I'm going with you. I asked my mom. She said it was all right."

"She did?"

"Well, she said no first. Like, six times. But then she said yes." He flashed a Salvador smile at me. "Rodeo said you could swing back and drop me off after. I wanna make sure you get it."

I smiled. Well, I assume I smiled. I couldn't actually feel much besides crying and sniffling and falling forward to wrap my arms around that Salvador in a fierce, grateful hug. Salvador hugged me back. Gladys bleated. I grabbed a seat, and we were off.

It was eight thirty on Wednesday morning. Up there, two hours away in a place I used to call home, they were probably firing up the bulldozers.

CHAPTER
THIRTY-EIGHT

*B*ehind us, the lights were flashing. The siren was singing its *wee-ooo-wee-ooo* song.

Rodeo's hands were clenched tight around the steering wheel. Yager rumbled and grumbled underneath us.

We weren't slowing down.

Me, Lester, Salvador, Ivan, Gladys, and Val were all shooting each other looks. It was a lot of looks.

"Hey, Rodeo?" Lester called out. "I, uh, think he wants you to pull over. Just a hunch."

Rodeo didn't answer. He kept driving, eyes on the road ahead.

"Rodeo?" Val said. "You hear that, right?"

Rodeo just shook his head and muttered something to himself.

Gladys bleated anxiously.

I stood up and walked to the seat behind him.

"Rodeo," I said, quiet and easy. "What's going on?"

Rodeo said something to me, but he said it so low I couldn't hear the words.

"What?"

He said it again, and this time I heard him.

"I promised you."

"Yeah," I said. "And we're almost there, so . . ."

"You know how the cops are," he said. "They ask questions, they make us wait, they make calls. It could be hours, honeybear. And I blew it, I gave us no time to waste. We don't have time to stop."

"It'll be all right, Rodeo. You were just speeding a little, I bet. We'll get a ticket, maybe even just a warning, be on our way, no biggie."

Rodeo shook his head.

"I gotta feeling about this one. And I *promised* you."

"Sure. But you *gotta* pull over."

The patrol car accelerated and pulled up beside us. The siren was earsplitting now.

"*This is the Chelan County sheriff,*" an amplified voice commanded. "*Pull your vehicle to the side of the road immediately.*"

I felt Lester settle into the seat next to me. We traded worried looks.

"Hey, man," he said to Rodeo, "I'm, like, *sure* he wants you to pull over now. And, no offense, but we aren't outrunning him in this old bus."

Rodeo didn't respond. The officer repeated his command over the loudspeaker.

"Rodeo, listen to me," I said, my voice rising. "If you don't pull over, you're gonna get arrested. And then we'll *never* get there. And you'll have broken your promise for sure. Please, Rodeo. Just pull over."

Rodeo just swallowed.

So I reached forward, and I flicked on the turn signal.

And, real easy, I pulled the steering wheel with one hand, just kinda easing us over toward the shoulder.

Rodeo blew out a deep breath. But then he nodded. And he took his foot off the gas and he tapped the brake and then we rattled to a stop there beside the highway. The cop pulled off on the shoulder in front of us.

Rodeo killed the engine. He was looking up ahead at that cop, who was grabbing his stuff and starting to open his door. I saw that Rodeo's hand was shaking.

The cop rapped on the bus door.

You know, some folks look like they start the day already half-pissed off. This particular officer of the law looked more like he started at a solid three quarters.

Rodeo jerked the door open and the cop stepped slowly up the stairs, one hand resting ready on the butt of his gun and his eyes darting quick around. In his other hand he held a crumpled piece of paper.

"Good morning, sir," he said to Rodeo, and there wasn't a word of it that sounded sincere.

"Mornin', officer. Is there a problem?"

The cop was taking his time, climbing up all cautious, and he hadn't gotten to the top step yet where he could see us all. He stopped, trying to peek over the railing, his hand still down by his weapon.

"How many passengers you got on board, sir?"

"Counting animals?"

"Excuse me?"

"Well, we got five people and one goat and one cat. If you count animals as passengers, which I would in these particular animals' case, then I guess the answer's seven passengers in total."

The officer's eyes narrowed. He stayed put on that second-from-the-top step.

"Any minors on board?"

"Yes, sir. Two minors on board. Coyote here, and Salvador in the back."

"Any weapons?"

"No, sir. Was I speeding, officer?"

"Nope," the officer answered, and stepped up to the top step. He looked toward the back, taking in Yager and her crew. If I was forced to describe the look on his face in one word, I'd have had a hard time deciding between "nauseated" and "hostile."

"I thought you said you had five passengers."

"I said *seven*," Rodeo clarified. "Counting Ivan and Gladys."

"Well, I'm seeing only four."

Rodeo and I both turned and looked.

There was Lester beside me, of course.

Salvador was sitting back on the couch.

Gladys was curled up in Rodeo's bed pile, nibbling at the corner of a blanket. I'm guessing the cop wasn't counting her.

"Where's Val?" I asked.

Salvador looked at me quick and gave a small shake of his head, but it was too late. I'd let the cat out of the bag.

The cop's eyes glittered at me.

"Val?" he said, and then his eyes slipped to Rodeo and he said,

"Don't move," and then he pulled his pistol out of its holster and walked down the aisle toward the back of the bus, gun held down low.

My heart thudded and my armpits flushed hot when he pulled that gun out. My mouth went dry. I'm just not a gun person, unless it's a water gun, and even then I'd rather just get wet on my own terms, thank you very much. I had a hard time breathing when I looked at the black, deadly thing . . . but I couldn't tear my eyes off it.

About halfway back, the cop stopped.

"Valerie Beckett?" he asked.

There was a resigned sigh. Then Val stood up from where she'd been crouched behind the Throne. She sat down in the Throne, her eyes wet and full and downcast. She was hugging herself like she was cold, even though Yager wasn't anywhere near chilly.

"Valerie Beckett?" the cop asked again, then held up the crumpled paper in his hand and darted his eyes back and forth between it and her. "It's you, isn't it? Are you okay, miss?"

Val didn't answer. She just swallowed and looked away.

The cop looked back at Rodeo.

"And why, *sir*, didn't you care to tell me about this minor?"

"She's nineteen years old," Rodeo said, but his voice was kinda thin-sounding.

"I'm sorry," Val said, and she didn't say it to me or the cop. She said it, her voice cracking, right to Rodeo.

"Oh, no," Rodeo said quiet, and closed his eyes.

"What's going on?" I asked.

"How long have you been transporting Ms. Beckett, sir?" the cop asked, gun still drawn, voice tight.

"Since Minnesota, sir, but she told me—"

"Minnesota? Are you aware that it's against the law to transport a minor across state lines without their parents' permission?"

"She told me that—"

"Her parents reported her missing two days ago. They suspected kidnapping. Then her cousin said she got a call last night, said this young lady was on her way to meet her in Seattle. Riding in an old school bus. We've all been looking for her."

"I'm sorry," Val said again, and Rodeo just sat there with his eyes closed, and I said, "What's going on?" again, but it was like no one could hear me.

The cop backed up so the wall was behind him and he could see all of us.

"Is anyone else also here against their will?" he asked.

"I'm *not* here against my will," Val protested, her voice small. "Officer, I told them that I was—"

She was cut off by a crackle from the radio clipped to the cop's uniform. He snapped it free and held it up to his mouth.

"Dispatch, this is Griffith. I have that Minnesota girl from the APB here in custody, and have apprehended the suspect as well. We're on Highway 4 westbound at mile marker one-zero-eight. Please send backup, over."

Rodeo shook his head, but it looked more like defeat than argument.

"Officer," he said, finally opening his eyes, "No one is here against their will. Val told me she was nineteen, and I—"

"That'll be enough, sir. I'm gonna need you to go ahead and stand up nice and easy and put your hands in the air."

I gasped and jumped up to protest, but I saw the cop stiffen and tighten his grip on his gun and Rodeo looked me in the eyes and said quiet but firm, "*No*, honeybear. Don't. It'll be all right," and then with just about the saddest eyes you could imagine, that brokenhearted hippie stood up slow and careful and put his skinny arms up in the air like he was some sort of criminal.

Lester put his hand on my arm, and it was just as quiet as Rodeo's voice and just as firm.

"Nobody move, now," the cop said, and then he made his way up to the front. "Turn around, put your hands behind your back," he said when he got up to Rodeo, and he clipped his radio back to his uniform and pulled a pair of handcuffs off his belt, real honest-to-god handcuffs.

Rodeo blinked. And then Rodeo, that crazy, beautiful, ridiculous freak, he looked that cop right in his eyes. Rodeo turned those magical eyes of his on the cop, looked right past his drawn gun and dangling handcuffs, and just looked him right in the eyes.

"Please," he said, "this is all a misunderstanding. I swear." His voice was tender, his face open, his eyes magnetic. "Please. I made a promise to my daughter. That we'd get to where we're going. And a promise is a promise, right?" He smiled a little when he said that, just a little. "Please."

Rodeo turned those magical eyes of his on that cop and just said, "Please."

The cop stood looking into Rodeo's eyes.

And then the cop smiled.

"Well, I didn't realize you made a promise to your daughter, sir," the cop said, and Rodeo's small smile grew. "And I couldn't care less," the cop continued. "Turn around and put your hands behind your back and do it now or I *will* forcibly subdue you. And quit staring at me like that."

I guess magic doesn't work on some sorts of folks.

"You can consider that promise broken, buddy. You aren't going anywhere, and neither is this bus or anyone on it 'til we get to the bottom of this. Y'all are done traveling today, and *you* are under arrest."

So that's what happened. Rodeo's smile faded to nothing and he shuffled in a circle and put his hands behind his back and the cop took his keys and slapped the handcuffs on, and I just sat there watching. It didn't seem real, didn't seem like it could actually be happening. It was, though.

Rodeo turned to look at me, and his eyes just about tore me apart.

"*I'm sorry*," he mouthed, and I just nodded.

The cop said all those words about the right to remain silent and all that jazz and then he walked Rodeo down the steps and barked at the rest of us to follow him.

Our quest was over.

Eight miles short.

CHAPTER
THIRTY-NINE

"This sucks," Salvador said.

"Yeah, man. You could say that," Lester replied, then spat in the dirt at his feet.

We were all sitting on a log that was about ten feet from the highway. The cop was standing off a ways, talking back and forth on his radio. Yager was parked and locked up, the keys in the cop's possession. He'd let us open most of the windows a bit before we got off, but I was still worried about Gladys and Ivan getting too hot in there.

By now, we'd figured it out, between what the cop had said and the pieces that Val was able to tearfully choke out to us. Val was not a nineteen-year-old community college student. She was a seventeen-year-old junior in high school. The rest was all true, though. The fight with her parents, them not accepting who she was. They hadn't kicked her out, exactly, but they'd told her basically that she could either be who she wanted to be, or she could live under their roof. Not both. They'd thought she'd surrender. Instead, she'd run away. When she didn't come home or show up at a friend's house, they were sure she'd been abducted by some creep on the mean streets of Minneapolis.

Val had said she was sorry about a dozen times until Rodeo

had finally said, his hands cuffed behind his back but his eyes and his voice gentle and sincere, "Val, it's all right. I ain't mad at ya. At all. I'm rooting for ya, kid. Okay?" and she'd blinked at him a couple times and then started crying again and said, "Okay," and then, "Thanks," and I remembered all over again why I love Rodeo (not that I'd ever really forgotten).

The cop stomped back over to us with a look on his face like he'd been chewing on lime peels.

"All right. We got a bit of a situation here and your job is to listen to what I say and then do it. Got it?" He shot a tough glare around at all of us like we were a group of hardened convicts or something. "Sheriff's office is a little understaffed at the moment, and the only other officer on duty is a couple hours away on a domestic call. I can't fit you all in my squad car, and I'm not about to sit around on the side of the highway for a couple hours. So." For a second I thought he was gonna let us all go and my heart started to flutter, but then he grimaced and shook his head at us like it was all our fault and said, "You," pointing at Val, "and you," pointing at Rodeo, "are coming with me. I'm gonna take you to the sheriff's office, where *you* will call your parents, and *you* will be held until such time as charges are pressed and bail is posted." His gaze slithered from Rodeo and Val to the rest of us.

"You," the cop said, pointing a finger way too close to Lester's face, "Lester Washington. You are gonna wait here. I'll be back in twenty minutes, and you *will* be here. I have your driver's license and I have your keys, and if you are not sitting right *exactly* here when I get back, you're looking at resisting arrest and fleeing the scene of a crime and criminal noncompliance and a heckuva lot more trouble than you want. Understood?"

Lester just pursed his lips and nodded and the cop took an angry step closer. "Understood?" he asked again, raising his voice. Lester looked at him. "Yes, *sir*," Lester said.

"And that goes for you two kids, too," he said, turning to me and Salvador and jabbing his ugly finger at us. "Got it? Right here."

"Aren't you gonna handcuff us, too?" Salvador asked flatly.

The cop narrowed his eyes.

"We don't handcuff kids, kid."

Salvador just rolled his eyes and looked away.

"Come on," the officer said, motioning for Rodeo to stand up. Rodeo gave me an apologetic look and rose to his feet, and the cop grabbed him by the elbow and started walking him toward the cop car. After just a couple steps, though, Rodeo skidded to a halt.

He turned and fixed me with a serious, heavy look.

"You gotta do this, little bird," he said. "Down through the clouds. Go to your roots. Remember Eureka."

My breath caught. My brain clicked and sparked and sputtered and whirred like Yager's engine roaring awake on a cold winter morning. I tried to look calm, but I knew my eyes were wider than Salvador's saved hubcap. To most folks, Rodeo's words would've sounded like some hopeless woo-woo hippie nonsense. I knew this for a fact, because the cop snorted and said, "I don't got time for your woo-woo hippie nonsense. Get moving."

But I knew exactly what Rodeo was telling me to do.

I gave him a quick nod, my mind still trying to find traction. He smiled at me, a small smile that had a little encouragement in it but plenty of worry, and then he turned and let that bully with a badge drag him off toward the police car, and he ducked his head and sat down in the back seat and the door slammed closed behind him.

Val, still sniffling, followed the cop's commands and sat in the front seat.

"Stay put," the cop shouted at us with one more angry point, then he got in and the cop car started up and peeled away with a spit of dust and gravel, lights and siren blaring.

We all sat there, watching.

"Nice guy," Lester said.

I looked at the glum pair of folks I was sharing that log with.

Lester looked troubled but stubborn, eyebrows furrowed in anger but chewing his lips anxiously.

Salvador looked kinda sad and kinda scared and kinda mad at the same time.

I'm guessing I looked kinda freaked out. Maybe a little excited. But mostly freaked out.

Because I wasn't totally sure what was gonna happen next.

But I *was* totally sure that when that cop and his pointing finger came back in twenty minutes, I sure as heck wasn't gonna be there.

CHAPTER
FORTY

"What do you mean, you're going?"

"I mean, Lester, that I'm going. On to Poplin Springs, like we planned."

Lester screwed his eyes at me.

"Girl. How in the *world* are you planning on—"

"You heard Rodeo," I said, standing up. "All that stuff he said? That was him giving me permission. In code."

"Code?"

"Yeah. 'Through the clouds.' That's the hatch up to the roof." I saw Salvador lower his eyebrows and nod, catching on. "I know how to drive her, Lester, I promise, but I ain't got time to explain it all. That cop is coming back and I need to be extra gone by the time he does."

I turned and started toward Yager, but Lester jumped up and grabbed my hand.

"Hold on. We can't do this. I'll be in trouble, like *serious* trouble, and—"

"I know," I said, pulling my hand gently free. "That's why you're staying. He's got your license, and you would be totally busted if you left. But I'm just a kid. Worst I get is a couple days in juvie or whatever, and I can live with that. I'm going, I'm going alone, and I'm going now."

"No." It was Salvador speaking up this time. "You aren't going alone." He rose to his feet. "I'm going with you."

"Whoa, whoa, whoa," Lester said, standing up himself and raising his hands. "Hold on a hot minute."

"Yeah," I said, tossing an are-you-kidding-me look at Salvador. "Hold on. What?"

Salvador shrugged, but his eyes were all attitude.

"You know you gotta do this. You *gotta*. And you know together is better than alone. So let's do it. Together." He looked at me, those eyes of his all intense and probing and sparkly. Then he said it. He didn't say it begging, or pleading. He just said it human. "Come on, Coyote."

Now, here's a thing. When someone you trust—maybe even someone you *love*, but not in *that* way—looks you in your eyes and talks to you and it sounds just like you talking to yourself, here's what you should do: You should listen.

So I did.

I mean, I glared at him and made my lips into an angry line and flared my nostrils. Obviously. But then I cocked an eyebrow and turned on my heels and walked off toward Yager.

I heard Salvador's steps start to jog after me, but then Lester shouted "Wait a *minute*!" with enough I'm-so-out-of-patience-it's-not-even-funny frustration in his voice that I *very* reluctantly stopped, huffed out a breath, and turned around.

"What?"

"Why do you two think that this is *your* decision to make?" Lester demanded. He pointed his finger at his own chest. "Hello? Grown-up? This is crazy, kid. I'm bigger than you and I'm stronger than you . . . Why shouldn't I just hold you and stop you from taking this bus and risking your lives and breaking, like, ten laws to go back and do this?"

His voice started out angry, but it ended softer. Sincere. Lester wasn't just bossing me around. He wasn't arguing. He was actually asking. And I had a feeling he'd actually listen. So I took three steps toward him, and I tried (and failed) to keep the wobbles out of my voice when I answered him.

"Because you're not my dad. Because my *dad* isn't even my dad, most days." Lester blinked when I said that, but he didn't argue. I think we were both a little surprised that I'd said it out loud like that. But, hey, the truth does a lot more good most of the time if folks have the nerve to say it out loud, even if it hurts. Especially if it hurts, maybe. "Because once upon a time, I had a mom, and once upon a time I had two sisters, and now I don't. I lost 'em. And I left 'em behind. And now I have to fight for them. I *have* to. Because they woulda fought for me. I don't know if I'm already too late, but I do know, I *know*, that if I don't try, I'll never forgive myself."

Lester shook his head at me. He rubbed a hand over his head. He closed his eyes for a solid five or six seconds, then he lowered his head and opened his eyes and looked up at me from under his eyebrows.

"You really know how to drive that thing?"

I shrugged.

"At least as good as Rodeo does."

He shook his head again.

"Oh, Lord." He waved me away. "Go on, then, hurry up."

Then he bent down, grabbed a handful of highway shoulder dirt, and rubbed it into the perfect white of his T-shirt chest.

"What'd you do that for?" I asked.

"This is from where I tried to stop you and Salvador pushed me to the ground," he said.

"Bull," I shot back. "That's from where you tried to stop us and *I* pushed you to the ground."

Lester cracked a one-sided grin.

"All right. Whatever. Just go. Before I change my mind."

So I went.

I scrambled up onto the hood and then up to the Attic and over to the hatch. I pulled it open and climbed down the rope ladder inside.

Salvador was right behind me every step of the way. When he skipped the last couple of rungs and landed with a thud behind me, I said to him, "You know you could've just waited and I'da let you in the door." He nodded thoughtfully and said, "Huh. Yeah. That woulda made more sense." Boys are idiots.

I pointed up at the painted sky above us, and the hatch in the middle of it.

"Down through the clouds," I said, and Salvador nodded.

Ivan, lying on my bed, just looked up at us and yawned.

Gladys, though, was happy to see us. She bleated and did a little hoof tap-dance and spun in a circle. I gave her a pat as I walked quick as I could up to the tomato plants, poked my hand through the pots, and grabbed my special one, the one painted all over with feathers. I picked it up and hugged it against my body. Then I grasped the thickest part of the plant's stem and tugged, twisting the plant just a little and rotating the pot until the whole caboodle slid out, the plant and its roots bringing all the dirt along with it in a big messy pot-shaped ball.

"Grab it," I grunted, "down at the bottom of the pot," and Salvador reached through my arms and scraped his fingers around in the pot and then pulled out a dull, dirt-covered key. I plopped the plant back in its home and slid it onto the shelf and took the key from Salvador and held it up in front of his eyes. "Go to your roots," I said, and Salvador nodded again and smiled.

Salvador followed me up to the front.

I sat down in the driver's seat. I wiped the key off on my pant leg. There was still some grit in the grooves, so I stuck it in my mouth and sucked it clean and then slid it into the ignition and gripped it in my fingers, ready to turn it. And then I stopped.

Not because I was scared. I wasn't.

Not because I wasn't sure I should do it. I was.

Not because I didn't know if it was the right thing to do or not. I did. And it was.

Nope. It wasn't anything like that.

It was the opposite.

I stopped because I knew *exactly* what I was doing, and *exactly* why I was doing it, and the absolute true-blue rightness of the moment darn near took my breath away. I wasn't doing this for Rodeo. I wasn't doing this to take care of anyone else. I was doing this to take care of *me*. And it was a good thing. When I fired up that old engine, I wasn't gonna drive us away from anything. I was driving us *toward* something. And that was a good thing, too.

There wasn't a no-go in sight. This was all *go*, and I loved it.

I turned the key. Yager roared and rattled and shook and then stood rumblingly ready.

The world waited for me out the windshield.

I looked out the window and saw Lester standing, watching us.

He gave me a loose farewell salute. I gave him one back.

I punched the power button on the radio and some rambling, shuffling rock song came blaring out.

Salvador was kneeling on the first seat, leaning over my shoulder. I cocked my head at him.

"Give me a howl," I shouted over the music.

"A what?"

"A howl!" I said, then threw my head back and belted out a wild, let-loose coyote howl. Salvador took only half a second to catch on and open his throat and add his own howl to mine, and I dropped Yager into gear, let out the clutch, released the hand brake, hit the gas, and launched us onto the highway.

CHAPTER

FORTY-ONE

The steering wheel vibrated in my hands. The gas pedal pulsed with the life of the monstrous engine it fed. The world whizzed by as we hit highway speed and raced down that black ribbon of asphalt toward destiny. I bobbed my head to the song on the radio.

Salvador said something, but I couldn't hear him over the music, so I clicked it off.

"What?"

"Aren't you scared?"

I swallowed.

"More scared than I've been in my whole life."

I focused on the yellow dashes of the highway dividing line and on keeping all my emotions out of my throat. Because I could feel them. And by "them," I mean my mom and my sisters. Out there in front of me, leading me home. And I could feel Rodeo, too, could see that look in those eyes when he said to me, *You gotta do this, little bird*. Because I did. Have to do it, I mean.

"So . . . what's Eureka? What'd that little clue mean?" Salvador asked me.

"Eureka is a city in California. That's where Rodeo taught me how to drive this old thing. He said he didn't know if or when

I'd ever have to get behind the wheel—you know, if he had a stroke or an aneurysm or something—but he figured I better know what I was doing. So in this big old empty parking lot at the edge of town, he ran me through the whole shebang. He was really kind of a drill sergeant, running me through everything over and over again until I had it down pat."

"California? I thought you were coming from Florida when you picked us up."

"We were."

"When were you in Eureka, then?"

"Oh, gee," I said, screwing closed an eye, trying to remember. "This musta been, lord, last summer, little over a year ago?"

"A *year* ago?!" Salvador squeaked. "You're driving us down the road based on one lesson you had a *year ago*?! You told Lester you were as good at driving as Rodeo!"

I shrugged. "Rodeo's not that good a driver."

Salvador sat down quick in his seat and gripped the back of mine with both hands, holding on like he was afraid we were gonna go careening off the road any minute, which was pretty darn unlikely.

"I'm telling you, man, I got this down. Once you're cruising, it couldn't be easier. I mean, we'll see how stopping goes, but for now we're looking good. Relax."

In the rearview mirror, I could see Salvador shaking his head. His knuckles were white on the seat back. Big baby.

He saw me looking and he tried to glare, but I shot him a big, teeth-flashing smile and he smiled back in spite of himself.

"This is crazy," he said to my reflection.

"Sure is," I said. "But it's the good kind of crazy."

"You look like a twelve-year-old."

"I got bad news for you, Salvador. I *am* a twelve-year-old."

"Yeah, I know. But twelve-year-olds aren't supposed to drive. Someone might notice."

I glanced around thoughtfully. I wasn't prepared to admit it out loud, but Salvador had a point.

"Hand me that hat," I said, pointing at a floppy-brimmed hat Rodeo had hanging on a hook on the wall. Salvador complied, and I slapped it on my head and then grabbed Rodeo's gold-rimmed aviator sunglasses off the dashboard and slipped them on.

"How do I look now?"

"Like a twelve-year-old wearing sunglasses and a hat."

"Well, what do you want me to do? Smoke a cigarette?"

Salvador shrugged.

"Do you have one?"

"Very funny. This'll have to do."

We passed a big green highway mileage sign and there was Poplin Springs, right there at the top.

Poplin Springs   6

Six miles away.

The highway wound along a little blue sparkling river. Both river and road curved between big hills that rose up toward the sky. The shapes of those hills felt familiar to me. I hadn't been here for five years, but I remembered them, or my eyes did, or my heart did. Their shapes, their curves and folds—they looked like something to me. Not something new, either. Looking at the shapes of those hills felt like when you wake up in the middle of the night and you're all dream-confused in the dark and you get up and go to the bathroom and you see your own face in the mirror, looking back at you. If *home* is a feeling, those hills looked like the soft edges of that feeling. I got all tingly, looking at those hills.

I turned the radio back on and let the rollicking music drown out any more conversation. I drummed along on the steering wheel and kept my eyes straight ahead on where I was going.

It was only, like, a minute later that Salvador shouted over the radio, "Hey! How long did that cop say it'd take him to get back there?"

"He said twenty minutes," I answered, "but I'm guessing more like twenty-five. He seemed like the type who always gives himself more credit than he deserves."

"Okay. And how long since he left us?"

I shrugged.

"I don't know. Ten minutes, maybe fifteen?"

I looked at Salvador in the rearview mirror. He was up on a knee, craning his neck to see behind us, chewing his lip nervously.

"Why?"

"Well. Don't freak out or anything. But there's a cop behind us."

"What!?"

"I said *don't* freak out."

"How could he be back behind us already?!" I looked in the

side mirror and sure enough, I saw the unmistakable shape of the authorities behind us.

"I don't think it's the same cop. His car was brown, right? This one's white. Just drive casual, okay? Their lights and siren aren't on or anything."

Before I could give Salvador the are-you-kidding-me side-eye he deserved, I saw something that took the spark right out of my sass.

It was the cop's turn signal. It blinked an on-and-off yellow warning, and then the cruiser glided over into the left lane and started pulling up alongside us.

"Uh-oh," Salvador said, but my throat had gone too dry to say anything back. In a matter of seconds that highway patrolman was gonna be right up next to me, looking in at little old twelve-year-old me behind the wheel. And I was all out of cigarettes.

I tightened my hands on the wheel, took a deep breath, and then pressed the gas pedal to the floor. Yager's engine whined, but she found some more "go" somewhere in her rattly gears and we shot forward with a little surge of speed.

"What are you doing?" Salvador hissed at me.

"Speeding up."

"Why?"

"If he pulls up and sees me driving, it's over."

"Um, yeah. That's, like, the stupidest thing I've ever heard."

Of course I knew that. But I mean, come on—when you got no other options, the one option you got left is just kind of automatically your best option. Isn't it?

The cop hit the gas, too. He stopped falling behind and started gaining ground again.

"Come on, Coyote. This is stupid."

I didn't respond.

"Didn't we just go over this with your dad?"

"That was different."

"How?"

"Because he had a good chance of being let go. Me, not so much. I hate to break it to you, Salvador, but I don't think I'm gonna be able to talk this cop into letting me go with a warning."

"Well, maybe not, but you're sure not gonna outrun him."

"I don't have to outrun him. I don't have to escape. I just have to get *there*."

"And then what?"

"Doesn't matter. I'm busted either way, right? So I'm gonna get there. And I'm gonna get that box. Then this cop can do whatever the heck he wants. But if I pull over now, this whole thing is over for good. And I've come too far for that."

It must've become obvious to the cop right about then that I was clearly not pulling over on purpose, because the lights on top of the car started flashing and that siren kicked in.

I kept my foot mashed on the gas pedal. The needle on the speedometer inched up above seventy.

Salvador and I were officially fugitives from the law.

The cop hit the gas hard, zooming up beside us. I looked down and saw an angry face behind sunglasses, and an arm waving me over violently. I waved back and tried to smile innocently. It didn't work.

The cop grabbed his radio thing and started barking something at me through his loudspeakers, but I just turned up the radio so I couldn't hear it. I was pretty well committed by that point, and I knew that whatever the cop was saying was probably just gonna stress me out.

The cop accelerated even more, starting to pull ahead of us. I gulped.

"Well, shoot," I muttered.

I knew what he was planning. And I knew it would work.

He was gonna pull in front of us and slow down. Block us.

Yager was a beast and Yager was reliable, but Yager was *not* particularly nimble. If that cop got in front and blocked us, I wouldn't be able to maneuver this eight-ton behemoth quick enough to dart around him. And I wasn't quite sure I was determined enough to actually *ram* a police car with a bus. I think Rodeo and I would both agree that that particular course of action was best left as a no-go.

But then I saw it. Coming right toward us, and not that far away.

The exit. *The* exit.

Poplin Springs.

Home.

It was coming up on the right side. Maybe a half mile away.

The patrol car inched past us. Its rear bumper pulled in front of our hood. The cop gave it a sudden burst of new speed and shot well past us. Gladys bleated out a cry of alarm. Yager, even giving it all she had, was no match for a highway patrol cruiser.

"Almost there," I said, eyeing the exit. Gladys bleated again.

Between the shrieking goat, the blaring music from the radio, the screaming of the siren, and the roaring of Yager's straining engine, it was a bit of sensory overload.

"This is crazy!" Salvador shouted. It would have been ridiculous to argue and unnecessary to agree, so I just gripped the wheel tighter and kept my eye on the exit, now a quarter mile away.

The cruiser slid over into our lane. The brake lights lit up. We roared toward its fender.

The exit was a hundred yards away.

We weren't gonna make it.

I jerked the wheel, faking a move to the left.

The cop fell for it. He sped up and matched me, blocking the move he thought I was trying to make.

That one move was all I needed.

I drifted back into the right lane and the cop drifted with me, speeding up to stay ahead of me.

We were there, at the exit. The white painted lines of the exit lane veered gently off to the right. I ignored them, staying straight on the highway.

"What are you doing?" Salvador yelled.

I waited until we were just past the white lines of the ramp entrance.

"Hold on!" I hollered. Then I cut the wheel hard to the right. Yager veered across the painted lines and over a gravelly triangle of highway shoulder and then onto the exit ramp. There was a jolting *crack* as we flattened a plastic reflector post, but all in all I thought I pulled the maneuver off pretty well.

By the time the cop realized what I was doing, it was already too late. When I swerved onto the ramp, he was already well past it and with the pedal to the floor. He hit the brakes and there was a squeal of rubber on asphalt, but the goose was cooked; the last I saw of him as we climbed up toward the overpass bridge, he was skidding to a dusty stop on the shoulder under the bridge a hundred yards past the exit.

"Woohoo!" Salvador whooped, jumping up out of his seat and raising a fist in the air. "You lost him!"

"Nah," I shouted back, though I was grinning so hard my face hurt. "He's just gonna back up on the shoulder. I only bought us, like, forty-five seconds. But I think that's all we'll need."

Poplin Springs had never been a big town, and even though Grandma had said it was growing, it still wasn't, like, a bustling metropolis or anything. It'd been years, but I knew exactly how to get to Sampson Park. As we came charging off the exit, I slowed to a city-street speed.

Houses and businesses whizzed past me.

The outdriving-a-cop-in-a-speeding-school-bus adrenaline drained slowly out of my body and a lump grew in my throat.

That familiar, almost-forgotten-home feeling that the shapes of the hills had given me a few miles back returned with a vengeance on the streets of Poplin Springs. There was a white house with green shutters that I kinda remembered. I'd gone to a birthday party there, I think. Back when my mama was alive. And a little convenience store on the corner—I remembered walking there with Ava to buy Popsicles on a sweaty summer day. Back before she died. And out in front of the grocery store, there was still that plastic horse you could ride that'd buck and rock if you put a quarter in. In my mind I could still see Rose sitting on top of it, holding on tight and smiling huge, bright-eyed with the little-kid thrill of it. But that was when she was still my little sister. Before she became just a memory.

Memory swirled around me, thick as campfire smoke, choking me and making my eyes burn.

This was it.

I was here.

My hands started to shake.

For a second, just a second, I totally understood why Rodeo had never wanted to come back. But just for a second. Because right on the heels of that feeling, and even overlapping and mixed up in it, was the feeling of knowing that coming back was maybe the rightest thing I'd ever done.

Because *they* were here. Memories swirled around me, as sweet and sad as a voice singing you to sleep at night.

I loved them. I missed them. And I'd been missing them for way too long.

I felt a tugging at my shoulder and realized that Salvador was saying something to me.

I flicked off the radio. Without the music and the siren and the highway noise, the world was surprisingly still. Peaceful, even.

"What?" I asked.

"Do you know the way?"

I blinked at him in the mirror. He was blurry. Come on, Coyote—everything was blurry.

"Yeah," I answered, then cleared the hoarseness out of my throat with a cough. "Yeah, I know the way."

I saw Salvador looking at me in the mirror and I looked away and cleared my throat again and Salvador didn't say anything, but he kept his hand on my shoulder, just kept it sitting there in the quiet stillness of that bus.

He's a good one, that Salvador.

Eventually the peace was broken by the sound of a siren coming up behind us fast. I wasn't worried, though. Nothing was stopping me now. Salvador looked back to check on the cop, but he still left his hand on my shoulder. Gladys clopped up to stand beside me, and she nudged my leg gruffly with her nose until I dropped a hand from the wheel to pet her. Ivan weaved between her legs and hopped up onto my lap. He rubbed his nose against my elbow and then settled his body in close to mine.

The road curved around a corner. And then it was there. Right in front of me.

There were the trees. And some grass. A big clearing.

And the machines. Big, yellow steel machines with treads and scoops and pistons and teeth. Some were parked, but some were moving, jerking and digging and scraping, kicking up dust. Workers tramped around among it all, wearing bright vests and hard hats and blue jeans and sunglasses. A pile of knocked-down trees sat off to one side.

"There," I said, or tried to, but it came out as almost a gasp, like I'd been punched in the stomach.

They'd already started.

CHAPTER
FORTY-TWO

"Get as close as you can and then just park anywhere," Salvador was saying, letting go of my shoulder and jumping to his feet. "Then just run. Go get it. Don't let anyone stop you. I'll take care of the cop."

I nodded numbly.

"Be careful," I said.

"What do you mean?"

"I mean be careful. That cop doesn't know you. He thinks we're crazy. Dangerous criminals, maybe. Just . . . keep your hands up and be careful."

"Yeah. Okay. I'll be careful."

There was a moment when I was almost paralyzed by all the madness I'd gotten myself into. A moment when I almost just kept driving, almost just cruised right by that torn-up park. It all just seemed like too much.

I guess sometimes life *does* seem like too much, especially during the big moments. But usually you can dig inside yourself and find what you need. You can find what you need to grow into those big moments and make 'em yours.

I saw my spot. A smashed-down patch of dirt that'd once been grass, just past a tore-up strip of gravel that had once been a sidewalk.

"Here we go," I said, and turned the wheel. We cut across the left lane of the road and bounced over the gravel, then came to a dusty skidding stop in the patch of dirt. Workers were pointing and shouting, and I saw one jogging over toward us. The siren got louder and pulled up right behind us.

"Go!" Salvador shouted.

I didn't need him to tell me. But it helped.

I didn't even kill the engine. I yanked on the parking brake, scooped Ivan off onto the seat I jumped out of, jerked the door open, and bolted down the stairs.

I hit the ground running.

There was a little plastic orange construction-zone fence, but I jumped it no problem and sprinted through the worksite toward that back corner of the park I'd traveled thousands of miles to get to.

This did *not* seem to be a popular move among the dudes working at the site. The kind of vague shouting and pointing turned into some pretty specific shouting and pointing once I cleared that little fence.

Behind me, I heard some yelling that sounded sort of police-ish and risked a quick look over my shoulder. Sure enough, there was the cop car parked all sideways behind Yager. And there was the cop, walking with all sorts of angry, uptight body language toward Salvador, who was walking back toward the cop with both hands up high in the air. The cop didn't have his gun out, thank the lord, but he did have one hand down on its grip sticking out of his holster. I couldn't hear his words, but I could tell that Salvador was talking, and that he was angling himself to stand between the cop and me.

God bless that boy.

I looked forward again, and just in time, too. A beefy guy in a flannel shirt was lunging toward me, hands ready to grab. I veered to the side, dodging him, but just barely. He took a couple of halfhearted steps in pursuit, but his belly outweighed his ambition and I left him gasping and swearing.

I bolted through where I was pretty sure there used to be a swing set and a slide but was now just a mess of dirt and holes and bulldozer tracks. I had some good memories about that swing set—memories of a mom's hand on my back, pushing me high; of Rose learning to kick her pudgy toddler legs; of jumping-off contests with Ava when I felt like I was flying, but lost to her long legs every time—but it was too late for the swing set now, and I wasn't here for it anyway.

I cut around a bench and then zipped sharp around an idling front-end loader and then I had a straight shot toward the back corner, the wild corner, the overgrown corner . . . the wooded corner where on a sunny spring day five years ago I'd knelt with most of my family and buried some memories.

But . . . it wasn't there. And I don't mean that just the box wasn't there. *None* of it was there.

There was no corner. There was no wild, there was no over-grown, there were no woods.

My steps faltered, my stride slowed, but I kept on charging forward because my legs didn't quite believe what my eyes were telling me.

There was no memory corner. There was, off to the side, a stack of stripped down logs and a ragged pile of leaves and branches. And there was a big ditch clawed into the ground. And there was a giant mound of soil and dirt and rocks. And there was a big, rusty backhoe, this one being moved by a man inside, scraping the bottom of the ditch with its enormous steel scoop and then pivoting with a lurch and dumping the load on the top of the mound.

"Hey, kid!"

I heard the shout and saw the man running my way on a diagonal. My brain was still catching up to the mess in front of me and what it meant, but I'd gone this far and wasn't gonna stop now, so I added some juice to my legs, stretching out my stride and surging past the guy.

I looked urgently around as I ran up to the scene of the crime, trying to size up where things were, where things had been, where things were supposed to be. I was out of breath, the sun was in my eyes, memories and desperation had their hands around my throat, and I was trying to compare the present torn-up, dusty wasteland with the green, wooded park of my five-year-old memories.

What I'm saying is, I was having a real hard time.

I squinted around, looking at the shapes of the hills, at the distance to the street, at the houses nearby, sizing up where I thought I was compared to where I'd knelt that day in memory.

I tried to place the ghost of my mama, the ghosts of my sisters, where they had been—laughing, smiling, touching, breathing, alive. I tried to find them there amid the root-ripped trees, the gouged ground, the torn trench. I listened for where their echoes might still ring.

That park was like my heart in some ways, I guess: scraped bare and scarred, alive mostly in memory.

But I was pretty sure I knew where I was in it.

I jumped down into the ditch.

I was at the part where I started digging for memory.

The ditch was waist-deep. The guy in the big metal digger was shouting at me, waving his arms, but his concern was no concern of mine. The machine fell silent and the guy stepped half out of it, yelling. But my ears weren't listening for his anger. They were listening for my ghosts.

I picked my way through the ditch, stumbling but not falling.

I wasn't seeing the dirt, the stones, the roots around me. I was seeing a tree-shaded clearing, and the shadows of two sisters, and a mama's face. And I was hearing her words.

"All right, now, everyone put a hand on the box. Yes, just like that, Rose."

I paused, turned, half-closed my eyes. I held the memory behind my eyelids, looked through it at the world around me, tried to find where my feet needed to be, where my hands needed to dig.

"Perfect. Now repeat after me." I could see the shared smiles we passed each other, the shining eyes. *"I promise," "I promise," "as a mother, as a daughter, as a sister," "as a mother, as a daughter,*

as a sister," "to hold my mother, my daughters, my sisters in my heart,"
"to hold my mother, my daughters, my sisters in my heart," "and I
promise to come back," "and I promise to come back," "to this very
spot," "to this very spot," "to retrieve this secret box of memories," "to
retrieve this secret box of memories," "ten years from today," "ten
years from today." "Amen. The end," "Amen. The end."

I breathed in, slow. Breathed out.

"I came back," I whispered to the dirt, to the memory, to the ghosts. To my mom and my sisters. "A little early, but I'm back. Promise kept." I opened my eyes, looked around. "So where are you?"

And there was no answer. And I almost, *almost*, had expected one. Come on, Coyote—ghosts aren't real. Memories don't talk.

It was just me, standing in the dirt, alone.

A gust of wind blew, spitting dust into my eyes. It brought with it the yells of the men, the sounds of a park being ripped out, the noise of the world going on with its business. And it almost, it *almost*, blew those memories away. I felt them, tugging loose from my heart's fingers, like feathers.

But, no. Heck no. Absolutely freaking not.

A promise is a promise. And I'm the kind that keeps them.

The rest of the memory played. Us lowering the little box into the hole we'd dug with a little spade, there between the roots. Covering it with dirt, then a big rock, then some leaves. Hiding our memories with care so they wouldn't be stolen. Rose, screwing her face up at my mom, asking, *"But what if we can't find it, Mama?"* And my mom putting on her playful serious face and answering, *"Oh, don't worry. We'll remember where it is."* And me nodding and smiling, saying, *"I'll remember!"* and Mom winking at me, bending down to kiss my forehead while she wiped her dirty hands on her jeans. *"There, see? Ella will find it. Ella will remember."*

I rubbed the dust from my eyes. Clenched my jaw. Looked up the trench I was standing in. Looked down it the other way. *Ella will remember.* Took three steps farther along. Two more. *Ella will remember.* Stopped. My feet in the dirt. My eyes looking up, looking for the memories of trees. Finding them.

"Here," I whispered.

Ella will remember.

I was there. I was in the memory place. I was on the ground in the place between the trees, the place where sisters knelt with their mom and buried a treasure.

But I was standing in a ditch that came up to my waist. We hadn't buried the box that deep. Not even close. The hole hadn't even been knee-deep, scratched out clumsily by kid muscles wielding a little spade.

It had already been dug up.

I looked at the backhoe operator, who was standing on his machine saying something to me, a look of pure pissed-off on his face.

"Did you find something?" I asked him.

He stopped whatever growling he was doing.

"What?"

"Did you find something? When you were digging. Right here where I'm standing."

He gave me a you're-ruining-my-day scowl.

"I found some *rocks*, kid. Now move it. I got—"

"That's it? You didn't find anything else? Like a box?"

"No, I didn't find no box. Look, it's a big shovel I got here. I could scoop up a microwave and not see it. Now you gotta—"

"Where's the dirt? Where's the dirt you dug out from right here?"

He gestured at the mound of dirt that towered over me at the ditch's edge.

"Where d'ya think?"

I turned and looked up at the pile. It was well over my head. It would've been over my head even if I hadn't been standing waist-deep in a hole.

It was a lot of dirt, is what I'm saying.

It didn't matter. I mean, it didn't matter at *all*, not one little bit.

I dug into the bottom of the pile with both hands. With *bare* hands. I didn't need gloves. I didn't need a shovel. I didn't need anything except to keep that promise.

"Hey!" the guy hollered, and then followed it up with something else (likely about stopping or knocking it off or getting out of the way or some such), but I didn't slow down and I didn't stop and I didn't turn to answer or explain.

The dirt gave way before me. It tumbled down into the ditch at my feet, but more spilled from above to take its place and I kept clawing at the pile.

I didn't stop to catch my breath or rest my hands or flip off the surly shouter, didn't pause for even a heartbeat until a pair of hands grabbed my shoulders and pinned my arms and then, strong but not in a mean way, spun me around.

I thought I'd see that cop glaring down at me, but instead it was just some guy, a guy with scuffed-up boots and a few days' worth of stubble on his cheeks. He was looking into my face, and he looked worried.

"Hey," he said, then said it again, "Hey. Hold on a sec."

I stood there in his grip, my breath coming in heaves.

"What's going on?" he asked.

"I have to find it," I said, and tried to shake loose.

"Find what?"

"There's a box and we buried it and I have to find it," I said in one breathless burst.

"Hey!" he said again when I struggled to break free and turn around. "Listen. Sorry, kid, but if you buried it here, it's gone. And you gotta leave, all right? This is a work zone. It ain't safe."

I shook my head.

"No. I have to find it."

"Well, you aren't going to. Sorry. You're gonna get out of this ditch and then get on home." He grabbed me firm, his fingers around my wrist, and started to walk, pulling me with him toward the end of the trench.

I dug in my heels and wrenched my wrist free and when he turned to grab me again, I raised both my hands up out of his reach.

"I have to find it!" I shouted, and I brought my fists down on his chest. He stepped back, taken by surprise, and I raised my fists again. I was *almost* ready to hit him again. Almost ready to hit and claw and scratch and kick and do whatever fighting I had to do, because what I was fighting for was worth fighting for.

But then I remembered Rodeo. I remembered how he talked to folks. How he didn't raise his voice, but talked soft. How he talked right into their eyes. Person to person. *Always kindness, Coyote.*

Folks like that. They like being talked to like people. Like they matter.

And at the end of the day, if you give them half a chance, people want to help other people. Most of 'em, anyway. They do.

So I lowered my fists. And I gave myself—and him—two breaths to calm down. And I lowered my voice. And I looked that fella right in his eyes. I looked long enough and close enough that I saw their color, a yellowy brown flecked with bits of green. And I talked right into his eyes, my voice as human and gentle as Rodeo's.

"Please," I said. "I have to find it. It's important to me."

And that fella, he paused. I saw it. And it was the kind of pause I'd seen a hundred times before when Rodeo talked with his Rodeo eyes and his Rodeo voice and won someone over, when he made them pause and then listen and then get on his side.

The man's eyebrows that had been scrunched-down angry rose, just a bit. The hard line of his frown softened, just a tad. He looked at me. I looked right back.

"Please," I said again. "Help me."

The man blinked. And he took one good, deep breath.

And then he said with a little shrug in his voice, "What kind of box is it?"

And I didn't smile because it wasn't a smiling kind of moment.

"It's a metal box. About the size and shape of a shoebox. We buried it right here five years ago."

"You sure it was right here?"

"Sure as sugar, sir."

The man shook his head, but then he kind of shooed me toward the pile with his hands.

"All right. We gotta hurry, though."

And I spun back to the dirt and started digging again, and that fella with the green-flecked eyes stepped right up at my side, and he started digging with his hands, too.

The backhoe operator started a fresh round of shouting, but the guy beside me barked at him, "Aw, chill out, Ed. It'll just take a minute," and then Ed said, "Dang it, Travis, I got a schedule to keep," and my new friend Travis answered, "Well, if you're in such a rush, why don't you get us a couple shovels?" and Ed snorted and spit, but a second later he was gone and a minute after that he was in the ditch with us, handing us shovels, and he started digging on my other side, and between shovelfuls, he asked me, "What are we looking for?" and I paused just long enough to tell him and his voice was rude and gruff, but I swear if I hadn't been so busy digging, I woulda hugged that man.

We tore into that hill of dirt, us three. There was nothing but the sounds of our breathing and the *clink*ing and *scritch*ing of our shovels digging dirt and tossing rocks.

Sweat was dripping into my eyes and I was wiping at it with my arm, so I don't know when exactly he got there, but I looked up and saw Salvador standing up at the surface, working at the side of the pile with a shovel of his own, his white undershirt smeared with dirt. He saw me seeing him and gave me a little nod, but he kept working, attacking the dirt.

An ornery bleat rang out and Gladys walked up to the ditch, flapped her ears, and peered down at me. I'd bolted out of Yager at a dead run and left the door standing open behind me, but I wasn't worried. Gladys could take care of herself.

Then, as if he could read my mind, Salvador said between breaths, "Don't worry. Ivan's still on the bus. And I closed the door."

I heard, somewhere, a voice still shouting and I glanced up just long enough to see it was the cop, hands on his hips and a frown on his face, taking turns snarling at Salvador and throwing some words at us down in the ditch.

Finally Ed, big old grumpy Ed, stopped for a breath and leaned on his shovel sweating and said up at the cop, "Come on, man. Give it a break. This girl is looking for something."

"What is she looking for?"

"Well, it ain't a *gun*, all right? So just give us a minute."

Ed was growing on me.

The cop seethed, but he zipped his lip and just stood there, rocking on his heels and looking nasty.

We hacked away at that mountain of dirt, me and Ed and Travis and Salvador, tossing the dirt over our shoulders and sending little avalanches of it crumbling down to our feet. The pile got smaller and smaller, and we got sweatier and dirtier. And all our shovels hit was dirt, or rocks, or roots.

Eventually, Ed gave up. He grunted and wiped his face and stepped back, panting from the work, and then sat on the opposite edge of the ditch watching us.

Beside me, I could tell that Travis was losing hope, too. His scoops got fewer and farther between, and sometimes he just kinda stood there, poking at the mound with his shovel.

Salvador never slowed down, though. Every time I glanced up, he was digging and scooping and throwing. His shirt was filthy now and stuck to his body with sweat, but he never stopped. I knew he wasn't going to stop until I did.

That's a friend, right there. That's the kind of friend you want with you.

My shovel dove and *plunk*ed, then scooped and lifted and tossed and then dove and *plunk*ed again.

And then, just like in some dumb movie, it happened.

My shovel dove and *plunk*ed, but it didn't *plunk* deep. It *plunk*ed shallow and stopped cold. I'd already hit plenty of rocks, but this *plunk* felt different. A little less solid. A little more hopeful. And it made a sound, too, a sound like a rock hitting a stop sign. It was quiet, muffled by dirt, but it was there. I knew I hadn't imagined it, because even Travis stopped his poking and his head snapped over to look at where my shovel had *plunk*ed.

I scraped the shovel nose back, but the dirt above came cascading down so quick that I couldn't see anything and I stabbed with the shovel one, two, three more times and each time I carved a little more dirt away and each time it made that little sound and each time that sound was a little louder.

And then, finally, the dirt that kept falling down didn't fall straight down; it split and poured down around the corner of something. The corner of something that was sticking out, just a bit, from that pile of dirt. The corner of something that was metal, and square.

I stopped. I mean, I just froze. I was looking at it. It was looking at me.

"That it?" Travis asked, and I couldn't answer. I dropped the shovel. I reached out with an unsteady hand. My fingers stopped, an inch away. My heart pounded in my ears and my lungs held on to their breath like it was their last. And then I touched it. I just touched it, lightly.

"*Mom*," I whispered, my finger on that box we'd buried there together.

Ella will remember.

CHAPTER

FORTY-THREE

I grabbed the jutting corner of the box and tugged. It didn't give.

There was a thudding crunch as Salvador jumped down beside me. He didn't say anything. He just scooped away the dirt around the box with his fingers while I wiggled and pulled at the box. Sometimes I stopped pulling and worked with him, scraping the dirt away. But he never took hold of the box himself, never yanked on it or tried to jerk it free, even though there was a distant chance he was stronger than me. He never tried to pull it out himself. I think he knew that moment was for me.

We got more and more of the corner showing and then another corner and we sped up, Salvador digging with both hands like a dog and me leaning back, putting my legs into it, straining to bust that box loose.

I was getting shaky, like when you're so super starving you can hardly stand it and then you see the plate coming, hot and salty.

And then it broke free.

It tilted and slid out into my hands and I was holding it. I was holding that box and it was just like I remembered—dirty and scratched up and dented—but other than that it was just like I remembered and it was in my hands. It was warm—I don't even know why—but it was warm. I held that box in my hands and I stopped breathing and I took every breath in the world. My mom. My sisters. My mom. My sisters. I held that box and I held them.

I held that box and every *the end* and every *once upon a time* that ever was rang out at the same time, all tangled up together.

With a slow, careful hand I wiped the dust off the top of the box. It was dinged up and dirt encrusted and rusty. It was perfect.

I realized I was kneeling. I had no memory of dropping to my knees, but there I was, on my knees in the dirt.

I rose to my feet. I tried to breathe. Tried to clear my eyes. I looked over at Salvador, who was looking back at me, his eyes deep and solemn pools. I nodded to him, once. He nodded back, once. He was still breathing hard from the chase, the digging, the finding. So was I, I think.

I looked up, out of the ditch, past the waiting machines and watching workers.

There was one tree left in the park. One, way over at the edge, that hadn't been ripped out. Maybe it wasn't in the way and would be spared. Or maybe they just hadn't gotten to it yet. But it was still there for the moment, still dropping shade like they all had on all those days all that time ago, and on one day in particular.

I stumbled out of the ditch, holding that box with two hands and one heart. I rose up out of that earth that was raw and torn up like a freshly dug grave. Salvador's footsteps scratched along behind me.

There were a few guys standing with crossed arms. I guessed they'd been watching the whole thing. They stepped to the side and let me pass. I made my way toward the tree that stood alone, all of its family ripped away.

Salvador's footsteps stopped at the line of workers and he let me go on by myself.

I heard one of the guys grumble, "What is it?" and I heard Salvador answer low, "It's a memory box. She buried it there with her mom," and then I heard someone say, "Well, where's her mom?" and Salvador almost whispered his answer, but I still heard it, "She's dead," and then there was a big silence, a heavy silence, an understanding kind of silence. And not one of those folks said a word. And not one of those folks complained about the interruption. And not one of those folks told me to hurry the heck up so they could get back to work.

"Hey!" The voice cut through the moment. It was the cop, of course. "Hey! Where you going?" His voice got louder as he spoke, so I knew he was jogging up behind me.

"Leave her alone, man," I heard one of the guys grumble.

"Leave her alone? Do you have any idea what she—"

"Oh, give it a rest, dude. You can wait one *minute*. I mean, she ain't going nowhere, right?"

The cop, though, would not give it a rest. And he wasn't gonna give me one minute, either.

"Stop!" he said, and I could hear his angry footsteps stomping up behind me. "Can you hear me? Stop!"

I could, and I didn't.

I was going to the shade of that tree, that last tree standing. And I was gonna sit down in whatever shade she offered. And I was gonna open up that box. And I was gonna spend a little time with my mom and my sisters. Right here in our park.

But the cop wasn't giving up easy.

He puffed up beside me.

"Hey," he said gruffly. "You need to stop."

I kept my eyes straight ahead and my feet moving. I didn't trust my throat to speak. The memories were all around me, the ghosts waiting under the tree; I didn't want to lose them. Ever again.

"Hey!" he said, and he grabbed my arm. "You need to stop. Now."

His fingers locked onto my arm. Hard. And he stopped me hard and spun me around hard. He was all hardness, that cop.

I didn't have it in me to deal with all his hardness, because there was nothing hard left in me. I was soft and broken and falling apart, right down to my middle. But I was ready to fight that cop to the end to do what I needed to do, what I was aching to do, what I was almost dying to do. I was ready to fight his hardness, because gosh darn it, the world is hard enough as it is without hard people making it even harder. I was ready to fight.

Turns out, I wasn't the only one.

I'd only gotten as far as opening my mouth when there was a coming-at-us-fast drumming in the ground. A little thunder rolling our way, for just a second, before it got to us. Well, before *she* got there.

She hit him from the side and she brought a cloud of dust

with her. Gladys came flying from our periphery, her head lowered and her horns ready, and she gave that cop a headbutting he ain't never gonna forget. Yeah, she rammed him. Hard.

That hard cop met the hard end of a hard goat. And the goat won.

There was a grunt and a coughing *whoosh* of breath when she hit him. He went straight down to the ground and skidded a bit on his butt, his feet kicking up in the air. When he came to rest in a little dirty cloud, Gladys stood over him, head lowered, pawing the ground with a hoof and clearly ready for round two.

The cop looked up at her, and I'd say the vast majority of the hardness had left him. His eyes were wide as quarters, his face pale, his mouth hanging open.

"I'm sorry, officer," I said quiet. "She's a good goat. And a goat is a loyal animal."

The cop just stared at me. I think he was still fairly rattled, and I can't say that I blame him.

"I'm gonna go over to that tree over there. And I'm gonna go through this box. Just for a few minutes. And then I'll go with you. You don't need your gun. You don't need your handcuffs." I looked at Gladys, who still stood trembling with ready indignation. "You probably *do* need to avoid eye contact and sudden movements, though."

Gladys snorted.

The cop twitched and flinched.

"Just a few minutes," I repeated, right into his eyes. "Okay?"

The cop swallowed, eyes still wide.

He nodded.

"Thank you," I said. The box felt heavy in my hands, and it felt weightless.

I turned and walked over to the tree and knelt down in the grass. I set the box on the ground in front of me.

There was a little metal clasp that clicked shut and held the box closed.

Slowly, I lifted it up. It was rusty and it was stubborn, but after a second it popped up and open.

I took a breath. One deep breath of air down into the very bottoms of my lungs.

I felt them. I felt them all around me. Looking over my shoulders. Putting their arms around me. They were there.

I opened the box.

FORTY-FOUR

*H*ere's a memory.

I don't know when it was, exactly. Not that long before we buried the box. Not that long before . . . everything.

It was spring, but the warm kind. The kind of spring that's already trying sometimes to be summer.

We went for a hike. All five of us. Just up in the hills around Poplin Springs. It was something we did.

We walked up the dirt trail, up out from the valley floor. Up to the tops of the hills, where we could see the distant mountains and the bends of the river and the town laid out below us all miniature. It was steep and it was long, but we could see forever up there, it felt like. And a chance to see forever is worth the work.

The slopes were green with spring's rain and sun, the grass long and bright, swaying like seaweed in the breeze. The fields were exploding with wildflowers: purple lupine and yellow balsamroot and little white ones I'd never known the name of. So much color, so much living, so much life up there that sometimes your eyes didn't believe it, and sometimes you even had to whisper to your own heart, *No, it's real.* It was heaven.

Rodeo was there. Back before he was Rodeo. Back when he was just Dad, and I was just his daughter. One of his daughters.

And Rose, her legs too little for the long climb, riding up on Rodeo's shoulders.

And Ava, long-legged and long-haired, talking with her hands.

And me, back when I was Ella. Just Ella. The daughter, the little sister, the big sister. The one in the middle. Never alone, back then.

And Mom. Oh, Mom. Mom with the voice like warm honey. Mom with the touches that made everything better.

I held my mom's hand as we walked. Hers bigger than mine, soft, warm, safe.

Near the top I dropped her hand and ran ahead, ran ahead of my family to beat them to the top.

The sun was just getting to setting, dropping down below the mountains on the horizon. The light was coming in long sideways beams, through the clouds, slanting sharp and golden through the grasses, through the flower blooms stretching up toward the sky.

I stopped there, in the middle of all the glory. I turned back to my family walking up toward me.

Mom came first, walking by herself. Dad and Ava and Rose were farther back, taking their time, talking and meandering. But Mom came first, following my footsteps, wading off the trail and into the grass and flowers to come my way.

She didn't come straight to me, though. Even though I wanted her to. She walked off to the side, just a little. Finding her own path. She stopped, off by herself, facing into the sunset. Her eyes were alight with the sun's fire. Her hair blew in wisps around her face. The sunlight hit her face and it was pure gold.

She looked off into the distance and I saw her take a breath, a deep breath, and let it out slow.

Then she turned her head and looked at me, looking at her. There was nothing but green and bloom and light between us. And she smiled at me. A sharing smile. A smile that was just for me. A smile that said all the most beautiful things that moms say to daughters. And I smiled back. A smile that said all the most important things that daughters say to moms.

You know what? I don't think I'm ever gonna see anything in my life more beautiful than my own mama smiling in the sun. I got a whole life ahead of me, but I just don't believe that I'll ever see anything more beautiful than that, and than her.

I loved her so much in that moment I could barely breathe. It almost choked me, how much I loved her. All I was in that moment was loving her. I loved her. I loved her. I loved her.

That's it. That's the whole memory.

That memory doesn't have any words.

It doesn't need them.

CHAPTER
FORTY-FIVE

The lid creaked open. I let it fall back until it hit the grass, so the box lay there wide open.

I looked inside the box.

My skin went all tingly and goose bumpy.

Oh, man.

It was there. It was all there. Just like I remembered it.

Just like we'd left it.

There was a pile of papers all jumbled together, and I could see the little-kid handwriting here and there, could see the crayon pictures. There were a few smooth rocks that we must've thought were special back then. And, boy, were they ever. I picked one up and held its cool roundness in my hand and closed my eyes and stopped breathing, just knowing that Rose had held it in her hand, had squeezed that very rock between her perfect little fingers.

I put the rock back in the box, laying it down gentle as a bird's nest, and picked up the top piece of paper. It was a drawing, scrawled in crayon with a four-year-old's care, sloppy and beautiful. It was a picture, I could tell, of me and Rose. Her hair was a spaghetti mess of curly lines, mine was done in short scribbles.

We had big wobbly smiles and round ghost eyes. We were holding hands.

Under the picture were a few lines of words, and I remembered what Mom had told us: *"Write down for each person what you love about them."*

The words were Rose's, but the writing was Mom's. Rose was too small to write, so she had told Mom her answers and Mom had written them down in big, clear letters so that Rose could see and start to learn. I ran my fingers over one line, felt the waxy crayon with my fingertips, and traced the words: *"I love my sister Ella because she loves me, no matter what."* I nodded, my breath hot in my throat, my eyes burning and blinking. "Yes," I tried to whisper. "Yes. It's true, Rose. No matter what."

Under that paper were more. Ava's papers, my mom's papers, the pages I'd done about each of them. I didn't need to read them all now, didn't need to read each word. I'd have time for that, I knew. Plenty of time. A lifetime of time. Besides, my eyes had gone too blurry to read.

I just wanted to feel the paper. To touch all the things that we had touched together. To see the shape of the handwriting and remember the hands that had written it.

I shuffled carefully through the treasures, past the letters we'd written. I found Ava's last school picture, saw her cheekbones and her blue eyes and her big, crooked smile.

It's funny. She always seemed so smart, so cool, so old. But, now, she looked . . . oh, she looked so young. Just a kid. Just a sweet, little, silly kid. And I realized—I was twelve. Twelve years old. Ava, my big sister, was only eleven when that truck swerved and tore the world apart.

I was older than my big sister. She was eleven forever. But, somehow, she would always be my big sister.

My shoulders shook.

Then, a little silk pouch stuck in a corner, cinched closed with a drawstring. I pulled it open and turned it over into my hand and a single twirl of gold fell out onto my palm.

It was a lock of Rose's hair, golden and shiny and wound into a perfect curly ringlet. I ran a fingertip around its smooth circle. We hadn't known if her hair was gonna stay curly; Ava and me had started with curls and then outgrown them. We were all waiting to see if Rose would keep her curls. And now, I guess, we'd never know. I held the ringlet in my shaking hand, blinked at it through burning tears. Rose would have her curly hair forever. I slid the curl back into the pouch, pulled it gently closed, and held it to my lips.

"Hey, Coyote," his voice spoke behind me in a whisper. My dad's voice. I hadn't heard him walk up.

I pulled a breath in, I let the breath out.

"Don't call me that," I said. But I said it asking, not snapping. There was a "please" in my voice, even if there wasn't in my words. I looked up over my shoulder at him. "Not now. I'm not Coyote right now. Okay, Dad?"

I knew he wanted to turn away. I knew he was hurting and aching and scared and sad and broken. I knew he wanted to turn around and walk away until I was Coyote and he was Rodeo again and we could just keep driving and never look back. I knew he couldn't stand to see what I'd found. He couldn't stand to see what we'd lost.

I knew. I knew he wanted to.

But here's the thing.

He didn't.

My dad nodded and his throat bobbed in a tight swallow. And he took one step closer, to stand beside me. And then he lowered himself to his knees next to me. And then he put an arm around my shoulders, and I could feel his whole self shaking.

And then he looked in the box with me.

That's my dad, right there.

CHAPTER

FORTY-SIX

I don't know how long my dad and I looked through that box. I know we looked at a lot of the treasures inside, but not all of them. I know there was a little bit of laughing, here and there, at funny pictures and silly stuff we'd put in. But not a lot. To be honest, it was mostly crying and plenty of silence.

It couldn't have been that long. I mean, we were in the middle of a construction zone, after all, and they were totally cool about the whole thing, but they did have a lot to get done. And Gladys gave that cop a bruise, but she didn't exactly give him an extra load of patience when she did it, so I bet it was really only a few minutes that we knelt there and, for the first time in a long time, shared some memories.

So I don't know how long it lasted, but I can tell you how long it felt like. It felt more or less exactly like five years. It felt like, breath by breath, we fell back and back and back. Back through all those years and all those miles, back away from Coyote and Rodeo and back to just me and my dad. And then I was kneeling there and I was a daughter again. I was a sister again. And Rodeo—or *Dad*, really—Rodeo had a wife again. A wife that he missed like oxygen. And he had three daughters again. Three daughters that he loved like . . . like . . . well, I guess just like a dad loves three daughters, which is big and strong enough all on its own and doesn't really need any comparison, really.

Eventually I pulled a photograph out from the stack. It was dusty and bent at the corners, but all the important stuff was there.

It was a family picture. It was me in a tank top, tiny and grinning, a big gap between my front teeth. Next to me was Ava, tall and pretty, one arm thrown casually over my shoulder, pulling me just a bit off balance so I was leaning on one foot toward her. Behind us was Dad. Lord, he looked different. I didn't even remember him ever looking that way. Normal clothes. Clean-cut hair trimmed short, a smooth-shaved face. You could see his chin and everything. He was squinting a little because of the sun, and he looked easy and happy and young.

Next to him was Mom. She was right behind me and you could kinda tell I was leaning back against her. She was smiling, and there was a little bit of laugh to her smile, like someone had said something funny just before the picture was taken. Rose was in her arms, one hand around Mom's neck, perched on her hip, one eye closed against the glare, showing off her baby teeth in a big smile.

I held the picture up and I could hear Dad breathing beside me, breathing like he'd just come up from the bottom of a lake.

I held up the picture and I pointed at Ava.

"Who is this?" I asked my dad, and we both knew I wasn't asking who it was; I was asking him to say her name, to say it out loud. To stop running.

It was hard. It almost felt cruel. But it was what I needed. And, I think, it was maybe even what he needed.

Rodeo swallowed and breathed through his nose.

"Who is this?" I asked again, even quieter than the first time. My voice wasn't slapping him, it wasn't pulling out splinters; it was taking him by the hand, it was pulling him up from where he'd fallen.

My dad rubbed his eyes.

He tried to say something but his voice caught and he cleared his throat and tried again, but there was still nothing there, so he took one more breath and tried again and on the third try he got it.

"That's Ava," he said. "That's your big sister."

I moved my finger to Rose, snuggled in my mom's arms.

"Who's that?"

"That's your little sister," he answered, and his voice was a scratched-out whisper, but it was there. "That's Rose."

My finger slid to my mom and the picture shook in my hand, but you could still see her despite the shaking, still see her smile, still see her shining eyes, still see my mom.

"Who's that?"

It took a couple tries again, but my dad did it.

"That's your mom," he said. "Anne." And when he said it, when he said her name, he reached out with one finger and he touched the picture. He ran his rough finger soft down my mom's arm.

Then I asked, "Who's that?" My finger was pointing at him, at my squinting, young, unbroken dad.

He sucked in a breath and blew it out with a sigh and shook his head and said, "That's me. That's your dad." He said it like he almost didn't quite believe it. He said it sad. He said it like he missed that smiling, clear-eyed man almost as much as he missed the other people in the picture. Well, maybe not almost. Maybe not even close. But still, he missed him.

My finger moved to the last face in the picture.

"Who's that?" I whispered. "Who's that, Dad?"

His arm tightened around my shoulders.

"Oh, honeybear," he said, and he kissed the top of my head. "That's you, baby," he murmured into my hair and then kissed me again. "That's my daughter," and another kiss, and then he said, "Ella," and he kept his lips pressed to my head.

We sat there like that, me and my dad. Me and my dad.

And then there was the sound of a throat clearing behind us, and I knew without looking that it was the cop and that our time was up. I appreciated that he only cleared his throat, that he hadn't growled or snarled or said something hard or officious or impatient.

I pulled away just enough to look my dad in the eyes and I was relieved to see that his eyes were there with me and they were whole; they were sad and red, but they weren't empty and they weren't far away at all. They were Rodeo eyes, open and honest and there, but they were Dad eyes, too. I woulda smiled, but it wasn't really a smiling kind of a moment. I don't know what kind of moment it was, really, but I know it was a big kind. And a good kind, in the way that big moments can be good without being happy, exactly.

I nodded to him and sniffled and he nodded back and rubbed his nose with his arm and then I put the picture back in the box, laid it in gentle like it was made of ash, and then I pulled the lid of the box closed and snapped the latch shut.

And my dad stood up. He reached down with his big ol' hand and took hold of my free one and helped me up. We turned and faced the cop together.

The cop was looking serious, but not sour. I mean, he wasn't gonna tell us a joke or anything, but he wasn't gonna slap hand-cuffs on us, either.

"All right," he said. "We're gonna need to go back and have you answer some questions about, uh"—he gestured back over his shoulder with his thumb—"the *bus* situation."

"Yeah," Dad said, and he said it soft and easy. "I'm sure we will, officer."

The officer walked off ahead of us and me and Rodeo fol-lowed. I nodded at the workers who were still standing there waiting and I said a few thank-yous, but I stopped in front of Travis and I looked him in the eyes and said a clear and true "Thank you, sir," and he just smiled and shrugged and said, "Heck, I needed a break anyway," and I smiled back and then he said more serious, "I'm real glad you found it, miss," and I decided right then that I was a big fan of rough, hard fellas who called girls "miss."

When we passed the ditch, Salvador joined us and walked by my side and I gave him a little one-arm side hug and he kind of gave me one back, but mostly he just looked away and blushed a little. I could hear Gladys clopping along behind us, and I liked that because it's good to have a friend you can trust at your back.

"How'd you get out?" I asked my dad as we walked.

"Easier than you'd think. Val got on the phone with her folks and it was all pretty clear pretty quick that there wasn't any kidnapping going on. That, plus that cop's boss finding out he'd hauled me away and left two minors sitting by the side of the highway, plus the news that you and the bus were gone . . . Well, that sheriff's office was pretty ready to get me out of there and get you two found and safe."

"Huh. Val okay?"

Dad shrugged.

"More or less. She still feels awful guilty even though I told her I totally get it. She ain't all that excited to go home, but it sure sounds like her folks might be looking at things a little different now. I think she gave 'em quite a scare."

I nodded. Losing something can sure make you realize how much you loved it, even if you knew you loved it all along.

"How'd you get here?"

Dad was quiet for a few steps.

Then he said, "Well, *she* gave me a ride," and he pointed up toward where Yager was parked and my breath got sucked out of my lungs when I saw her standing there, a little grayer and a little older, but still no doubt and no mistake my grandma. I gave my dad the box and I took off running, brushing past the cop without slowing, I ran back toward the street, right up to my grandma, and I wrapped my arms tight around her, so tight I'd have been afraid of hurting her except that her arms were around me just as tight and we stood there, tight together and not bothering or needing to say a word.

Five years is a long time.

And she said "Ella" a few times into my hair like my dad had a minute before and I said "Grandma" a few times, too. Then she held me out, her hands on my shoulders, and looked at my face and I looked at hers.

"Oh, I *missed* you," she said, and I did a little laugh-sob thing and said, "I missed you, too," and really it was a pretty stupid thing for both of us to say. Because, I mean, *obviously*. But it's okay to say stupid things sometimes, especially if they're true.

So on that day at that tore-up construction site, I got to be a daughter again and I got to be a sister again and I got to be a granddaughter again, and I tell you, those are three pretty fantastic things to be, sadness and all.

You know what? I kinda wanna take that last sentence back. It *feels* like the truth but it isn't, or at least it isn't the *whole* truth, because a thing like that—it doesn't happen that easy. It just doesn't. But I can say this: On that day at that tore-up construction site I got to *start* being all those things again. And that's just fine. 'Cause I can tell you for a fact that it's a heckuva lot better to *start* being those things than it is to *stop* being 'em. And starts are important. Once-upon-a-times are important.

CHAPTER
FORTY-SEVEN

I can spare you the rest. There were quite a few conversations with various authorities. There were an awful lot of stern looks and wagging fingers and dire warnings. There was also a fair amount of apologizing and explaining and promising on the part of me and Dad, a.k.a. Rodeo, a.k.a. that freaky, big-hearted hippie.

We'd broken our share of laws. Well, to be fair, *I'd* broken my share of laws. Rodeo was actually surprisingly innocent in the whole affair, apart from kinda sorta encouraging me to do it, but even that was under duress and in code. Either way, though, the folks in charge couldn't just look the other way. I mean, it wasn't like they could just say, "Sure, an underage kid stole a bus and raced it down the highway and ran away from the cops but, hey, she's got kind of a sad story, so no big deal."

So they looked into it. There were cops and a prosecutor and a judge and even a counselor I had to talk to. It all took a few days, and to tell you the truth it got a little old. But in the end, they decided that I was not a deeply troubled threat to society. And that Rodeo was without a doubt a certified weirdo, but not the dangerous kind and in fact maybe kind of an okay kind, really.

So neither one of us had to go to jail, and no one talked about taking me away from my dad or anything. Things worked out like they should have. Despite the badges and the titles and regulations and all the paperwork, it was all being handled by human beings, after all. And for the most part, human beings try to do the right thing, if they can see what that is.

They did make us pay for the reflector post I ran over, though.

And there were goodbyes. To Val, first. Her parents drove out to get her, and they took turns driving, Rodeo-and-Lester style, so they made it by the next night. I wasn't there for their reunion, but when I said goodbye to Val the next morning, she seemed okay. And sometimes you gotta take okay, because it's way better than terrible and can sometimes turn into pretty darn great. She gave us her address and her phone number, and I can guarantee that keeping in touch with that girl is right near the top of my list of things to do.

And then, a day later, we took a little drive back to Yakima and said goodbye to Salvador. That one was even tougher. And you know what? I don't think I'm gonna get too much into describing that one. I will say that Salvador told me, "I'm not *not* gonna miss you, Coyote Sunrise," and I said, "I'm not *not* gonna miss you, too," right back to him and we both laughed a little and there was a quick hug and, yeah, it was super awkward. But awkward's not always bad.

I worry about Salvador every day. But I never feel sorry for him. A promise is a promise. I've got his phone number. We'll be talking. He is my best friend, after all. Sure, he's also my *only* friend, but hey, "best" is still best no matter the number. And I'm pretty sure that even if I had a hundred friends, Salvador would still be the best one.

Rodeo convinced Lester to let us buy him a bus ticket back to Tampa and the Strut Kings. When we dropped him off at the bus station, Lester gave me a good, long hug and said, "You're still crazy, girl," and I said, "Yeah, probably. Don't go marrying any security guards," and he laughed, and that was that.

We said goodbye to Gladys, too, of course. There weren't any tears for that goodbye, but I did miss her as we drove away. She was a good goat, that Gladys. I was happy to see her back with her family.

And, eventually, we said goodbye to Grandma. Not for a while, though. We stayed for about a week. She and I went for walks, and she roasted a chicken for dinner once and we went out for ice cream, and a couple nights we sat together on the couch and ate popcorn and watched a movie and, boy, it was something. It was really something.

But even though we didn't talk about it, I knew all that week at Grandma's that we weren't there for good. We did laundry and ate breakfasts and got into a sort of routine, but I knew it wasn't a forever routine, and Dad spent the week changing the belts and oil and spark plugs in Yager, and you don't do that when you're getting ready to park it for good. You do that when you're getting ready to hit the road again.

So one night, when Grandma was in cleaning the dinner dishes and Rodeo and I were sitting out on the back porch watching bats flit and dart through the dim evening air, I asked him, "When we leaving?" and he waited just a few seconds before answering, "I was thinking the day after tomorrow," and I nodded to myself and looked away, off toward the shadowy shapes of those hills that had welcomed me home.

But then he did something else.

He said, "Would that be okay, Ella?"

He asked me. And he called me by my name.

And I just looked at him for a second, surprised by the question.

"I don't wanna keep doing this forever. This driving around, I mean," I said.

Rodeo nodded and sighed.

"I know. I just don't think I can stay here, and—"

"Me, neither," I interrupted him. His eyebrows went up in surprise. "Coming back here was . . . something I had to do. And I'm glad we did. But it's hard, being here. I don't think I could walk past that torn-up park every day.

"But I want to take them with us. Mom. And Ava. And Rose. I'm not leaving 'em behind, not ever again. We're a family again. Okay?"

Rodeo's eyes were red and watery, but he looked 'em into mine and nodded.

"Okay."

"And I don't just wanna leave here. I wanna go somewhere. Not running away. Looking. Looking for a home. A home without four wheels. That's what I want. Okay?"

Rodeo blinked at me. Then he nodded, a deep, slow nod.

"Okay," he said. "Okay. We'll find it."

And I leaned over and grabbed my dad in a hug, and my dad hugged me back.

"Good," he said. "Now, let's go in and help your grandma with the dishes." He let me go and stood up and walked away from me, toward the back door glowing warm with yellow light.

"One more thing, Dad." He turned to me and I said, "For god's sake, will you cut off that beard now?"

My dad took a step back toward me and he leaned down and said into my eyes, "Absolutely not," and then he smiled and I knew I was smiling back.

CHAPTER
FORTY-EIGHT

And so here we are now. Rambling still, but maybe not roaming. Wandering, but also looking. We ain't drifting so much as waiting. Like a dandyflower seed, blown free by a breath from the sweetest little girl the world ever saw, floating with the sunshine but looking for soil, looking to take root, looking to flower. That's us. That's me and Rodeo. That's me and my dad.

And you know what? Driving toward something is better than driving away from something. Way better.

I do cry sometimes. But I don't have to hide it anymore. When I feel sad, when I miss my mom or my sisters, I can just cry. And my dad puts his arm around my shoulder. And sometimes he cries with me. And it's awful. And I love it.

Yeah. Maybe I'm a little broken. Maybe I'm a little fragile. But I think of Val, and Salvador, and Lester, and I think it's all right. Maybe we're all a little broken. Maybe we're all a little fragile. Maybe that's why we need each other so much.

Every morning, Rodeo asks me where I want to go. And if I have an opinion on the matter, I tell him. And I know that the next time I tell him I want to visit Poplin Springs, Washington—and there *will* be a next time, absolutely—then that's where we'll go.

I don't take care of my dad anymore. We take care of each other.

Back in my room, under my bed, there's a box. Inside the box is a treasure. A whole pile of treasures, actually. Sometimes I sit and look through them. Sometimes we sit and look through them together.

I started a new tradition for us, too. Most nights before we go to sleep, we each tell a memory. One a day. A memory about our family. It can be a big memory or a small memory, a sad memory or a happy memory. It doesn't matter. Sometimes, I write them down and put them in the box.

I remember the night before we made it home. How I was afraid that once I got there, my mom and my sisters would feel *gone*. Well, they are gone. But, lord, they aren't gone at all. Not even close. Not anymore. Not ever again.

And then one day, we see it. That green highway road sign with the name of a town on it. A town we visited years ago, and liked. Loved, even. A small town, with nice folks. A town we've maybe been working our way toward but pretending we weren't. A river runs through it, always moving, but always there. It's got a bakery with big, round sourdough loaves that are absolute heaven with a smear of butter on 'em. It's got a middle school with a big soccer field. And, over by the laundromat, it's got a taco truck. There's even a drive-in movie place in the summer. It's a fine place. A place that's worth a shot, maybe.

And the sign, it's telling us that town is ten miles away.

The sun is coming sideways through Yager's windows, and

she's humming all around us. To be honest, there's still a faint smell of goat to the place, but we're used to it, and even if we weren't we wouldn't mind, because she was a darn fine goat and traveling companion.

Ivan is sitting on the dashboard, eyes half-closed, gazing out at the highway.

The sun is thinking of setting, but she won't just yet. She's gonna light our way right into town. She's gonna leave us enough light to get there. And then there'll be the coolness of night. And then we'll wake up to a new day.

I look up at the Holy Hell Bell, and it's gleaming like St. Peter's gates up there in a sun ray and I think about standing up and ringing it, but I don't, because it ain't that kind of moment. It's just not. It's rich and it's full and it's a certain deep kind of happy, but it's already ringing with its own quiet music.

And then my dad says, "Give me a once-upon-a-time, Ella."

And I smile. And I rub my eyes. And I take a little breath, and then a big one.

And I'm almost silenced by how much story there is to tell in this world. Almost.

I stand there, looking out at the world we're driving into. None of it had to happen. Not one bit. Sunrises and sunsets and ice cream cones never had to exist, shooting stars and acoustic guitars and holding hands, good books and warm blankets and goodnight kisses—none of them ever *had* to be. Mama and Ava and Rose never had to live and breathe; they could've never come to be. Rodeo and me and Yager and Lester and Grandma and Salvador and Val and Ivan could've never come to be. All of it, every little bit, could've never happened, and I could've never seen it and I'd never even know I hadn't.

But it did. And I did. Oh, I did.

There is so much happiness in the world.

There is so much sadness in the world.

There is just so *much* in the world.

"Well," I say, and I squeeze my dad's shoulder, "once upon a time, there was a girl and her dad."

ACKNOWLEDGMENTS

The biggest fiction in any book is that there is usually only one name on the cover. I'm in debt to so many folks for all their help and support along the way in getting this story out into the world.

Thanks to my agents, Pam and Bob, for finding Coyote a home and fighting for her every step of the way.

To my amazing editor, Christian, whose yes made this book possible and whose intelligence and sensitivity made the story immeasurably better.

To all the hardworking folks at Henry Holt and MacKids, thanks for making lots of beautiful books, including this little one.

To Celia Krampien, for bringing Coyote and Ivan to life and giving my story such a wonderful, perfect cover.

To all the other kidlit writers and storytellers with whom I've connected in real life or online . . . it's so great to be in a community with you, doing this work.

To all the teachers and librarians out there who share books with their students, and who make it possible and joyful to make a living writing stories for young people.

To all you readers who pick up a book when there are so many other things you could be picking up—you kids reading on buses and sidewalks and park benches and couches and beaches, in cars and beds and classrooms and airplanes and restaurants: I see you and I am you and I thank you.

And last, but not remotely least, to all my friends and family, who have always been in my corner. Thank you, times a million.

DISCUSSION QUESTIONS

1. Coyote says that this story begins when she meets Ivan—even though her adoption of Ivan is long before she ever thinks about going home. Why do you think this is where Coyote decides to start her story? What does Ivan mean to her?

2. If you lived on Yager, what three questions would you ask someone before letting them on? Who would you bring along on a road trip?

3. Describe Rodeo's appearance, his personality, and his strengths. How do outsiders view him? Why does Coyote love him? What are some of the problems for her in having him as a father? What are some times that he comes through for her even when it's hard for him to do so?

4. Rodeo and Coyote have a close father-daughter bond, but there is still a lot they have trouble talking about. Why do you think some things are hard to talk about even with loved ones?

5. Many promises are made throughout the novel by the characters. What are some of the promises made and why were they made? Why is it important to keep promises and when is it right to break a promise?

6. Summarize the scene when Coyote and Salvador are on the roof of the bus. What is the point of shouting up there? What do the two learn about each other? Why do you think Salvador thanks Coyote at the end of that scene?

7. What role has friendship played in Coyote's life in the last five years? Why is Coyote's friendship with Salvador so important to her? What do the two of them have in common? What makes them become good friends in such a short time?

8. What are some of the benefits of having a good friend? What are some of the qualities that make someone a good friend?

9. Coyote says of Salvador and his mother, "They were pilgrims on a quest, just like me and Rodeo" (p. 117). What quest are Salvador and his mother on, and why are they on it? How about Rodeo and Coyote? Are Lester and Val on quests, and if so, what are they?

10. Each of the characters that join Coyote and Rodeo on their journey have a problem or situation that they are trying to overcome. How do their journeys affect each other, and what lessons do you think they learn from meeting and traveling with one another?

11. Coyote is trying to balance her own needs with her feeling that she should take care of her father. In the scene when she finds him on a sandbar, she reflects, "My job wasn't to take care of him. Not anymore. My job was to take care of me" (p. 264). Explain those statements. How has she been "taking care" of him throughout the book? Talk about how and why she changes her approach.

12. When the story opens, Rodeo and Coyote never talk about her mother and sisters. Why does Rodeo think that's the best way to deal with the past? How does Coyote feel about that approach? Explain why she comes to believe that "remembering them and being sad about it is way better than forgetting about them" (p. 254). Do you agree with her? Why or why not?

(Questions #3, 6-9, 11, and 12 were provided by Kathleen Odean, a school librarian for 17 years who now offers workshops for educators on new young adult books. She chaired the 2002 Newbery Award Committee and served on earlier Newbery and Caldecott committees.)